TARYN'S HAUNTING

A TARYN'S CAMERA BOOK

* * *

REBECCA PATRICK-HOWARD

WANT MORE?

Want access to FREE books (audio, print, and digital), prizes, and new releases before anyone else? Then sign up for Rebecca's VIP mailing list. She promises she won't spam you!

Join me at

www.rebeccaphoward.net

DIVE INTO

TARYN'S HAUNTING!

Rebecca uses music and imagery to write her novels.

Want to check out the songs that inspired *Taryn's Haunting* and the ones that are referenced throughout the book?

Check out Rebecca's Google Music playlist for

Taryn's Haunting.

Taryn's Haunting playlist

Or http://bit.ly/2njrxhB

Want to see images and links that helped Rebecca write the book? Check out her Pinterest board for *Taryn's Haunting*!

Taryn's Haunting Pinterest board

Or

https://www.pinterest.com/rebeccapatrickh/taryns-haunting-book/

For Robbie

And "Matt"

NEW HAMPSHIRE, 2017

Nicki was now 100% convinced that there was something wrong with her best friend, Taryn. Only a nutter would not only have cheerfully moved into the creepy, old house but could have actually enjoyed living there.

Yep, Taryn was crazy, Nicki thought to herself as she turned up the speakers to drown out the unnerving creaks and groans ("house settling" her hiney) that had plagued her all night.

Then she immediately burst into tears.

Taryn is gone, Nicki reminded herself. Taryn wasn't a crazy nutter and she certainly didn't have anything wrong with her brain. Taryn was the best friend Nicki'd ever had and she'd been gone for almost a year. God, she missed her.

"Nobody is ever gone for good," her mother used to tell her. "They live forever in your heart, love."

Nicki snorted. "Bull."

What was the point of someone living in your heart, the point of memories, when you couldn't talk to them or touch them? Couldn't call them up to chatter on about Joseph Fiennes on Hulu or ask for advice when your boyfriend tried to dye your hair platinum blonde and it came out a jolly orange?

She didn't want Taryn in her "heart." She wanted her right there in the room with her.

When her phone started buzzing and vibrating on the bed beside her, Nicki exhaled noisily with relief. Sometimes she got lost inside her own head. She turned the volume back down on the ancient boom box, snuggled deeper into her duvet, and answered.

"You alive there, duchess?"

Her husband, Shawn, was a thousand miles away in Western Canada but, thanks to modern technology, sounded like he was right there in the room with her. Isolated as the old house may be, the new cell phone tower they'd installed on the edge of the property had finally guaranteed regular service. She couldn't have stayed there, not alone anyway, without it.

"Barely," Nicki snorted. "I almost went and got a room for the night in town."

"Scaring yourself?"

Nicki glanced around the big, airy bedroom and nodded as though he could see her. "There are very strange noises here."

"Old house and old pipes," he sang cheerfully.

She, in turn, cheerfully wanted to strangle him. Of course *he* could be nonchalant about it–he never had to stay there alone.

"It's more than that," Nicki retorted. "I feel like I keep seeing things out of the corner of my eye but by the time I turn around, they're gone. And no matter where I am outside, I have this constant feeling that someone's watching me from the house. And today?"

"Yeah?"

He was humoring her, she just knew it.

"Today I thought I heard someone laughing," she finished stiffly.

"Is that all?" he asked.

No, it wasn't, but she wasn't going to give him the satisfaction of more conversation if he was just going to make fun of her.

"It's fine."

"I'm sorry," Shawn said, sounding like he might be speaking to a five-year-old, "but Nicki's a big girl now! She can fight off those big, bad ghosts!"

"Shawn..."

It was a warning–a warning that, as a Welshman, she knew curses and insults that could have him cowering in the corner of his comped hotel room.

"I'm sorry," he apologized again, this time sounding like he meant it. "I honestly don't think there's anything there, though. At least, nothing bad."

"Oh yeah? How do you know?"

"Well, I was with you for months and I didn't see or hear anything that would give me cause for concern about leaving you there alone," he replied. "If it would make you feel better, though, then why not come up and join me? Or go get yourself a hotel room for a night–four nights if you want. Stay away until I get back and we'll tackle this together."

Well, she was certainly feeling less frightened but now Nicki found herself feeling silly. She *was* a "big girl" and it seemed foolish to waste money on a room at an inn when she had a perfectly fine place to stay for free. More than fine, even. The historical, stone house was big enough for a family of six or seven and she had it all to herself.

A gift from her friend. Taryn's Aunt Sarah's house, a place that she'd inherited herself. A place that she'd then willed to her "sole family member, Nicola Hogg." Though they weren't family, at least, not by blood. Just by heart.

"I'll be okay," Nicki sighed at last. "I guess I'm just projecting some of my feelings onto the house and hearing and seeing things that aren't there."

"There are only two logical people who could be haunting it," Shawn pointed out gently, "and neither one of them would hurt you."

Nicki continued to think about that after their conversation ended and she'd hung up the phone. *Only two logical people who could be haunting the house...*

And even though her logical sensibilities tried to prevail, they failed and Nicki found her eyes welling with tears. Soon, the entire room was blurry and unfocused.

"Oh, Taryn," she sobbed into her duvet, "if you're here then please come out. Please! I promise I won't be scared."

And for the first time all evening, the house was totally silent.

ONE

HGA library

HAZEL HILL, KENTUCKY, 2014

Taryn wasn't sure that she'd ever seen a sadder place. And that was saying a lot, considering that she'd made a living out of painting and photographing structures that were basically on their last legs.

It wasn't just that the group of dilapidated buildings were crumbling down around her, vandalized both by people and the elements. No, the sadness came from their emptiness. She could all but smell the former vibrancy of the Hazel Hill Academy's campus; the fact that the sense of deterioration competed with it troubled her. Few things were as depressing to Taryn as an abandoned building that continued to yearn for the past, for *life*, but knew that it was bound for destruction.

"Sorry fellas," she apologized, taking in the group of sorry-looking buildings with unhappiness. It was almost like a little village up there on the hill, a self-contained world for the children of the mountains at one time.

As depressing as her job usually appeared on the outside, Taryn generally tried to remain positive when she entered a new worksite. Many of her jobs were offered by people who planned on renovating the structures–most of which were historical and on the register. She was used to working with architects, providing the visuals for their technical renderings. Those were the good jobs.

Taryn was technically an artist. That's what she got paid to do, to paint. When individuals or organizations needed a rendering of a structure that was caving in or gone altogether, they hired Taryn due to her ability to "see" the past. Taryn could look at the most dilapidated, rundown house and see past the decay and ruin to visualize what it must have been in its heyday. And then she'd paint it. Months, or sometimes even years, later she could revisit the site and see a total turnaround as construction brought the place back to life. She liked to think that she played a small part in the revitalization.

That's not what was happening here at Hazel Hill Academy. Nope. Out of the six remaining structures (a girls' dorm, boys' dorm, administrative building with classrooms, gymnasium, library, and greenhouse), all but two were being razed to the ground. A freak tornado and electrical storm had done their work on the dorms, rendering them beyond repair, and simple time and neglect had taken care of the others. The academy had been closed for more than thirty years and only basic maintenance had been kept up over that time.

If someone even cared enough, or had the right vision, to come in and restore it all, it would cost millions and millions of dollars. A rough estimate of $4 million was given at one point but most agreed that was conservative. That was before the girls' dorm's roof got molested by a tree.

It didn't matter, Taryn now thought sadly to herself. Nobody was coming.

Hazel Hill, Kentucky was in one of the deepest pockets of Kentucky's Appalachian Mountains. The town lacked both interstate (I-64) and Mountain Parkway access and the Appalachian Regional Commission who, if nothing else, was known for improving the region's infrastructure wasn't going to be connecting it to the rest of the world any time soon.

The former boarding school, created as one of the region's first college preparatory schools back in the nineteenth century, was now a health hazard. From asbestos to loose boards and rotten floors, it was only just a matter of time before someone wandered in out of curiosity and broke a leg or worse. It all had to come down.

"Maybe, once we get it all down, someone will be interested in doing something with the land," Clark Reynolds had told Taryn when she'd arrived. Clark was church elder and president of the Academy Guild and he had *not* sounded optimistic.

The First Christian Church of Hazel Hill, a red brick building at the foot of the academy's hill, had bought the school for $1 from the national Disciples of Christ. Many of the church members had attended the school themselves; some were former staff members. All had deep affection for the place. They'd had big plans to restore it, to perhaps re-open it as a school of sorts. That was twenty-five years ago, however. Their plans were big, their pocketbooks shallow.

Clark, after giving her a tour, had quickly left and locked the main gate behind him. She was completely alone.

Now, standing alone in the parking lot (a barren expanse of crumbling concrete and willful weeds), Taryn surveyed her surroundings. It was certainly peaceful there, that was for sure. Off to the west, the sun was starting to sink lower in the sky, disappearing behind the orange colored gymnasium. Dark shadows fell across a neglected tennis court–once green, now black from muck and mildew. Long branches from a lone weeping willow tree in the ravine below her slowly swayed back and forth, scraping the overgrown ground.

"Bob WHITE, Bob WHITE," the sudden call for the elusive man startled Taryn out of her reflections.

She wasn't completely by herself, then. She had the Bob White and the man it continued to look for but never seemed to find. And she had the past. If there was one thing Taryn had learned, it was that as long as a place held onto its past, she was never alone.

And the past was very much alive at Hazel Hill Academy. She could all but smell the former joy, excitement, and life it once held.

And the death, too. Taryn shivered and folded her arms across her chest. There, just an undercurrent beneath everything else, was always the scent of death. It never truly left a place, either.

TWO

NEW HAMPSHIRE, 2017

Taryn's aunt had been a practical recluse during the last few years of her life–as in, the last twenty or so years. For a long time she'd been a well-respected school teacher and then a principal but at some point she'd given all that up and gone hermit. Nicki wasn't sure why, wasn't sure that Taryn had known either.

It was weird being in someone else's house. She felt like an intruder. The only thing that comforted her was the fact that Taryn had spent so much time in the house before her death, making it her own. Although the house had belonged to Sarah for many years, it was Taryn's at the end and Taryn's it still felt.

"Maybe it had always been Taryn's," Nicki said aloud.

She paused and shook her head. *Where had* that *come from?*

It was settled, then. She'd started talking to herself, so she was clearly going crazy. Everyone should have seen that coming.

The New Hampshire farm consisted of more than one-hundred acres at the edge of the Ossipee Mountains. There were no nearby neighbors; it took her nearly fifteen minutes of driving just to get to the paved road from the house. She was certain that she'd seen a bear on the gravel driveway twice already that week. God only knew what else was out there.

Nicki was used to living "in the middle of nowhere", so to speak. As a historical landscaper, she was often hired to work at out-of-the-way properties that still seemed locked in time. However, what Nicki was learning was that "out of the way" in Wales and "out of the way" in America were two totally different concepts. Back at home, even in the most isolated location she'd worked at, she could be at a high street with a choice of pubs in twenty minutes, tops. Along the way, she'd pass many smaller villages and farms for sure.

She'd gone for a drive earlier that week and had literally driven for thirty-five minutes in the mountains without seeing a single house, business, or farm. She'd heard there were other places in the United States that had even *more* isolated spots, though she wasn't sure about that. This was only her second trip here. The first had been for Taryn's funeral.

"What the hell were you thinking?" she asked.

Nicki hadn't worked for several months. She was taking some time off for her mental health. She'd thought that staying in the old house, being cut off from the rest of the world, and generally just spending some time with her thoughts would be good for her. And it *was* good, for the most part.

Damn, though, she was bored.

"Gotta start my daily rituals!"

Since she'd decided that she was going crazy, she figured she may as well embrace it.

In the daylight hours, the house felt okay. The noises were always more muted then. Nothing really ever came out until nighttime.

Nicki didn't have cable up there at the old farm house, but she did have two televisions with DVD players and several old stereo systems. She kept one of those blasting on every floor. While her original idea had merit, Nicki had decided that being completely alone with her thoughts wasn't healthy; she needed something to drown out her own inner voice every once in a while.

To keep her mind busy, she had created a schedule of sorts. It started with her getting up at around noon. (Mostly because she had trouble sleeping there alone at night and usually didn't fall asleep until the first drops of sunlight began brightening the bedroom.)

She started with a tedious bathroom procedural that included washing her face, exfoliating, applying moisturizer and balm, flossing/brushing/rinsing her mouth, and plucking any facial hairs that sprouted up overnight. From there, she got dressed and then began her cleaning.

Oh, the cleaning...

If anyone had thought that she was just sitting around, being a lazy git, then they were dead wrong. Nicki rarely stopped moving. She *couldn't* stop moving. If she did, then she might not re-start.

Sarah's house was bigger than anything she'd ever managed on her own before. In addition to the multiple bedrooms (five, depending on what you were counting), there were also three living spaces (a formal parlor, living room, and family room of sorts), a formal dining room, bathrooms, a library, a kitchen, and a bunch of little rooms that had been turned into various things over the years (craft room, music room, office, and two junk rooms).

The house, in other words, was huge.

Taryn had a housekeeper when she lived there but Nicki had let her go. She and Shawn just didn't have the funds to keep her on, which was too bad because she really could've used the help. Nicki had learned that even when the rooms were shut off and not being used, they still managed to find ways to destroy themselves. The basic upkeep was exhausting.

So, Nicki cleaned.

She swept, mopped, polished floors, polished *silver*, dusted, cleaned windows, washed linens, ironed linens, oiled hinges, cleaned dishes, and beat old rugs every single day.

And that was just basic upkeep and didn't count the straightening that she did after she made her own messes.

And Nicki was, in general, a messy person.

"You just have to walk through a room and it looks like a cyclone follows you," Shawn was fond of saying.

Yeah, well, it was true.

How had Taryn kept up with all of that? Even with a housekeeper, it would've been difficult. Taryn was not well in the last year of her life. Indeed, that was why she'd retired to the farm house, though nobody in her life had been aware of just how serious her health situation truly was. If they'd known, if Nicki'd known...

Nicki paused on her hands and knees, the sponge dripping soap and water onto the floor.

"If I'd know, I would've been here," she said between clenched teeth.

But Taryn was a young woman, still some years off from being forty. Who could've known that her aneurysm was going to burst when it did, how it did?

Taryn knew, Nicki sighed to herself. Of course, Taryn had known. That's why she'd come up here–to die alone and in peace.

Nicki was trying not to take that personally.

THREE

HGA dining room

HAZEL HILL, KENTUCKY 2014

"Have you done any exploring yet?"

Taryn had just stuffed a greasy French fry in her mouth and now she quickly chewed and swallowed before answering. It went down her throat like a rock.

"Not yet," she replied. God, she could still feel it sliding down to her stomach. It was physically painful.

"Why not?" Nicki demanded.

Taryn rolled her eyes and laughed. Damn, the woman was pushy. But in a friendly way. She also knew Taryn, knew that Taryn normally couldn't wait to get into the thick of things.

"I got here kind of late," Taryn replied. She took a long sip of peanut butter milkshake to help work the rest of the fry down. "Too late to see anything tonight. No power on in any of the buildings."

"Was it a long drive?"

Taryn nodded, even though Nicki couldn't hear her head rattle. "Took six hours from Nashville and I got a late start."

That was a lie. Taryn had left at six that morning, hoping to reach Hazel Hill by early afternoon. She'd made half a dozen stops, however, along the way. Between the constant bouts of nausea and vomiting and the extreme dizziness that kept overtaking her, she'd been afraid that she wouldn't make it at all.

"God, what's going to happen if I just can't do it?" she'd cried in panic at one point. She'd be stuck there, at a Stuckey's, no less, on the side of the interstate for God knew how long. Who would come and get her?

Matt would, of course, but he was in Florida.

It was this fear of being dependent upon people that set her resolve. She'd forced herself to vomit one last time, promising herself she wouldn't do it anymore that day, and had then washed her face with a paper towel and rinsed her mouth out with a sample of Listerine that she kept in her backpack.

"No more," Taryn had sworn. The redhead in the mirror had gazed back at her with determination, though there were dark circles under her eyes and her face was white.

She wasn't going to worry Nicki about any of it.

"Where you staying then?"

"A no-stars motel in a place called West Liberty," Taryn replied. "No motels or anything in Hazel Hill."

"Is it close, at least?"

"About twenty minutes. Not bad."

"You eating?"

Taryn would say that Nicki was as bad as her mother, except her own mother had never worried over Taryn the way that Nicki did. Maybe as bad as her *grandmother*...

"I'm eating right now, as a matter of fact," Taryn said as she took another swig of her shake. God, it was good.

"Where at?"

Now Taryn knew that Nicki wasn't being nosey–she was being curious. Nicki loved to eat, maybe even more than Taryn and Taryn was crazy about food. Much of their time in Wales had involved consumption of something.

"Well, we call them 'Frosty Freezes' here," Taryn smiled as she looked around the small restaurant. "They're basically fast food places that sell cheeseburgers, chicken strips, onion rings, fries, pizza bread, mozzarella sticks..."

"Nothing healthy?"

"Not a thing."

"My favorite kind of place," Nicki swooned.

"And lots of ice cream," Taryn finished.

"Now you're talking!"

She'd eaten in places that were much cleaner and more fashionable, but she'd had fewer milkshakes that were anywhere near as good. The frosty freeze had been there for more than sixty years, or so the owner had told her when he'd delivered her basket of burger and fries to her booth, and it contained the original furniture. Taryn believed it. There were six booths in total, with three Formica-topped tables in the middle. A half-wall separated the dining room from a smaller room in the back. She could hear the Pac-Man theme song and hear the occasional clank of balls from the pool table. There were three other tables currently dining with her and the whole place smelled like grease and cigarette smoke.

But, oh, the fries. They were heavenly. She would eat here again.

"So how does it feel there?"

Taryn knew Nicki wasn't talking about the frosty freeze.

"Sad," she answered. An image of the red-bricked girls' dormitory, with half its roof caved in from a marauding tree, flashed through her mind. The library with its door blown open from the wind and piles of books scattered across the floor visible from the weedy sidewalk. "Depressing."

"Aw, that sucks."

"Yeah."

"You gonna be there long?"

The food was good, but Taryn couldn't eat another bite. She'd gone five hours without vomiting and she wasn't going to chance it. Now, she leaned back in the booth, when its cracked plastic seats and wobbly table, and closed her eyes.

"A month," she said. "More or less. The buildings aren't coming down until June or July, so I have plenty of time."

It was April now. After a long, brutal winter Kentucky was finally starting to awaken to spring.

"Well, I know you're trying to eat so I won't bother you anymore," Nicki said, "just take care of yourself. Okay?"

"Will do."

She could tell that Nicki was still lingering on the other end of the line, however, with something on her mind.

"Yes, dear?"

"Have you, uh," Nicki's voice faltered as she struggled to get out what she was trying to say.

"Yes?"

"Been to the doctor lately?"

"All the time," Taryn smiled. "She's my new BFF. After you, of course."

"Anything new?"

"Nothing new," Taryn assured her. "They increased my pain medication, but I don't take it when I know I'll be driving. I'm okay. I'm doing everything they tell me to."

"Okay." Nicki's sound of relief was had Taryn setting her lips in a grim smile. "Just as long as you're okay."

Once she'd hung up the phone, Taryn reached into her knapsack and pulled out her camera, Miss Dixie. She set her up on the table and studied her.

"You ready to do this?" she whispered quietly.

Miss Dixie regarded her drolly.

Taryn reached over and patted her lens cover.

She was hired by individuals and organizations because she had degrees in historical preservation and art and because she had an acute ability to visualize the past the use her skills to interpret missing floors, structures, and architectural elements.

What she wasn't hired for was her ability to actually *see* the past. Although it didn't happen every time, and she had no way of controlling it, Miss Dixie was her conduit to other time periods. When something needed looking into, when a place had something to say, it showed Taryn through her camera. There had been many times when she'd taken photos of rooms that looked perfectly normal through the viewfinder, only to pull back seconds later and see an entirely different room on the LCD screen.

It was her own way of time traveling.

Even after she'd thrown away her trash and paid, Taryn remained in the dingy little diner. It was fuller now, packed with everyone from young parents with kids to elderly couples on canes. She'd need to leave soon, need to give up her booth to someone else. Sometimes, however, she liked the feeling of being a part of something–even if it was just an illusion.

FOUR

NEW HAMPSHIRE, 2017

At times like this, when Nicki was feeling at peace with herself and the sun was sinking behind the mountains and over the lake, she sort of understood what drew Taryn to Sarah's house and what had made her stay. In an old rocking chair, wrapped up in a quilt on the front porch, Nicki gently rocked herself back and forth and listened to the night sounds begin their evening symphony.

"God, but it's peaceful out here," Nicki murmured.

Although she'd lived in London during graduate school, and Cardiff for undergrad, she'd always been a bit of a country girl at heart. And, like Taryn, she had a thing for the past. Of course, she didn't have Taryn's gift but, in her own way, she loved thinking about what things might have looked like, how they could have been. She was open to endless ridicule by Shawn but in college Nicki had enjoyed larping and attending Renaissance weekends back in the U.K.

The old wooden boards creaked under the rocking chair's movements. It was almost musical. Nicki closed her eyes and imagined her friend sitting in that same chair, feeling the cool spring breeze on her face. Had she sat out there on nights when she couldn't sleep? Listened to the night sounds and wind blowing through the trees?

Nah, probably not, Nicki decided.

Taryn was kind of afraid of the dark–ironic, considering that she didn't think a thing in the world about exploring old houses and diving headfirst into some of the creepiest places Nicki had ever seen.

Somewhere upstairs, in the deepest recesses of the house, a door closed. It didn't slam shut, which would have startled Nicki but not scared her, but slowly fastened to in a way that was obviously deliberate. The smoothness of the act, the consideration in which it was done, had her jumping to her feet with her heart in her throat.

Someone is here with me, she thought.

With the purple sky growing darker around her, Nicki left the safety of the front porch and entered the house. The foyer was full of shadows and stillness. The house had grown dim while she'd ruminated outside; the only light she'd left on was in the kitchen at the back of the house. Nicki glanced up the master staircase and listened. It was quiet again. If there was someone in the house other than her, they weren't making themselves known now.

"Hello!" Nicki called out. Her strong voice belied the shakiness she felt inside.

In reply came the long, slow creak of a door slowly opening.

Which room, which room, which room, she thought wildly.

She wasn't familiar enough with the house to know which doors and boards made which noises, but she was certain it had come from one of the bedrooms. Maybe the creepy one across the hall from the master–the one she never went into because it was mostly for storage and had the weird dolls.

For a moment Nicki cursed herself for not being the European television version of an American–the paranoid redneck with the arsenal at her disposal. Nicki was smart enough to realize that was a stereotype, that not all Americans walked around packing heat, but she wished it were kind of true now. The closest thing Taryn had to a weapon in the house was a fireplace poker.

Still, it was better than nothing. Gripping it in one hand, Nicki pulled out her phone with the other and quickly dialed up Shawn.

"Hey, what's up?" he asked jovially.

"Shhhh," Nicki hissed. "Something's in the house. Stay on the line with me."

"Want me to call the police?" he asked, his voice suddenly formal and to the point. "I'm in the production trailer."

"Yes," she replied.

She waited until he'd picked up the extra line and dialed the number. Once he assured her they were on the way, she considered the staircase again.

"I'm going up," she said at last.

"Oh no you're not!"

Nicki set her mouth in firmness. "Well I'm certainly not going to go sit outside in the car like a ninny."

"Nicki, go get in the car and drive to the end of the gravel road," Shawn instructed her. "Whoever's in there could have a weapon. They could hurt you."

"Shawn," she whispered, "what if it's not a person at all. What if it's..."

"Taryn wouldn't scare you," Shawn assured her. "She'd have made herself known by now."

"But–"

"It's not her," he repeated, his voice gentle.

Ignoring him, Nicki gradually climbed up the stairs, her gaze fixated to the top. It was so dark up there that she couldn't see beyond the landing. There were no other noises, no movements, and yet...

Nicki knew she was being watched. Someone else was up there, was close, and they were as aware of her presence as she was of theirs.

"Who's there?" she called out.

"Nicki!" Shawn's exasperation was palpable.

"I know you're up there!"

"Oh my God," he muttered, his voice muffled against the phone. "You're going to get your damn self killed."

She raised herself another step then paused. *Was* she being stupid? Was Shawn right?

Before she could make up her mind, a blast of bitter wind coursed through her. It wasn't the coldness that had her quickly moving back down the stairs and towards the front door, but the stench–the awful, horrible smell that had her gagging and dry heaving. It was the smell of rotten food, the taste of rancid milk, the stench of something rotten.

The smell of something that had been dead for a very, very long time.

FIVE

Girls' dorm attic

HAZEL HILL, KENTUCKY 2014

The girls' dorm was still mostly intact, it just had a tree through the roof.

"That just happened a few months ago."

Taryn looked up from her camera and acknowledged the older woman standing before her. She was probably fifty, but carried herself as someone much younger. Her short hair was bleached platinum blonde, her mini blue jean skirt showed off still-shapely legs, and she wore full makeup. She looked like she was on her way to a night on the town, only, Hazel Hill didn't have a nightlife scene. Only a gas station that served biscuits and gravy in the morning. Taryn could see a little red LeBaron convertible parked next to her own vehicle. It looked out of place against the shabby backdrop.

"Storm?" Taryn asked.

The other woman nodded. "Bad storm. Flattened some of the houses around here straight to the ground. I think it was a tornado. Tornados are funny like that, you know. They'll hit one house, jump right over the next and not even touch it, and get the one on the other side."

Taryn knew all about that. She'd seen it happen in Nashville.

"I'm Rosa, but the way." When the woman smiled, she revealed perfectly straight, glistening white teeth. They were so perfect that they just had to be caps. Taryn was jealous.

"I'm Taryn," Taryn replied in return. She stuck out her hand and the one that gripped hers was smooth and soft. This was a woman who took pride and care in her appearance. Taryn was fascinated.

"I just came up here to see if you needed anything," Rose explained. "I'm church historian but I do a little of everything down there." She gestured to the south of the academy, towards the bottom of the hill. Taryn couldn't see the little red, brick church from where they stood but she knew that it was there. She passed it every time she drove in.

"I'm okay," Taryn replied. "Was just getting ready to go in there and take some shots."

Oh," Rose said, looking at Taryn's camera quizzically. "You're a photographer too?"

"Yeah, I usually start with pictures," Taryn said. "This here's Miss Dixie. She's my second set of eyes."

Oh, if Rosa knew just how true that was...

"I like taking pictures myself," Rosa said. "Every couple of months I take my mother on a tour and I always come back with hundreds. Fill a whole memory card!"

"What kind of tour?"

"All kinds," Rosa shrugged. "There's a company out of West Liberty and they do bus tours all over the United States. We've been to New York City twice, Pennsylvania Amish country, Nashville, Branson, New Orleans..."

“Sounds like fun,” Taryn said. She tried to imagine what it would’ve been like to have traveled with her own mother, but she couldn’t. Taryn’s parents had been virtual strangers to her, even before their deaths.

“It is,” Rosa agreed. “Mother is getting up there in years. She’s ninety this year, but she still gets around. She likes to get up and go.”

“So you all are from around here?”

When Rosa nodded, her blonde hair bobbed up and down. It looked as soft and fluffy as cotton candy. “Both of us born and bred. Neither one of us ever lived anywhere else. I went to college at Morehead, but I moved back here. After college I took up as librarian at the elementary school down the road. Still there.”

Taryn understood what it was like to have lived in the same town for your entire life, but she imagined that Rosa’s ties to Hazel Hill were much stronger than her own ties were to Nashville. Taryn had lived around Nashville for more than thirty years and she hardly knew a soul; Rosa probably knew everyone inside and out.

“What’s it like to live here?”

“Quiet,” Rosa laughed. “Everyone looks out for each other, but nobody bothers you.”

“That’s nice, that sense of community,” Taryn said.

Rosa nodded. “Don’t get me wrong, sometimes it’s too quiet. I always had a dream of moving to Nashville, listening to the music in the bars. I like to get out, do things, see people. I guess you could say that I’m a midnight girl in a sunset down.”

Taryn smiled at the reference to the Sweethearts of the Rodeo song.

“But, this is home. This is where Mother wants to be. The mountains get in your blood, you know? Leaving isn’t easy, not for any of us.” Rosa’s laugh this time was a titter. “Maybe that’s why we go back for generations.”

Fear of movement was real, Taryn understood that. The chains that held you back were usually all in your head.

“Well, listen to me,” Rosa laughed again, “I’m keeping you from work.”

“Oh, it’s okay.”

“No it’s not,” Rosa chastised her. And then, to Taryn’s surprise, she walked over and took Taryn in her arms. “You take care of yourself, you hear?”

She pulled back and Taryn nodded.

With one last squeeze on Taryn's shoulders, Rose offered another grin. "And you come over for dinner one night. I'll be planning on it."

As Taryn watched the little red sports car fly over the grass and gravel, she felt a little pang of loneliness. For a moment, anyway.

* * *

The girls' dorm technically had three stories, although the top was really an attic. There was a basement, too. Taryn had a vague idea of what each building was used for, but she didn't have any specifics. She didn't know, for instance, what classes were taught in which rooms. Clark's "tour" had consisted of little more than pointing in vague directions and rattling off generic names.

Once she walked around and got a feel for the place on her own, she'd look up Clark Reynolds, or maybe Rosa, and get more details. In the beginning, however, she liked to form her own impressions without the hindrance of influence.

Taryn was going to start at the very top.

The two staircases on either end of the building were solid oak. There was nothing ornate about them, no intricate carvings or embellishments, but they were still beautiful in their own way. Although cobwebs now clung to the spindles and the wood was starting to crack and splinter from the exposure to the elements near the top, they were solid works of art to Taryn. As she slowly climbed to the top, she looked down at her feet, paying careful attention to the places where hundreds of feet had rubbed smooth spots into the wood.

She tried imagining girls in long skirts and patent leather shoes, taking the stairs two at a time, chattering to their friends and calling out to one another with laughter as they scurried to their bedrooms.

The building was so quiet now, it was hard to think of it as having ever been full of life. But, of course, it had been once. Young women, some as young as ten years old, had filled those empty rooms. They'd come from wealthy families who sought higher education for their children and from poor families who'd applied for scholarships. This would've been a big deal, coming here to live and study.

The last flight up to the attic was narrow and stuffy. The air was so still, so thick, that it felt like it hadn't churned in years. When she reached the door at the top, however,

Taryn was met with a gust of wind. She was also met with the slap of a tree branch; she was under the hole.

The attic stretched the width and length of the building. The tree, which had been uprooted from the field behind the dorm, was laid crossways across the left-hand side. Taryn couldn't see over it very well, and she certainly wasn't going to try to climb over it since the floor was undoubtedly rotten from exposure, but she still gained a better idea of the attic. Though it was nothing but a big, open space she could still see several twin beds pushed against the walls.

"The overspill area?" Taryn mumbled.

Miss Dixie was slung around her neck and she picked her up now and turned her on. Miss Dixie was her second set of eyes–in more ways than one. Whenever Taryn started a new job, she always walked around the property with her camera first. Long before she began sketching or painting, she took pictures. Sometimes hundreds of pictures of details so small that most people would barely notice them. Things like angles of walls and copper plating and eaves. Support beams. Later, back in her hotel room or rental house or wherever she was staying, she'd sit down at her laptop and patiently go through each picture, one by one, and study them. Only once she had a good feel for what she'd be working with would she begin to paint.

Her paintings were for her clients; her pictures were for her.

Now, as Taryn stood at the edge of the once-stuffy room with its single window and eight-foot ceilings, she wondered what the girls would have thought about staying up there. Did they hate it? Was it a punishment or a reward? Away from the prying eyes of their dorm mother, was this highly sought after?

She'd ask Rosa. It was something only a female would know the answer to.

Taryn took half a dozen shots of the room, but she didn't glance down at her viewfinder. She'd look at the pictures later. To do it now might ruin something.

On the second floor, Taryn walked through each tiny dorm room, taking shots of the old metals beds and mattresses with their rats' nests and mildew. The rooms were mostly devoid of furniture, although here and there she encountered a small bedside stand or chest of drawers. No closets. Would they have had wardrobes? Each room looked like it held two girls.

She was surprised to see that there were only two bathrooms on each floor, one at either end. The bathrooms held a single tub, a sink, and a toilet. Two toilets for what looked like eighteen girls.

"That would've been interesting," Taryn chuckled.

Her laughter echoed and returned to her in a canned whisper.

The first floor was set up exactly the same way, except it only had one bathroom. Instead of the second, there was a much larger room with several chairs and stained-glass window. A little brass sign on the door read "Parlor."

Taryn stood back, took a shot of the sign, and smiled.

"The old socializing room," she said, nodding her head in approval.

The girls' dorm was on one side of the campus, the boys' on the other. Each afternoon, the boys would have been allowed to come to the girls' building, to come calling. They would've met in that room. And done what, she wondered? Played cards and board games? Talked? Helped one another with homework.

God, it sounds so innocent and wholesome, Taryn thought to herself.

It sounded nice.

When she was finished with the first floor, she attempted to find the door to the basement but couldn't. Try as she might, it just didn't appear to exist.

"I *know* there's a basement," she complained. She'd seen the windows when she'd walked around the building.

Despite the chilly spring air outside, she was starting to work up a sweat and her legs were beginning to ache. She'd need to rest. If she overdid it, then she might be out for a good two or three days recovering, and she couldn't afford to lose time.

If she really overdid it then she might be out for a lot longer than that, Taryn reminded herself.

Still, she was going to finish that building. One a day, she'd promised herself.

"I guess I'll just look outside," Taryn shrugged. She pushed open one of the heavy double doors and stepped back into the sunlight. The air felt much fresher and cleaner out there. Taryn took in a deep breath then began circumventing the building.

All the way around on the other side, entrance obscured by an overgrown honeysuckle bush, she found a narrow concrete staircase. It led almost straight down to a plain-looking door with green-chipped paint. There was nothing to suggest that the entrance was to anything that mattered.

"Must be here..."

The door didn't easily give but, after putting her hip into it, Taryn was finally able to push it open. With a grunt and a curse, she fell inwards and almost lose her balance. Miss Dixie swung against her, beating her chest.

"Please don't kill me," Taryn said with a wry grin. "It's too early in the game for that."

The air down there was stale and sour. The long corridor that she stood at the end of was dark, almost pitch black, and the linoleum floor beneath her was squishy from moisture.

A small ray of pale light tricked out from a room on the left so she followed it now, the flashlight app on her cell phone providing a flicker of radiance.

The room she entered was long, reaching the length of the building, and narrow. Small, ground-level windows that had been boarded up over the years lined one wall. Taryn was short, but she could almost touch the ceiling. It smelled entirely of dampness and mold.

I probably shouldn't be in here, Taryn thought. The last thing she needed was to get an infection of some kind.

Rickety round tables and broken chairs were scattered throughout the room. Various animals had made nests on them and she could see the faint outlines of carcasses that had been left behind. Their bones stuck out from clumps of fur like needles in rolls of yarn.

She was standing in the middle of the cafeteria.

It couldn't have fit more than thirty people, at least not easily. Taryn was having difficulty imagining the entire school fitting into the room, or any kind of festive dinner being put on there. True, it was dark and neglected, but it looked like it would've been depressing even back then.

She took a couple of pictures and then left.

There was only one other room downstairs and it was across the dark corridor.

No rays of light infiltrated this space. A quick glance around with her flashlight revealed only one small window and it was boarded up. When she stepped completely inside the room, she was startled as the heavy door clanked to behind her.

"What the..."

Feeling the slight stirrings of panic brought on by claustrophobia, she hopped towards the door and blindly felt for the knob. It was sticky in her hand, but it turned.

Taryn heaved a sigh of relief. She didn't relish the idea of being locked in there alone all night. An old bucket against the wall caught her eye and she used this now to prop the door open.

Now convinced that she was safe, Taryn turned back to the room again and studied it. Long metal tables filled the center of the room. Along the far wall, she could see two sinks and two refrigerators. A row of stoves and ovens flanked the opposite wall. Another door, leading to what she imagined to be the freezer, was in the corner. She wouldn't press her luck and try it.

Taryn was surprised to see that the room still contained supplies–vintage mixers and colanders and food processors that would probably fetch a pretty penny one eBay. Forks and spoons were gathering dust on a table. Thick plastic bowls were stacked neatly on the counter, ready for breakfast cereal. Garbage cans were pushed neatly against the wall; some contained empty bags ready to be filled.

It was almost like they all just walked out of the room one day and never went back.

Huh, Taryn thought. *Seems like someone should've wanted some of this stuff.*

She wanted to hang around, nose around some of the stuff, but the pain in her legs and now her hip (from pushing open the door) was really starting to get to her. She needed to get back to her motel room and take some medicine or else she wasn't going to be good for anything.

"Okay Miss Dixie," Taryn sang. "Last time, I promise."

The flash filled the room like a nuclear bomb. Suddenly, all the dark corners disappeared, and she was standing in a bright vacuum, the blinding light sending a flare of pain through her eyes.

"Ow!"

And then it was dark again, almost more so than before, but something had changed. She no longer smelled the dampness and mold and accumulated grime. She smelled...

Milk? Taryn sniffed the air and paused. Did milk have a scent?

Cold liquid. Cold and thick and sweet. It was definitely milk. Taryn wasn't sure she'd ever smelled coldness before, but she smelled it now.

Milk and cold, Taryn thought to herself. What did *that* mean?

And something else. Taryn sniffed again, then swallowed hard. Fear. Fear had a scent; it was one Taryn was familiar with. And this room was full of it.

SIX

NEW HAMPSHIRE, 2017

She should have buried the camera.

Each day, before she'd even had her morning pee or opened the curtains, Nicki picked up Taryn's camera and held it in her hands. It was heavy and that was good; the weight was a solid reminder that Taryn had once been there.

“I’m sorry, dude,” Nicki whispered.

She’d meant to bury it with her friend, had intended on leaving it in the casket with her. But, in the end, she hadn’t been able to. It was ultimately Shawn who had gently reached into the coffin and lifted it from Taryn’s clasped hands right before they closed the lid.

“Take it,” he’s whispered to Nicki. “It’s okay.”

He’d known that she needed it.

“Taryn wanted you to have it,” he’d added. “You know that throwing something so expensive into a hole would piss her off.”

They’d smiled, and Nicki had even giggled a little, but it had been a watery laugh and only lasted for a second. After that, Taryn’s coffin had been closed and Nicki hadn’t smiled for a very long time.

Nicki was not much of a photographer. She enjoyed taking pictures, but she didn’t know what she was doing. Before Taryn’s camera, Miss Dixie, she’d mostly just used her smart phone. She wanted to learn, though. It would be nice to give Miss Dixie something to do again.

Nicki flipped the camera open and looked at the memory card. It was still in there; she hadn’t the nerve to remove it. She had no idea what pictures were on it, or if there were even any on it at all.

"What are you waiting for?" Shawn continued to ask her. "Put it in the computer and look. Might be interesting."

She wasn't ready to do that, though. Not yet. Once she saw those pictures then there would never be anything "new" of Taryn again. She was already grieving the fact that they'd never have another conversation, that she'd never heard her voice. Never get an email or direct message or a "like" on a Facebook post.

She was saving those pictures for a rainy day. Once she looked at them and saw them all, Taryn would be gone for good.

Shawn would be home in two days. At that point they were going to have The Conversation–the one in which they decided what should be done about the house. Nicki wasn't ready for that, either.

The long drive into the neighboring town gave her time to think.

Like I need more time to do that, she thought wryly. That's all she did anymore–think.

It was good to get out of the house, though. She hadn't been out for more than a week. It was crazy how much time could fly by when you weren't even doing anything. Now that she wasn't on a job, Nicki found that the days just all kind of blended in together.

The drive through the countryside was a peaceful one. The White Mountains climbed high in the distance, their tops white against the blue sky. Hazy. She'd heard about the Kancamagus Highway, about how beautiful that stretch of road was. Nicki liked places and things with weird names. Maybe she'd go for a longer drive tomorrow. Or when Shawn came home.

For now, she was just going to lunch.

The little restaurant that looked like a house from the outside was called a "tavern" but, once she was inside, Nicki knew it for what it was: it was a pub.

Suddenly feeling at home with the dimly lit corners, oak-paneled walls, salty smell of fish and chips, and smattering of hushed conversation, Nicki took herself to a corner table and sat down. There were only a few people in the restaurant and they were mostly at the bar, watching a football (American, not British) on a television screen. Still, it was nice to get out in public.

The server who brought her a menu barely gave her a second glance. Despite the nearly empty dining room, she looked frazzled.

Nicki took that as a challenge.

"What's good?" she asked cheerfully.

"Everything," her server replied flatly.

Okay...

"Something fishy?"

"Lobster bisque," came the brusque reply.

"That and some chips," Nicki replied.

The server paused now and peered over her writing pad. "Our kind of your kind?"

"Uh, mine I guess."

"Fries it is." With that, she turned on her heel and marched towards a door in the back.

Eh, well, nothing she could do about a bad mood that wasn't hers...

Nicki had brought a book with her, a fantasy novel by David Eddings, and she took it out and began to read while she waited. The tavern was toasty warm and cozy and, despite her server's shortness, Nicki was feeling pretty good about being out. She thought that she might go walk around the lake when she finished. Maybe get some ice cream. She should do something...

When the server returned with her food, she decided to make one last effort.

"You from around here?"

The server, who was not wearing a nametag, nodded. "Born and bred."

"I'm from Wales," Nicki told her. "I inherited a house here. From my friend."

"Lucky you."

Dang, this was rough.

"Yeah, my friend passed away not too long ago. I'd never been to the US before her funeral.

"Um hmm." Her server appeared ready to dash back to the kitchen, but Nicki wasn't through with her just yet. She was dying to have a conversation with someone.

"Yeah, she lived in this big old stone house way out in the country," Nicki continued. "I like it out there, it's pretty quiet, but I was going kinda stir crazy."

Suddenly, her sever stopped tapping her toe and for the first time since Nicki sat down, appeared to actually see her.

"You're the artist's friend, right?"

Nicki nodded, pleased that both she and Taryn were known.

"Yeah, I knew her," the other woman said. "She used to come in here a lot. Always liked to order desserts. Well, up until the end anyway. Not so much then."

Nicki felt a pang in her chest. "Did she...?"

"Look sick?"

Nicki bobbed her head again.

"Yeah, she didn't look well," she told her. "I could tell something was up because she never finished anything. Never asked for pie. I didn't know it was that bad, though."

"Nobody did," Nicki assured her.

"So you're living in that house?"

"For now anyway," Nicki said. "My husband is working on a television program at the minute. He hosts a show about old houses. It films in Canada for HGTV. I'm hanging out here while he's on location."

"That's awesome!" Now her server really did appear interested. "What's the name of the show?"

Nicki told her and the other woman squealed. "I love that show!"

"We're hoping it gets picked up for another season."

"I bet it will," she smiled.

Then a shadow passed over her face and she kind of bent over a little, like she was trying to close the distance between Nicki and herself. "Say, uh, speaking of old houses..."

"Yes?"

"Did your friend say anything to you about hers? About her aunt's?"

"Not much," Nicki replied. At least, nothing she was going to share with the server in public. "Why?"

She straightened and shrugged. "We had some conversations about it. There were some questions she had. Some...things that were bothering her. I guess it was no big deal after all."

But Nicki knew better than that.

"She heard things, saw things," Nicki prompted her.

"Well, yeah." The server blushed. "But then she died an I thought that maybe she was just, uh..."

"That it was her illness and she was hallucinating maybe?" Nicki smiled at her gently.

"Yeah, something like that," she mumbled, her face blushing pink.

"Taryn had a gift," Nicki said. "One that probably nobody else in the world has. If she told you things, they were probably true."

As Nicki sat at the table and ate her lobster bisque, she thought about her server's words. So Taryn had talked to her about things going on in the house. And Nicki was hearing and seeing things. She remembered some of the conversations they'd had, about the feelings Taryn was having about the house.

Something had been going on there. Something that had worried Taryn.

Nicki glanced down at Miss Dixie in the chair beside her and frowned.

"Do *you* know what was going on?"

If Miss Dixie knew, then she wasn't talking.

At least, not yet anyway.

SEVEN

Girls' dorm

HAZEL HILL, KENTUCKY 2014

Three of the classrooms in the admin building were ruined almost beyond repair. Roof damage had caused massive leaks and Taryn was pretty sure that the stuff growing up the walls was black mold. She didn't even enter those rooms, just stood at the doors and took pictures from a distance.

Her favorite part of the academy, so far, was the auditorium. It seated around one-hundred people and still had the original velvet curtains, all the fold-out seats, and even the upright piano pushed against the stage. To her delight, props and crumbling scenery from a production of "The Wizard of Oz" were growing dust on the stage.

Taryn stood in the middle of the stage and gazed out upon the invisible audience. After peeking around the room, ensuring that she was truly alone, Taryn cleared her throat and began to speak.

"Welcome everyone!"

Somewhere offstage, a bird ruffled its feathers.

"Thank you for being here with me today!"

She closed her eyes, imagined a polite road of applause.

"Oh, I think we could do better than that!"

The audience erupted with a thunderous ovation which had Taryn prancing back and forth along the old, pine floors. She waved her hands in the air, bringing them together over her head. “Yeah! That’s more like it!”

Then, she did something she never did in public: she began to sing.

Her rousing rendition of Brandi Carlisle’s “The Story” had her off-key voice bouncing off the walls and coming back to her like a musical boomerang. She didn’t care. She sang and sang, adding dance movements where necessary, and strutted around like Madonna herself.

When finished, she paused, took a deep bow, and then clapped for herself.

“Thank you, thank you very much!”

Giggling, Taryn hopped off the stage and began her exit. She loved music more than just about anything, even more than taking pictures and painting. Growing up in Nashville, she’d had the opportunity to be around music her whole life. She’d have been a singer if she could have carried a tune. It was one of her deepest regrets.

If it was true that Heaven was whatever your imagination could think up, an assortment of things you loved and saw during your time on Earth, then Taryn hoped she lived in an old plantation house and sounded like Emmylou Harris.

For a moment she'd been happy, almost giddy at the act of being silly, but now Taryn felt herself growing melancholy. The pain shooting through her lower back, the aches in her legs, were reminders that she was falling apart just like these old buildings. Nothing could put her back together, either. Her aortic aneurysm was too big for them to safely operate on. The only thing they could do was provide pain management for her in an effort to control her blood pressure. And each day seemed to bring more and more pain.

She thought of the song she'd been singing, the line about being made for someone, and Matt flashed through her mind. *Matt.* He deserved something, *someone*, better. Someone who was going to be around for a long time, forever. Someone who could commit to him. They'd been friends for most of their lives. Before Nicki, she'd considered him her best friend, sometimes her only friend. That they'd started dating hadn't been a shock to the universe–it might have even been fate.

Falling in love with the person with whom you'd had a crush on since you were a child–didn't that make a great story?

Yes, Taryn thought to herself, *but is it* my *story?*

The admin building had a sub floor, a basement of sorts, that had contained extra classrooms. Although it didn't look particularly inviting with its bleak concrete walls and smell of water, she headed down that way anyway.

The hallway wasn't very long, maybe only fifty feet or so, but Taryn found herself hesitating at the foot of the stairs. At the end of the corridor there were two double doors. They weren't shut all the way and she could see a sliver of deep darkness protruding from the one on the left.

"Something's in there," she whispered aloud.

And then, *Damn Taryn. You're spooking yourself.*

The moisture under her feet softened her footsteps as she began to walk, her shoes making squishy noises with each step. Green chalkboards lined the walls, and someone had come in and written vulgar words on them with permanent markers. Posters advertising ancient ice cream socials and cheerleading tryouts still hung on doors.

Without understanding why, she ambled towards the doors with curiosity, ignoring the rooms on either side of her. The closer she grew, the wider the sliver of darkness became. It grew and grew until the door was completely open.

A bright ball of flight flickered once, then twice, and then a shadowy figure appeared beyond an opening. Taryn stopped, gasped, and felt her blood run cold. She tried to turn but her feet felt rooted to the ground. As she watched in horror, the shadow defined itself, taking on a more human form.

Taryn closed her eyes, willing herself to snap out of it and run, when the catch of a breath that did not belong to her filled the space between them.

"Oh my goodness!"

When Taryn opened her eyes, she found herself facing Clark Reynolds. He stood there before her, holding onto a tiny flashlight and looking as frightened as her.

"I'm sorry, I didn't know you were here," Taryn said in a strangled voice.

"I heard you upstairs," he said, his voice shaky. "I thought I'd meet you up there. I didn't hear you come down. You walk like an Indian, soft footed."

Oh God, he heard me singing? Taryn cringed with embarrassment.

But if he'd heard her, her made no mention of it.

"Kind of spooky down here isn't it?" he asked, mopping his face with a handkerchief.

Taryn wasn't sure that she'd ever actually seen someone carrying one. She dug it.

"Were you in there in the dark?" she asked, gesturing to the pitch-black room behind him.

He nodded. "Power's out and the windows are boarded up. Someone called earlier, asking about some basketball trophies. We used to have a pretty good team. I was trying to find them in the storage room."

"No luck?"

He shook his head sadly. "No luck. Lots of theft and vandalism over the years."

That's funny, Taryn thought, *because I kind of thought that it looked like everything was still here.*

Still, if basketball trophies were taken then it must have been by someone who wanted them. Good for them. Better than leaving them to rot.

"I thought you were a ghost," Clark admitted. He began walking towards her and, as he passed her, she realized that she was meant to follow.

"You get a lot of those here?" she asked with a smile.

"They say they're here," he called over his shoulder.

"Old buildings get that a lot," Taryn said.

He nodded and began his ascent up the stairs. "Been saying that about this campus since I was a student here in the sixties."

"Anyone in particular?"

"Oh," he laughed, "you know, the usual."

"Lady in white, woman in black, sick child, etc.?" Taryn asked.

"You've got it."

He might have been forty years older than her, but he took the stairs much faster. He was at the top before she'd made it to the first landing.

"I met Rosa yesterday," Taryn said when they'd reached the first floor.

"Oh yeah?" He paused, looked in on the auditorium, and then started walking down the hallway. Taryn guessed he was finished with the building. He certainly seemed to be a hurry to get out of there. "I've known her most of her life."

"Was she a student here?"

"Too young," he replied. "By the time she come along, we'd done away with the younger grades."

Taryn counted back quickly and realized that the academy would've closed about the time Rosa was old enough to enter it, if she was figuring her age correctly.

"Did you go here?"

"Since I was twelve," he answered.

Now Clark stopped in the middle of the hall, looked around at the walls, and smiled proudly as though they were still the hallowed walls of his youth. "Best years of my life."

"You love it here."

He nodded, his chest swelling with pride. "Best place in the world. My wife died a few years ago and she was buried with her family up in Menifee County. Family plot and it was already paid for. She asked for two stones. One, where she is, and the other here in Hazel Hill. It says, 'My body may be resting someplace else, but my heart is in Hazel Hill.'"

"Was she from here?"

He shook his head. "No, just went to school here like the rest of us."

He began walking again but before he reached the end he stopped and glanced back at Taryn, “Haven’t figured yet where I’m gonna be buried. Be nice to be with Julia but I don’t reckon I’m ready to leave here yet.”

Damn, Taryn though, *what kind of school was this?*

She didn’t even go to her high school reunions.

EIGHT

NEW HAMPSHIRE, 2017

Shawn was coming back tomorrow. Nicki was relieved. She'd thought about traveling down that scenic highway, just to do something different, but had decided to wait for him. Things were more fun with him.

"I need to get out of this funk," Nicki sighed.

She'd been blaming her bad attitude on Taryn's death but, in truth, she'd been depressed for a while now. Wasn't it funny how life just got in the way sometimes? Lately she had been throwing pity parties for herself every chance she got. She was tired of her job, of her lack of close friends, of her financial situation (though that was improving), and of all the bad news she was constantly being exposed to every time she got on Facebook. Everything was bringing her down. She didn't know how to shake it.

I don't know where I belong, Nicki thought as she gave the foyer rug a good beating with the broom.

She'd enjoyed traveling as part of her work but the constant moving around was getting to her. She had no roots, no place to call "home." As a child, they'd moved around so often that there wasn't a single place that she referenced as being from. Someone asked her where she was from, she'd answer "Wales." To a Welsh person she might say, "Cardiff." Truthfully, though, she'd lived all over England and Wales. No place for longer than six months.

She was good at her job, loved working with historical homes, but it wasn't bringing her the joy she'd once had.

"Maybe I'm just tired of doing stuff for other people," Nicki sighed.

That might be it. She'd spent the past several years landscaping for clients; she never got to enjoy the fruits of her labor. Once she finished, it was time to move on and start the next assignment. Now Nicki stopped and looked around the property. She saw great potential there. A vegetable garden, for starters. Some shrubbery. Some fruit trees–a small apple orchard maybe? Boxes here in the front...

Realistically, they probably weren't going to be staying there for very long. When Shawn's television show wrapped, they'd most likely head back to England. Nicki didn't have the proper visa to stay there for very long. But...it wouldn't hurt to try, right? To do something fun for herself?

When she stepped back inside the house, Nicki stopped in her tracks. The sound was faint, like it might have been a memory of a dream, but she was certain she heard the muffled tinkling of music. Nicki closed her eyes and held her breath, listening as hard as she could.

The slow, mournful cry of Otis Redding reverberated throughout the house. It was soft at first, barely discernible, but the longer she stood there, the more pronounced it became. Nicki placed her hand on the doorknob to steady herself, then she closed her eyes. If she didn't move, didn't make a sound, maybe it wouldn't go away.

The song wasn't a part of her world, she knew that. It belonged to someone else's universe, maybe someone else's time. But it was definitely there.

From up above in the master bedroom, the floorboards creaked. In a rhythmic pattern they groaned in time to the music, not just one set of feet but two. Slow and measured.

Someone was dancing.

Nicki didn't even think twice.

Forgetting her pledge to remain quiet, she let the throw rug fall to the floor and took off up the stairs, two at a time. With a burst of energy she didn't know she'd possessed, she sprinted across the landing to the bedroom and flung open the door.

The room was empty. The music had stopped.

Someone had been there, though, she was sure of it. The air molecules were still disrupted, the currents still trying to rearrange themselves back to their original positions. There was a faint scent of something left behind, too. Something floral, maybe. Nicki didn't know. She didn't wear perfume.

More disappointed than scared, she leaned against the dresser and smiled. So she *did* have a ghost after all. It couldn't be bad, though, if it listened to Motown.

How luckier could she get?

But that thing that had happened to her the other day, what had that been about?

She had a lot to discuss with Shawn.

NINE

HGA administration building

HAZEL HILL, KENTUCKY 1963

Ellen Rose lingered in the doorway, her thick, plastic tray clutched tightly between her fingers. There was a line of pushy kids behind her and she was being nudged inch by inch into the noisy lunchroom. Still, she held her ground. She was afraid to take the initial steps that would take her further into the room, afraid to cross the threshold that would leave her no choice but to move forward. She was afraid, period.

She didn't know where to sit.

When she'd been assigned a "friend", a sophomore who paid her little interest and gave her a half-hearted tour around campus, she'd been told nothing about the lunchroom.

"That's where you'll eat," Julia had said with a vague wave towards the concrete stairs leading down to the basement.

That was it. No further instructions.

Ellen had never been in a lunchroom before. At her old school, the two-room building back in Magoffin County, her own mother had been the cook. They'd eaten at their desks. She'd known everyone in her school; indeed, many of them had been her own cousins and siblings.

She didn't know *anyone* here. Not only were the faces that now studied her with interest complete strangers, but they all appeared to be so much bigger, so much older. The other girls, with their full skirts and Mary Jane flats and flips, looked like grownups. Ellen still felt like a little kid–a little kid walking into the house at Thanksgiving and being told to sit at the kiddie table.

Only, Ellen didn't know where the kiddie table *was*.

"You going to stand there all day?" the girl behind her snapped. She gave Ellen another little budge forward and Ellen almost lost her balance. She tightened her grip on the tray, steadying her glass of milk.

She glanced wildly around the room, eagerly studying the faces that were looking in her direction, hoping that someone (anyone) would give her an inviting look.

Nobody did.

"Go *on*!"

She didn't look back to see the face that the male voice belonged to, but her ears and cheeks turned bright red from the command.

Move, she did, but only to the left a few inches. Now, plastered against the wall, the other kids were able to squeeze past her and file into the room. Even though it was the first day of school for everyone, she was the only one that looked nervous. Everyone else was laughing, calling out for friends, scooching over to make room for each other. They chatted animatedly as they filled one another in on their summer adventures, as the boys tugged on the girls' hair and the girls gave mock squeals in protests.

They were all friends here, everyone knew each other.

Ellen didn't know a soul.

Finally, she saw an empty round table in the far left corner.

Ellen made a beeline for it, walking quickly with her head down, hoping nobody saw her or got to the seat before she did.

Once seated, she busied herself by placing her napkin in her lap, just as her mother had taught her before she'd left, and arranging her spoon and fork on the table. Lunch consisted of a bologna sandwich, jello, and cheese slices.

It's okay, she thought to herself. *I like baloney.*

But suddenly the tears in her eyes threatened to spill over again. Sure, she like baloney–she *loved* baloney. Her mother's fried baloney. With eggs.

Oh, she was homesick! She'd cried herself to sleep the night before, stuffing her face in the pillow and keeping her sobs silent so that her roommate (a freshman from Morgan County) wouldn't hear her and think she was a baby. She'd never been away from home before, not without her family.

Sure, they'd spent the night at her grandmother's house in West Liberty and on her uncle's farm in Campton, but her parents or a least one of her siblings had always been with her.

Last night was the first time she'd ever slept alone in a bed, too. Without cold feet pushing against her bottom or a head full of someone else's hair in her face, she liked not to have fallen asleep. It was strange being alone. And yes, even though she was surrounded by people, she felt very much alone.

Ellen had just taken her first bite of sandwich when she became aware of the shadow looming over her.

A nice-looking brunette with a perfect flip stood next to a blonde with a sleek beehive. They both wore pastel dresses cinched tightly at their waists with matching belts. Ellen thought they looked like movie stars.

At first, she began to smile. *Oh good,* she thought, *someone is coming to sit with me!*

Her day was starting to look up.

But then they spoke.

"This is a senior table," the brunette snapped.

The blonde nodded in confirmation, gazing at Ellen as though she was a piece of gum on the bottom of her shoe.

"I'm sorry," Ellen whispered.

"You should be!" The brunette slammed her tray down on the table, drawing the attention of the people at the table next to them. "You can't sit here."

Ellen rose clumsily to her feet and picked up her tray. "I'm sorry," she whispered again. "I'm sorry."

There was no place else to sit. All the chairs were taken.

Not knowing what else to do, Ellen returned her tray to the kitchen. Before she handed it over, however, she grabbed her sandwich and milk glass. The sandwich she stuffed in the pocket of her printed, cotton dress.

"You okay?" the woman who took her tray asked.

Ellen nodded, trying to keep her head down. "Just a little tummy ache."

She quickly left the room before anyone could say anything.

There was a group of maple trees in the lawn next to her dormitory and she made for them now. She wasn't sure if she was allowed to be out there or not, so she slunk behind the one with the thickest trunk and tried to make herself small as she slid to the ground.

It had rained the night before, so the ground was still a little soft and moist. She knew she'd have stains on her dress, but Ellen didn't care. The feel of the dirt was familiar; it reminded her of home.

Now, she slowly removed the sandwich and began to eat. The thick, chewy meat was also familiar and when Ellen closed her eyes she could almost pretend that she was back on her farm, taking a rest from the garden.

"Happy Birthday to me, Happy Birthday to me," she sang quietly in between bites.

Today was her first full day at Hazel Hill Academy. It was also her birthday.

She was eleven years old.

TEN

NEW HAMPSHIRE, 2017

The room was darker than she'd remembered. She'd lit a fire before going to bed but now she couldn't even see the embers.

It must have gone out in the night, Nicki thought.

A harsh chill was in the air, sending goosebumps up and down her arms and legs. Nicki shivered and began to rise, to stoke the fire or at least turn up the heat.

She couldn't move.

The room was not dark because it was night, but because something was covering her. Something was pressing down upon her, flattening her to the bed, smothering her. Something dark and heavy and acrid.

Gasping, Nicki opened her mouth to shout, to call out or something, but no sound would come. Though she screamed bloody murder on the inside, barely a whisper came through her lips. She struggled to sit up, and realized she couldn't. Arms flailing, she pulled at the sheets and blanket, scratched at the mattress. She couldn't see anything above her, but it was definitely there. She was paralyzed, stuck to the bed as though she'd been tied down.

Help, Shawn, she cried frantically to herself. *Help me!*

Only Shawn wasn't there, of course. Not until tomorrow.

Time and time again she opened her mouth, tried to make a sound, and couldn't. The heaviness on her chest was suffocating. As her legs kicked and she fought, it was becoming increasingly difficult to breathe.

The stench assaulting her nose was almost worst than the pressure. It was a rotten, pungent smell–a combination of raw sewage and spoiled meat. Nicki gagged when she felt the stomach acid rising up her throat.

She was frightened, yes, but also livid. That something would assault her when she was at her most vulnerable angered her. As the rage built within her, her strength increased. At last, with one mighty thrust, she flung her upper body upwards and let out a ferocious yell. The invisible bonds that had been restraining her broke and dissipated as though they'd never been there at all. The moonlight was streaming through the room again, sending a pale beam across the bed.

She started to run across the floorboards, to fly through the door, but she stopped short of moving.

On the far side of the room, standing as stoically as a statue, was a figure. It was neither man nor woman; although it was nude, there were no genitalia. It was as smooth and generic as a Ken doll. In the moonlight its alabaster skin glistened like gemstones. As she focused in on it, however, she realized that while the figure itself was motionless, its surface was not. The veins and blood vessels under its nearly-translucent skin were crawling with the progression of a million tiny ants. Nicki watched in horror as the skin rippled, the tiny bulges traveling up and down its arms and chest in rapid secession.

It was watching out the window, its dead eyes fixated on something she couldn't see, but when she sharply inhaled it turned its hairless head and looked straight at her. Hot pain seared through her.

Nicki closed her eyes and screeched.

She was once again alone in the bedroom. The awful stench was gone, leaving behind nothing but a faint whiff of earthy fertilizer. The figure, whatever it had been, vanished. There was no sign that it had ever been there. Downstairs, she could hear the rhythmic ticking of the grandfather clock in the foyer.

Whatever had been there with her was gone. Nicki knew that she'd be okay for the rest of the night; nothing else would bother her.

She didn't care.

As soon as she thought her legs could stand, she bounced from the bed and began scampering around the room, throwing things in her duffle bag.

Screw this, she thought.

She was going to the Holiday Inn.

ELEVEN

Girls' dorm

HAZEL HILL, KENTUCKY 2014

"Hello, my queen."

Taryn paused, the charcoal pencil held in the air, and smiled down at her phone. They talked every day, usually more than once, but she was almost always glad to hear from Matt. The "almost" being that, despite his insistence of being cosmically linked to her, sometimes he called at the most inconvenient times–like when she was about to take a bite of cheesecake or when she was just about asleep.

"Hey there," Taryn replied. She looked down at her sketch of the gym and sighed. It wasn't going well anyway. She needed a break. "What's up?"

"Taking a break," Matt replied.

Matt worked for NASA. He was an aeronautical engineer who had graduated from one of the top schools in the country. He'd wanted to be an astronaut since they were kids and although he hadn't made it to space, he was always quick to point out that he hadn't been "yet." He was still working on it. Still, he'd made it far. Taryn was proud of him.

"I'm meant to be sketching this gym but it's not going well," Taryn admitted. "I don't know why. Basic lines, basic architecture. Boring, really."

"Just not into it?"

"Guess not," she answered.

Her ex-fiancé, Andrew, had died in a car crash many years ago. He'd been an architect and they'd worked together on several jobs. Sometimes, when she was feeling particularly melancholy, she remembered how they'd sit there in the grass together, sketching and listening to music. She still couldn't listen to Dave Matthews and Emmylou Harris singing "My Antonia" without thinking about him. The line about not knowing that she'd ever see him in this world again killed her.

Now she sketched on her own. Although she was a loner by nature, and an introvert, it was becoming harder and harder. Lonelier.

"Got things on your kind?" Matt asked.

Well, maybe he really could read her...

"This place is sad," Taryn replied. "Sadder than usual. I keep thinking about all the kids that used to go here. This was their place, you know? Not just one person's home but many. And their school..."

"You're talking to the wrong person about that," Matt laughed. "You and I hated our high school."

Well, that was true enough.

"I got a call from the lawyer this morning," she said at last. "The house is finished, more or less."

"You still thinking of selling?"

Taryn didn't have to be psychic to detect the note of hopefulness in his voice.

"No, I am not selling my aunt's house."

"Come on Taryn," he said patiently. "It's going to go into ruin if you don't get someone in there. All the work you've done on it will be for nothing."

Taryn thought of the big stone house up in New Hampshire, about her beautiful little aunt whom she'd loved just like a mother, and something softened inside of her. Selling it? No. She hadn't grown up there, had barely visited in the past twenty years, but it was the closest thing she thought of as a "home." She certainly didn't think of the cookie cutter subdivision house she'd lived in with her parents. There had been nothing cozy, warm, or inviting about it. And her grandmother's house, where she'd lived after her parents' death, well...that had belonged to her grandmother. It was her's...

Sarah's house was Taryn's. She known it all her life. It had spoken to her as a child. She wasn't going to let it go.

"Maybe I'll live in it," she said.

They'd had this conversation before. Matt didn't like it.

"But..."

He didn't need to finish the sentence. She knew what came next. What about *him*?

"I don't know," Taryn murmured. And she didn't. She wanted to think about Matt, wanted to think about what it meant for their relationship, but she kept putting it off. What if she made the wrong choice? Go down to Florida and live with him and share that life together or go to New Hampshire and try something on her own? Both had sacrifices, both had possible rewards.

The fear of making the wrong choice had her delaying making any choice at all.

"'You're the One I Love.'"

"Huh?" Taryn was startled enough to drop her charcoal.

"It's this song I heard in a movie the other day, or a movie trailer," Matt explained. "I reminded myself to tell you about it, because I thought you'd like it, but I kept forgetting the name. It's 'You're the One I Love.'"

"Oh," Taryn said, feeling more disappointed than she would have reckoned. "I'll have to, uh, look it up."

Matt often told her he loved her, but they'd been telling each other that in a casual, offhand way since they were eleven years old.

"I was thinking of taking some time off and coming up there."

She started to tell him that she was busy, that she had a lot to do and a short amount of time to do it in, but then she stopped herself. There was such a hopefulness in Matt's voice that she couldn't tell him no, wouldn't hurt his feelings.

"That would be nice," Taryn said at last. "I could use the company and it would be good to see you."

"I'll start looking at flights then!" Matt replied cheerfully. She was sure that he was already envisioning spreadsheets and pie charts with glee. Matt never made any decision without first analyzing it to death. She would accept the first cheap flight that she found; Matt would weigh the pros and cons of all of them.

I guess, in their own ways, they both did that. Wasn't what that she was doing to their relationship herself?

* * *

Taryn's camera, Miss Dixie, was burning hot. She'd used the heck out of her today.

"Sorry girl," Taryn apologizes as she gently placed her on the motel bureau. "Take a break."

Taryn was doing things a bit backwards today. She normally spent the first few days walking around, taking pictures and studying them before she started sketching. She was feeling out of sorts, however, and was in the mood to draw so she'd spent the afternoon doing a preliminary of the gym. Her talent was in painting, but her heart was in photographs. Sometimes she had to do whatever was calling to her, however.

"Ooooh," Taryn moaned as she flopped down on the bed. She tried not to imagine what kinds of germs and other yucky things were clinging to the slick, cheap bedspread beneath her. Best not to think about such things. Because of the amount of time she spent on the road, she refrained from watching those exposes on 20/20 and 60 Minutes–the ones that took a light to motel rooms and showed you all the nasty stuff that clung to the surfaces.

Taryn was quite happy in her ignorance.

She'd planned on going back out to eat but now she didn't feel like it. The ache that had plagued her legs all day had now turned into a sharp stabbing sensation traveling down from her hip to her toes. She could barely put weight on it.

Taryn flipped over on her side, scooted up to the headboard, and opened the drawer on the bedside table. Probably wasn't safe to stash her medication in such an obvious location but she didn't want to carry it around with her, either.

She'd been on the "hard stuff" for a couple of years now. When it had first been prescribed to her, she could get by with taking a couple of pills a month. She tried to refrain from taking them at all, because they mostly knocked her out and gave her a hangover upon awaking. As her condition progressed, however, and the pain began to take over she found that she needed them every day. She didn't take them every day, because sometimes she had to drive, but she could.

"Damn genetics," Taryn muttered as she popped one in her mouth and swished a mouthful of Ale-8 around. Now it was certain that she wouldn't be going back out. She'd order a pizza.

Something was eventually going to kill her. Her Ehlers-Danlos Syndrome, that rare connective tissue disorder that she'd never heard of until she was diagnosed with it herself, was eventually going to cause irreparable damage. She'd already lost a kidney and her appendix from ruptures. Next, it might be something that she couldn't afford to lose. Like her liver. Her intestines. The aneurysm.

The pain medication wasn't meant for her discomfort; it was meant to keep her blood pressure down so that something else didn't explode.

And to think, Taryn thought to herself, *all those years I'd just thought that I was extra talented with my bendy legs and fingers.*

Alas, her hyper-flexibility and double-jointed arms and fingers had simply been symptoms of her EDS.

It didn't take long for the little, white pill to start working. A soft, gentle warmth spread from her stomach to her extremities and Taryn closed her eyes as she began to enjoy the first few minutes of lessened pain. She'd never felt "high" from the medicine but she often felt a bit happier; decreased levels of pain were enough to relieve her and take a load off her mind.

A hazy pink strand of light from the approaching sunset somehow found its way through her thick motel-room curtains and fell upon Miss Dixie. In the flash of light, she appeared to wink at Taryn–a sign that she wanted attention.

"I know, I know," Taryn grumbled.

Feeling better enough now to at least sit up at her laptop, she removed the memory card and opened her photo editing program. She hadn't looked at any of her pictures since taking them, considered that bad luck, but it was time.

The last few shots were of the gym, just some she'd casually taken that afternoon as she was sketching. The dark brown, brick building looked as sad in the pictures as it did in real life. The floors were in shockingly good condition, the Hazel Hill logo monogrammed in the middle with what could have been fresh paint. The floor was flanked by opposing bleachers. The basketball nets still hung, and even a deflated ball rested in the corner of the room under the antique scoreboard. She'd taken a trip into the locker rooms and found a row of lockers. Someone had trashed the visitors' locker room and she'd found herself wading through piles of empty Styrofoam cups and fast food wrappers. The whole thing had smelled like burnt food, old sweat, and rotting wood.

Her pictures depicted all of this in its mistreated glory.

Taryn was starting to feel a little nauseated and almost put her computer aside for a break when, suddenly, her eyes fell upon the set she'd taken on her second day on the campus. The girls' dorm.

The tree was gone from the roof. The missing bricks were replaced, and it looked as though the whole building had been recently power washed. Broken windows in present day now gleamed, raised to welcome the sunlight and framed by frilly white curtains that blew gently in the breeze. The caution tape was missing from the back steps; the crumbling concrete stairs were intact.

A little wrought iron bench was positioned by the stairs leading down to the cafeteria. It wasn't there in present day. The honeysuckle bush that was currently trying to take over the front was still there, but was trimmed neatly back and climbing delicately up the twenty-foot dinner bell that was situated in front of the steps.

Taryn felt her heart begin to quicken, the tinges of early excitement. Although it had happened numerous times before, it never got old.

Despite what it inevitably meant for Taryn, despite the warning bells ringing in her head, she couldn't stop her stomach from doing flip flops in anticipation.

It was a message to her, a summons. Taryn straightened her back and sat up a little straighter. She now knew that she was there in Hazel Hill for a reason. Everything she saw and did from here on out mattered.

Seeing the past come alive through the lens of her camera never got old.

TWELVE

NEW HAMPSHIRE, 2017

Shawn shut the door to the last closet and then turned to face Nicki. “Okay,” he said, “the whole house has been checked.”

Nicki’d made him start from the cellar, that spooky place that she never visited on her own, and work his way all through the house.

She still wasn't completely satisfied.

"I'm telling you, Shawn," she complained as they began their descent back to the first floor, "you're not going to find anything by looking for it."

Shawn paused on the third step and glanced back at her. "Then why did you make me look?"

She shrugged. "I don't know. Just in case?"

Nonplussed, Shawn continued down the stairs and towards the kitchen, Nicki right on his heels. "So, what do you want to do?"

"I was scared Shawnie," she admitted, her voice breaking a little, to her embarrassment. "I really was."

"No kidding." Although his head was in the refrigerator, she could tell that he wasn't laughing at her.

"Maybe more frightened than I've ever been," she said.

He peeked at her over his shoulder. "Even more than at Ceredigion House?"

Ceredigion House. The old Welsh mansion where she'd not only met her future husband but her best friend as well. They'd all been hired to help restore the amazing estate to its former glory. Some of the best, and worst, times of her life had been spent there. And yes, she'd been scared there. Nicki had seen things that she still couldn't explain, still couldn't wrap her head around. But Taryn and Shawn had been with her. It was different.

"I was by myself," she said at last.

Shawn put down the hunk of cheese and jar of Mayo that he held in his hands and crossed the room to her. "I know," he said, resting his forehead on hers. "I'm sorry that I wasn't here. You come with me next time?"

She reached up and ran her fingers through his unruly black hair. "Uh huh."

They stayed like that for a few more seconds and then he moved away and returned to his sandwich. "In the meantime, what do you want to do?"

Nicki leaned against the stove and sighed. Here, in the sweet little kitchen with the few of the mountains through the windows and Shawn beside her, it felt silly to be worried. "I don't know."

"We can sell," he reminded her. "That amount the lawyer told us wasn't anything to sneeze at."

No, it wasn't. Nicki thought about that amount all the time, thought about the things it could do for them.

“When your visa comes through we could settle someplace here in the US or move back to the UK,” Shawn said. “We’d have our pick.”

She nodded. They’d be able to buy just about anything they wanted. And yet...

Through the kitchen door, Nicki could see the framed picture of Taryn and her aunt Sarah hanging on the wall. Sarah’d had them all throughout the house when she’d lived there, Taryn had told her. Though Taryn had removed most of them, said that it made her nervous to see pictures of herself, she’d kept that one. She was a little girl in it, probably no more than five years old. Her red hair was fiery red, and she was laughing at something funny her aunt was telling her. They were sitting on the front porch, snapping green beans. Nicki, too, had left it.

“Just doesn’t seem right. Taryn left it to me.”

“Taryn would want you to do what was best for you,” Shawn said quietly. “She wouldn’t want you to feel tied to a place that you didn’t like. Or want.”

But Nicki *did* like it–she was just afraid of it.

* * *

Nicki liked it when Shawn was home. He did most of the cooking. He did most of everything, in fact. Shawn had itchy feet and couldn't sit still for very long. He had to keep moving.

Nicki alternated between itching to get back to work and enjoying her time off. She didn't necessarily miss her job, but she missed having something to do–something that wasn't just cleaning house. Maybe she needed to find a hobby.

Her K-3 visa was still processing so, technically, she shouldn't have been in the United States at all. Because England participated in the Visa Waiver Program, however, she could stay there as a tourist for up to ninety days. She'd already been there that long, had taken a trip back to England twice already to reset the whole process. Checking on her visa status and participating in the Visa Journey forum had become her new part-time job. Every time someone on the site got approved, the whole forum erupted in virtual applause.

Shawn's music had changed to Canadian singer Krista Hartman's "Til the Air." Nicki wasn't sure how Shawn found some of these people, some of these singers who seemed to come from out of nowhere, but she appreciated his diversity and effort.

Krista's voice was soft and melodious. Nicki leaned back in the rocking chair and closed her eyes, letting Miss Hartman's song wash over her like a gentle blanket. She might have snoozed a little, enjoying being taken away to a gentle place where she was weightless and blissful, but suddenly Nicki felt herself stiffening.

She didn't open her eyes at first, didn't move. Though her muscles tensed, Nicki remained still.

Someone was watching her and they were very, *very* close.

The air around her seemed to shift slightly, to almost part down the middle. Nicki was left in the center of an airless vortex where breathing took great difficulty and the atmosphere was heavy and dense.

Slowly, Nicki brought her rocker to a halt and tightened her grip on the armrests. She could no longer hear a thing, not Shawn rattling around in the kitchen, not Krista lamenting about the lover who'd disappointed her, not the night sounds that she was starting to find comforting if not familiar.

There was nothing.

When the soft tuft of air blew on her ear, she knew its owner wasn't human. It was curious, possibly checking her out to see what she was all about, but it didn't belong to a person–Nicki knew that with certainty.

Or, at least, not to anyone who was alive.

She opened her eyes now and pushed herself further into her chair, as though trying to melt into the back. The sky, which had been dull lead colored just moments before, was not pitch black. The mountains that surrounded the farm, the woods, the lake at the foot of the hill–even their vehicles and the end of the sidewalk–were all gone. Instead, she could see nothing but impenetrable, gray fog.

It rolled in from the west like billows of smoke, stained dirty with thoughts and actions that reeked of shame and despair. Nicki, generally a cheerful and joyful person, felt a wave of hopelessness rotate through her just as the fog rolled closer.

The thing that had been close to her remained. She could feel it to her left. When she turned her head, however, she saw nothing but a solid black wall.

Sadness she'd not felt since the long, drive home from Taryn's funeral swept through her, replacing the hopelessness. There was nothing frightening about the black thing that watched her, nothing scary about the fog that thickened around her and threatened to cut her off from the rest of the world, but the despair coming from them was almost worse.

"What do you want?" Nicki whispered, her lips trembling. "What's your business?"

Cold tendrils broke free from the wall of blackness and licked at her feet and fingers. They felt like ice. She recoiled, surprised by the sharp spasms of pain.

"You go away right now," she snapped, suddenly feeling proprietary. This was *her* house–Taryn's house.

The air was filled with uncertainty now, as though surprised by her unexpected reaction. What was it to do?

For a moment the fog hesitated, and Nicki was afraid that it would move right through her and overtake her. And then what?

She'd be dead. She knew it.

But then it apparently changed her mind and as quickly as it had appeared, it began dissipating.

Soon, the air was clear again and she could make out the outline of mountains and trees in the background.

"What's going on?" Shawn asked, poking his head out the screen door. "I got a weird feeling."

"Something was here," Nicki told him.

She started to rise but her legs were so shaky that she didn't make it. Shawn was out the door and holding onto her before she could fall.

He sniffed once, then twice, and his nose crinkled.

"What is that?" he asked. "What's that smell? What did you see?"

"Death," Nicki answered weakly. "It was death."

THIRTEEN

Girls' dorm

HAZEL HILL, KENTUCKY 1963

Ellen sat stiffly on the bleachers, her skinny little knees knocking together. The hem in her skirt needed to be fixed and her blouse had a chocolate syrup stain on it from the ice cream social they'd had the week before. She couldn't do a thing in the world with her hair, which always seemed to be frizzy and tangled, so she'd put it up in a ponytail. Now, looking at the other girls with their bobs and flips and pixies, she felt like a little country bumpkin.

"Who's ready to go first?"

The junior girl who stood before them down on the gym floor wore the green and gold skirt and matching cheerleading sweater. Her poms lay at her feet like two little mountains. She wore clean, white shoes and her red lipstick could be seen halfway across campus. She also wore thick mascara. Ellen's mother would have called her a hussy; Ellen thought she was beautiful, like someone from a magazine.

Hazel Hill Academy had rules when it came to makeup and clothing but some of the girls pushed those rules as close to the edge as they could. Ellen wouldn't have dared. The idea of getting in trouble was too terrifying.

The girl sitting next to her, a freshman, was faintly humming "I Fall to Pieces" while she picked at the polish on her fingernails. The girls in her dorm were still talking about the plane crash that had killed her last March. Some had ripped pictures of her from magazines and taped them to their headboards. Others had posters of Ricky Nelson and Elvis. Ellen's roommate had made fun of her kitten poster.

"Come on now, I need someone to go!"

Two girls sitting in front of Ellen finally raised their hands and volunteered.

It was easy to see that they'd been practicing together, Ellen thought with nervousness. As she watched them perform a perfect routine, the jealousy that swirled through her actually made her sick to her stomach.

"Envy's a sin, Ellen," she could hear her mother and grandmother saying. She didn't care. She wanted to look like them, to sound like them.

To have a friend she could practice with.

Another two got up and did a different routine but, at the end, they both did cartwheels. Ellen gasped as their skirts lifted above their knees and threatened to show their bloomers before they righted themselves. The other girls offered them rousing applause.

"Okay now," the cheerleader in charge said as she pointed to Ellen, "you and you." She indicated the girl next to Ellen. She must have been nervous, too, because her polish was almost all gone.

"But we haven't practiced together," Ellen hissed.

"'s'okay," the other girl whispered back. "Let's just do the one they taught us."

Standing on the gym floor, in front of all those other girls, and having everyone staring at her was a lot different from rehearsing in the trees behind the library or discreetly in her room. Still, with her face burning red and her ears scorching fire, she held her head high and made sure that she projected her voice just as she'd heard the other girls.

Ellen didn't make a single mistake. She brought her hands together when she was meant to, stomped her foot in time with the other girl, and made sure that her splits at the end was straight.

Pleased with herself, Ellen grinned with accomplishment as she rose to her feet.

Nobody said a word, though some of the girls gave them a polite round of applause.

“I’m sorry,” the girl in charge said. “What grade are you in?”

“Sixth,” Ellen answered, unable to remove the smile from her face.

“You have to be at least in the eighth grade to be a cheerleader,” one of the other girls called out from the judges’ table.

“Huh?”

Ellen looked around in confusion. Nobody else had told her that. It wasn’t on the tryout posters.

“Yeah,” the head cheerleader said, shrugging her shoulders. “Sorry. Come back in two years.”

And, with that, she was dismissed.

Ellen left the gym with her head hanging low. She’d spent the past two weeks doing nothing but practicing. And she’d *been* good!

When she heard the footsteps behind her, she didn’t even stop, assumed they weren’t for her.

“Ellen!”

Upon hearing her name called, Ellen slowed down and looked behind her. It was her English teacher, Mrs.

Lykins. She liked her, even though her class was super hard and there was a lot of reading in a short amount of time.

"You did well," her teacher assured her. "I'm sure you would've made the team if you'd been older."

"I didn't know about the grade thing," Ellen sighed. She felt like she might cry.

"Well, we don't have any age requirements for the theater club if you'd like to join us there," Mrs. Lykins said brightly as she patted Ellen on the shoulder. "I'm sure you'd enjoy it."

Ellen thought about standing on a stage in front of a bunch of people, trying to memorize lines. It sounded scary but, then, wasn't that basically what cheering was like?

Besides, maybe she'd make some friends. She had to have someone to introduce to her parents and siblings when they came up for family weekend.

"What do I have to do to join?"

FOURTEEN

NEW HAMPSHIRE, 2017

Nicki gave Shawn a half-hearted swat as he peered over her shoulder.

"You sure you want to do this?"

"Go away," she commanded without looking up at him.

"Once you look at these you won't be able to see them again," he said, "at least for the first time again."

"I said scat."

"She was *my* friend too," Shawn grumbled as he stomped away, his heavy boots making the old bedroom floor shake.

Nicki looked up from the laptop and tossed her long, auburn hair back over her shoulder. Afraid she may have hurt Shawn's feelings, she motioned him back over. "Do you really want to see them?" she asked.

"Nah," he grinned. "Just giving you a hard time."

"You can stay if you want." Nicki patted the bed side her and gestured for him to sit.

Now that she thought about it, having him by her side while she went through Taryn's pictures sounded kind of nice. Maybe this *wasn't* something that she should be doing on her own...

"I think this is something you should do on your own," he said.

Damn. The man really could read her mind...

"What are you going to do?"

Shawn finished buttoning his flannel shirt and then raked his hands through his wild hair. "I'm going to take out these storm windows," he said. "We don't need them anymore."

"Okay," Nicki said, but her voice trailed off. The pictures had all finished uploading and were starting to appear on her screen.

Shawn, realizing that his wife would be lost in her own little world for a while, shrugged and sailed out the door. Nicki heard it close lightly behind him, but she didn't glance up.

Taryn would've already seen these, of course, Nicki knew. Taryn would've taken the pictures, uploaded them herself, and spent time editing them before she even started painting and sketching. She hadn't opened Taryn's own laptop, however. Felt it too intrusive. She already felt a little weird every time she opened a cupboard or took something from a drawer–like she was invading her friend's privacy. Going through her computer felt wrong.

"Hazel Hill Academy," Nicki read the words on the old, wooden sign. "'Organized 1880. Only college preparatory in the area for years. Many of its graduates have gone on to prominence.'"

Well, sounded interesting anyway.

As Nicki began flipping through the images, she couldn't help but smile. Taryn would've loved the dilapidated buildings, the comely mountains that surrounded the former boarding school, the wild flowers poking up through the sidewalks and parking lot. Where other people would've seen decay and ruin, Taryn would've seen possibility and beauty. She'd loved history–enjoyed living in the past much more than she'd liked the present. It was one of the things that she and Nicki had bonded over.

With each passing photo, Nicki's smile grew bigger and bigger. A cracked window here, a purple iris there, a torn basketball net, crumbling red bricks, vines growing through a chain link fence–it was as though she was right there with Taryn, seeing these things with her at the same time. Or like she was borrowing Taryn's eyes.

Nicki wasn't sure that she'd ever felt closer to someone.

"These are great," Nicki murmured. And they were. They deserved to be printed off and hung up someplace. Sold. A whole photo book made for urban explorers. Taryn was a talented photographer. Nicki knew that her pictures shouldn't be locked away on a memory card.

But Taryn was gone, and Nicki didn't feel right making those decisions for her.

She'd been holding her breath a bit, partly afraid of what she might come across, but Nicki was relieved to find that the images were all ordinary. Good, of course, but not extraordinary in subject matter. Not like they could've been. Not like Taryn's sometimes were.

She wasn't sure how long she'd been up there, an hour at least, when there was a soft rap on the door.

Nicki looked up and felt her neck crack. She'd stiffened with her head bent forward for so long.

"Yes?"

"Need a snack?" Shawn called.

He came in bearing a plate full of cheese and crackers and fruit. A steaming mug of European hot cocoa, what Nicki called "chocolate mud" balanced in the crook of his arm.

"Thought you could use some calories," he added as he placed the plate on the bed and handed her the drink.

"How long I been at this?" she asked as she took a nibble of a cheese slice.

Shawn glanced at his phone. "A little over two hours now."

Dang, Nicki thought. *I really* did *lose track of time!*

"Finding anything?" he asked, peering over her shoulder.

"Rub my neck," Nicki commanded. He obliged.

"These are good."

She nodded. "They really are. We should call Ruby Jane and see if her art exhibit friend wants anymore."

Taryn had done a few showings at an art gallery down in Nashville. She'd been nervous at first, but the papers and rags had been all over the exhibit, raving with positive reviews. It had been good for Taryn's ego and she'd made a few bucks in the process. Taryn was always worried about money.

"Know anything about this place?"

"Just the stuff that Taryn told me on the phone," Nicki said. She continued to flip through the pictures, this time a little faster. "She liked it there. Said it was peaceful. I think she made a friend, but I can't remember her name. Or his name. She got a bit quiet there at the end. I just assumed she didn't feel well."

Shawn patted her on the shoulder. "She probably didn't."

"These are all fairly normal," Nicki told him. "I mean they're good but they're not..."

She hadn't even finished the sentence when she suddenly stopped flipping and paused on image #431.

"Well.," Shawn said. "Huh."

"Yeah," Nicki agreed. "Huh."

They both leaned forward, until their heads were touching side-by-side and just inches from the screen.

"Can you make that bigger?"

Nicki zoomed in on the thing they were both focused on.

"Huh," Shawn repeated.

"What is it?"

Taryn had taken quite a few shots of the girls' dormitory.

Nicki spoke softly. "It could've meant anything–that she liked that building the most, that she was having trouble with the sketching and needed more details, that was situated in such a position on campus that it naturally showed up in most of the shots..."

"Or that something was calling her to it," Shawn finished for her.

Or that.

It had been a cloudy, overcast day when she'd taken this picture. Everything was gloomy and gray, even the grass. The bricks, usually crimson in the sunlight, were rust-colored. Nicki didn't have Taryn's gift but, in the other shots, she could almost imagine what the building would've looked like when it was alive and full of life. Not in this one, though. It looked bleak and sad, as if nobody had cared about it for years.

Worn curtains blew through broken glass. Black holes existed where entire blocks of bricks were missing. Skeletal tree limbs poked through gaps in the roof.

And, in the basement, a pale-faced girl stared through the ground-level window, her mouth open in a silent scream.

FIFTEEN

HGA gymnasium

HAZEL HILL, KENTUCKY 1963

Ellen was free. For the past two weeks, she'd been doing the grunt work in the kitchen: washing dishes, taking out the garbage, etc. It's what they made the scholarship girls do.

It's also what they made the high school girls do. Miss Mollett, her dorm mother, had mistaken her for a freshman all this time. She'd had no idea that Ellen was only a sixth grader.

When Mrs. Lykins had finally filled her in upon witnessing Ellen lug a fifty-pound garbage bag up the stairs, her dorm mother had flushed with angry embarrassment. She was apparently rarely wrong and never apologetic.

"You'll be mopping the lunchroom floors from here on out," Mrs. Lykins told her. "It's not ideal but it's better than what you were doing."

"At least I won't smell like spoilt milk every day," Ellen had said happily.

Her new job didn't start until tomorrow, after lunch, so now she had the whole afternoon off. She'd done her homework, had picked out her clothes for the next day and pressed them, and had tidied her room.

"Well, what am I meant to do now?" Ellen asked herself. She stood in the middle of her dorm room and surveyed her surroundings. Everything was neat and tidy; she hadn't given Miss Mollett a single reason to write her up or complain about her.

Since she had hours until the dinner bell and nothing else to do, Ellen decided to take herself for a walk. She hadn't done a lot of exploring around the campus, had really only traveled between the buildings, and it felt like a good day in which to branch out.

"Just stay away from the boys' side," her roommate cautioned when Ellen met her leaving the building. "You'll get in trouble."

The boys' dorm was on the other side of campus, separated from her side by a ravine and a bridge. The only other thing over there was the music building, the barns, and a few houses for the school's employees. She had no reason to go since she didn't ride horses and wasn't taking music.

Hazel Hill Academy set high on a high overlooking the town of Hazel Hill. Ellen didn't know much about the town, she'd only passed through it on the way to school when her mother had dropped her off, but she'd heard that there wasn't much to it. It boasted a general store, a gas station, a small clothing store, and a restaurant. Most everyone had to travel to West Liberty or Morehead for shopping and stores.

Ellen did not head into town. Instead, she took the path that ran down behind the administration building. The one that went into the woods. There was a soccer field down there, and the baseball diamond, and she wanted to see them. Ellen enjoyed playing sports, had always liked baseball with her cousins.

Oh, I miss them terribly, she thought with a pang.

They'd hardly know her when she saw them again. Her mother had said that it would be summertime before she got to come home, and it wasn't even Christmas yet!

The path down the mountainside was steep and the soft pine needles beneath her shoes were slippery. She held onto the saplings as she slid down the slope, doing her best to keep her balance.

The forest around her was thick with trees and bushes and vines. A hush fell over the mountain and soothed her. Away from the laughter and chattering of the students up on the campus, she relaxed under the hushed stillness and solitude of the woods. It was almost like being back on her ridge, on her farm. She could walk for what felt like miles there, never seeing another person. Ellen enjoyed being away by herself, being alone with her thoughts.

I'll probably get in trouble for sneaking off, she thought to herself as she neared the bottom, *but I don't care.*

Then again, they probably wouldn't even miss her.

When her feet touched the last pile of yellow pine needles, the trees opened and she was standing in an open valley, a flat blanket of green grass for as far as she could see. Sports' fields took up the middle and since there was nobody else around, Ellen headed towards the familiar shape of the baseball diamond.

Her white canvas shoes grew dusty from the dirt they kicked up on the field, but she didn't care. She was just so happy to be out of the dorm, out of the smelly kitchen, and outside in the sunshine.

Ellen stood on Homeplate and begin to swing an imaginary bat. "She pulls back, she swings, and she makes contact!"

Laughing, Ellen began running the bases, her hair streaming behind her and coming loose from its ribbons. Her skirt flew around her knees, lifted in the soft breeze as she completed her homerun and inwardly cheered herself on.

"And the crowd goes wild!"

Ellen stopped in her tracks and looked around. She'd been alone, right?

The red-haired boy languidly emerged from the dugout, tossing a baseball from one hand to the other. He looked like he might be her age, maybe a year or two older, and his britches were dusty and torn. He had a nice-looking face, though, and a huge grin that spread from ear to ear.

"I didn't know anyone was here," Ellen said shyly, suddenly overcome with embarrassment. "I didn't see you."

"Waiting for friends," he said, pointing to where he'd been sitting, "but I guess they ain't comin' today."

Ellen began slowly backing off the field. After what she'd just done, she knew she couldn't stick around and look at him. She was mortified at what he'd just seen her doing–playacting like she was a child.

"Hey, don't leave!" He gave her a look of disappointment but then his face brightened as he thought of something else. "I got my bat with me. How's about we play?"

"Really?" Ellen stopped moving towards the trees and gave him a look. "You want to play ball with me?"

"Sure," he shrugged. "Why not? You can run, anyway. Can you hit?"

"I can hit," she said with a nod. "I hit real good. I never strike out."

Now looking genuinely happy, he slapped his hands together. "Well alrighty then!"

She waited while he popped back into the dugout and emerged with his bat and glove. “I’ll pitch first, okay?”

He handed Ellen the bat and she skipped happily to Homebase.

“I’m Ellen, by the way,” she called out to him as she took her place by the plate.

“Logan,” he sang out in reply.

The day had gone remarkably well for her, all in all.

SIXTEEN

NEW HAMPSHIRE, 2017

Someone was in the room with her. Nicki could feel it as soon as she awoke. The sense of not just being watched, but being studied, was overwhelming. It was daylight, she knew it because even with her head under the covers she could still see the rays of sunlight filtering through the duvet, so she shouldn't have been scared. She knew by instinct, however, that whoever watched her was not her husband.

What kind of fresh hell is this? she wondered to herself.

There was a rattling sound that she couldn't place, like metal objects clinking together, and then pressure on her side of the bed.

Nicki gasped and bit her lip so hard that a trickle of blood leaked into her mouth. Someone wasn't sitting down by her, they were getting up. How long had someone been on the bed with her? Been just inches away?

She waited, listening for them to leave, and tightly closed her eyes. Shawn was there, he must have been in the house with her. He would know if someone was trying to hurt her.

The house was silent, however. She could not hear the sounds of her husband downstairs nor the hopeful and expected sound of whoever was in her room walking away.

Well to hell with this, Nicki thought suddenly.

She wasn't going to lie there and be a victim.

Hoping to have the impact of surprise, Nicki quickly pounced from under the covers and sprang to the floor. "Ahhggh!" she cried, making herself as menacing as possible.

Nothing. The room was empty. Nobody was there.

Again.

How many times is this going to happen? Nicki shook her head in disgust. She couldn't keep living like that, couldn't keep scaring herself. Maybe she was going crazy. Maybe her grief or guilt or depression or whatever it was she had was making her hallucinate.

"Maybe I need to be heavily medicated," she grumbled to herself.

She quickly threw on a pair of yoga pants and a sweatshirt and bounded down the back staircase. Shawn was in the kitchen, frying bacon, and he looked up and smiled when she entered the room.

"I was letting you sleep in," he began, "but I was hoping that later today we could go into North Conway together. Maybe get something to eat? Watch a movie?"

She nodded as she headed to the refrigerator for a Pepsi. Nicki wasn't one much for conversation until she had some sugar and caffeine in her.

"Sounds good," she said after a long drink from the can.

"How'd you sleep?"

She pulled out a chair from the breakfast table and perched on the edge. "Awful."

"Yeah?" The sizzling of the bacon was a homey sound, a reassurance that things were back to normal, however briefly. Plus, it smelled good. She was famished. She couldn't remember if she'd eaten the day before or not; she'd been engrossed in Taryn's pictures for most of it.

"I woke up and could have sworn that there was someone in the room with me," she said. "It was empty."

"I got spooked today myself," Shawn admitted.

"Yeah?"

He nodded as he slid slices of bacon onto a plate layered with paper towels.

"Came downstairs and swore that I saw a man standing in the foyer. Just standing there, looking out the front door," he said. "He was so real that I actually called out to him. I thought someone had wandered in."

Remembering the sensation of someone getting up from her side of the bed, Nicki shuddered. "What happened?"

Shawn shrugged. "By the time I made the turn and came to the bottom step, he was gone. I searched the house and couldn't find anyone."

Nicki shook her head. "Damn."

Shawn walked over to the table and handed her a plate of scrambled eggs. "I did, however, smell the faint aroma of a smoking pipe for the next hour. And I was *not* imagining it."

Nicki took a bite of eggs and then reached for a slice of bacon that he'd placed on the table between them. "Shawn?"

"Yep?"

"Do you think Taryn brought something home with her? Something from that boarding school?"

"What do you mean?" he asked, mouth full.

"Well, we were always concerned about the stuff that happened to her on her jobs. What if, this time, it was something bad? Something that she couldn't shake off and leave behind?"

"You think there's something in the house that she brought with her from a jobsite?"

Nicki nodded. "Maybe. And if it was bad enough do you think that maybe..."

Shawn swallowed hard and then reached over and took her hand. "Nicki?"

"Yeah?"

"Taryn was sick," he said gently. "She had a rare and progressive connective tissue disorder that caused her internal organs to rupture. She had an aortic aneurysm that was inoperable. She was a ticking time bomb. It wasn't a ghost."

Nicki felt her face flush, tears fill her eyes. "I know, I just thought that..."

"You're trying to reason her death out, look for an explanation," he said, still holding onto her hand. "Unfortunately, there's not going to be one."

"Okay," she said stiffly.

She felt foolish, silly. Of course the paranormal wasn't responsible for Taryn's death. That was crazy, right?

To her surprise, Shawn got up from the table and left the room.

Well, okay then, she thought to herself, a little miffed.

When he returned, however, he was carrying a flash drive.

"I found something that might help, though," he said as he sat back down.

"I opened her laptop today," he began.

"Shawn!"

"I know, I know," he said, holding up his hands in defense. "But there are things about the house that I needed to find, some emails from her attorney. It was necessary."

Nicki leaned back in her chair and crossed her arms over her chest. He might have been Taryn's friend, too, but that didn't give him the right to go snooping through her stuff.

"She kept notes about that last job," he explained, sliding the flash drive over to Nicki. "And about living here. It's not a diary, exactly. There's some budgets and some drafts of emails, a few entries here and there about what was going on."

Nicki opened her mouth to protest, but he cut her off. "I didn't read it all, I just looked enough to get the gist. I thought you'd be the one to read it. That's why I moved everything to this."

"I couldn't read her stuff."

"You should," Shawn said, giving the flash drive another push. "Those email drafts? They're to *you*."

"Oh." That made a difference, of course.

"It might give you some answers," Shawn said, "but it might not. Don't expect too much."

She picked up the little piece of plastic and held it within her fisted hand. There were words in there, words to her. She felt downright giddy now, where she had felt dismay at the invasion of privacy.

"I think there's something else we should consider," Shawn continued.

"What's that?"

"There's something here," he said sincerely as he glanced around the kitchen. "I feel it too, and while I don't think it killed her, it might have contributed to...well, *you* know."

Nicki nodded; she knew. So did others. People who had spoken to Taryn in those last few weeks, the few who'd seen her...there were rumors. Rumors that Taryn hadn't been quite in her right mind. Of course, she'd been attacked (not by a ghost but by an actual person) in her own home and she'd had the drama of sorting out her personal life as well, but there'd been something else...Nicki remembered those conversations, recalled the evasive answers her friend had provided to the inquiries about her life. Remembered some of the things that Taryn had perhaps hinted at.

She knew her best friend, knew she wasn't crazy. She'd been physically sick, not mentally.

"I'll read the stuff on here," Nicki said at last.

"And I'm going to do some research on the property," Shawn told her.

"We'll figure this out."

He reached for her hand again and squeezed it. The bacon grease on his fingers made her smile. He always made a mess when he cooked.

"We will."

They always did.

SEVENTEEN

Tennis court and boys' dorm

HAZEL HILL, KENTUCKY 2014

Taryn's easel was anchored to the ground with ropes and tent hooks. The wind was particularly strong that day and she was worried about her canvas flying away, but Taryn was determined to work on the painting of the admin building. She'd been neglecting it, in favor of the gym and dorm, and it was high time that she focused on it.

On her iPod, she blasted Miranda Lambert and danced around to "Little Red Wagon" while she dipped her brush in linseed oil and splashed color on the canvas. Even though she hadn't been sleeping well lately, she was in a good mood.

"I think I was born in the wrong time," she told her tube of burnt ember.

In the admin building, she'd come across a yearbook from 1957 and had spent the morning rifling through it. She knew that it was glorifying a period that probably wasn't any better than her own, but the images of those girls in their poodle skirts and little sweaters and boys with their slicked back hair and sideburns had sent her into a "Bye Bye Birdie" spiral. She'd been wishing to time travel all day.

Like a lot of people, Taryn's idea of the 50's and 60's involved images of sipping on milkshakes at diners, playing Elvis on the jukebox, and going to drive-in movies in convertibles.

"Screw reality," she sighed happily when Miranda was finished. She much preferred her own fantasies about what life might have been like.

"I agree."

Taryn quickly pulled out her ear buds and turned around. Rosa stood before her, a Tupperware container in hand. She wore tight jeans, a low-cut top, and heels. Taryn thought she looked great.

"Sorry about that," Taryn apologized. "I talk to myself. A lot."

"Don't apologize to me," Rosa smiled. "I bet you get lonely up here."

"It's not so bad," Taryn said as she looked around. "It's peaceful. I was actually thinking that this was the kind of school that I might've liked."

"It was very insular," Rosa said. "They had everything they needed right here. Hardly had a reason to leave campus."

"And to travel through school with the same people for, what, seven years in some cases?"

Rosa nodded.

"They must have felt like family by the time they graduated," Taryn said. That sounded nice, too.

"We still have Homecoming for the graduates," Rosa said, "though the crowd gets smaller and smaller each year. People return to this very place every August and talk memories with each other. It lasts all weekend. For many of the students, this was the only home they knew."

"Did it have orphans then?"

"Not in the literal sense," Rosa explained, "but some of the kids were more or less abandoned here. Their parents couldn't afford to come and see them, or they moved away and left their kids here. Some rarely went home throughout the school year."

"What happened during the breaks?"

"The school closed down over the Christmas holidays. The kids who didn't have anywhere to go were divvied out amongst the staff. It was a different time," Rosa grinned. "Could you see a teacher today bringing students home with them to spend the night?"

Taryn laughed. "Probably not."

"Oh, here," Rosa handed Taryn the rectangular Tupperware container. "I made some banana bread, brownies, and chocolate chip cookies and had some left over. I thought you might like them."

"Heck yeah! I love food!"

"Good! It's nice that they won't go to waste."

Taryn had questions she wanted to ask Rosa, lots of questions actually, but she wasn't sure what the proper segue was to them. "Is this place haunted" seemed a little crass, "Did someone die here" inappropriate.

Finally, she just went with a tiny version of the truth.

"I don't mean to be weird or anything," Taryn began, "but I've had some strange feelings around the girls' dorm. Did anything happen there?"

Rosa turned around and regarded the building behind them. She cocked her head to the side, her fluffy yellow hair bouncing with the movement, and then shrugged.

"Not that I know of," she said at last. "No deaths or anything that I've ever heard tell. But you're not the first to mention that."

"Really?"

Well, that is interesting, Taryn thought.

Rosa turned back around. "There were girls, older girls, who I knew in the seventies before the school closed and they talked about the building being haunted." She laughed, revealing perfect teeth. "I just assumed they were trying to scare me."

If you want to be scared then you should look at the picture I took a few days ago, Taryn thought wryly.

"I'm probably just hearing things," she said aloud.

"I can ask Mom about it. She's been around the school forever. If anyone knows anything about it, she would."

"So what does your mom think about what's happening here?"

Rosa sighed and rubbed at her temples. "It breaks her heart. She can't hardly come up here anymore, can't even look at the dorm when she does. Too many memories. She went to school here, you know, and then stuck around here and worked. It's been a part of her whole life. She can't stand to see it in this shape. Wants to remember it as it was."

"That's understandable."

"I was brought up to believe that this was Heaven on Earth," Rosa said, "that no place else was better. The people were better here, the scenery better, the air itself better. Lots of folks believe that about Hazel Hill."

Well, it *was* a lovely place.

"When I was little, my mother was convinced that I was going to be a successful business woman, or at least marry a millionaire. She thought I'd have all kinds of money, told people at church and in town that I was going to buy the academy and fix it up. Re-open it." Rosa smiled sadly. "I guess I let her down. I'm just a librarian."

"You left and went to college?"

"Came back, though. Daddy died and she was having trouble on her own. Asked me to come back and stay with her," she replied. "Now that she's older, she won't live in an assisted living facility. Won't leave Hazel Hill. I take care of her."

So she wanted Rosa to go out and marry a millionaire or to become a successful business woman, yet she made her return to this town and kept her here? Taryn didn't think that made any sense. And now makes her feel guilty for not buying it and re-opening it?

"What about your parents?"

Taryn braced herself for the reaction she usually received. "My parents died many years ago. I lived with my grandmother until she passed away as well."

"Oh honey!" Rosa immediately went to her and engulfed her in a hug. Taryn could smell Elizabeth Arden's Red Door on her. "I'm so sorry!"

She backed away and Taryn smiled gently. "It's okay. It was a long time ago."

"Any other family?"

"Just an aunt," Taryn replied. "But, uh, she passed away a couple of years ago. She lived in New Hampshire and I hadn't seen her for a long time. She didn't seem to get along well with my mother, her sister."

"My God," Rosa cried, "you've sat back and watched your whole family die! You poor thing!"

Taryn wasn't sure if she should tell her about her fiancé, Andrew, who had died in a car crash. That just seemed excessive.

"I've lost a lot of people," she agreed.

"I bet you're tired," Rosa said, shaking her head.

Taryn thought about that for a long time after the other woman left. Alone, sitting on the ground by her easel and nibbling on homemade banana nut bread, she let Rosa's words run through her mind again. "You must be tired." That was a good way of putting it. She hadn't been particularly close to her parents but losing them had still been difficult. And her grandmother's death had been horrible. Andrew's almost unmentionable. And Sarah's...

No wonder I won't let go of Matt, Taryn thought sadly. *He's all I have left of that life before adulthood, the only reminder that I have of being a child–of being someone else.*

Yes. She was tired.

* * *

Taryn really needed to get back to the motel before the storm set in. She could see the storm clouds rolling over the mountaintops and the sky was already turning black. She'd quickly loaded up her car, packing the basked goods even before her painting supplies because food was important, but now she waited around, thinking.

The dorm was calling to her.

"Maybe for just a minute," she murmured.

As she walked towards the little staircase, she thought about the picture she'd taken there. About the small face staring forlornly out the window. It was a child's face, she could see that, but how old? It was hard to tell. Could've been anywhere from ten to seventeen. Since all she could see was a head and some hair, there was no way to determine time period.

"It means something," she repeated. She'd been saying that to herself for the past few days. "It has to mean something."

It always did.

The first few fat drops of rains splashed on her shoulder the minute she opened the door. Taryn quickly jumped inside to avoid getting wet and closed the door behind her.

God, it's so quiet in here, she said to herself. *Like a tomb.*

The thought made her shiver.

The face had appeared from the kitchen, pressed up against the one tiny window above the sink. Taryn went in there now, her flashlight already on and ready.

She'd expected it to be dark, but hadn't counted on the storm adding an extra layer of dimness. Now, with the thunder clashing outside and the rain pattering on what was left of the roof, she could barely hear her own thoughts. The black room closed in around her, cooling her skin with its dampness.

For the rest of the buildings to be so light and airy, this kitchen was a dismal place. An awful spot to spend a lot of time in.

And so small, Taryn thought. *Why such a tiny kitchen to feed so many people?*

She didn't see a thing, nothing but the remnants of a room that had once been used and was now abandoned, and was about to turn around and leave when she was unexpectedly stunned by the scent of blood.

She'd smelled blood before, had smelled her own in fact. It wasn't something that you forget. When she'd thought she'd smelled it in here before, she'd talked herself out of it. Had decided that she'd been wrong. Now she knew she wasn't. The thick, bitterly sharp aroma filled her nostrils and made her gag. There was something else, too, something primal about it. Something besides blood. A mixture of freshly mown grass and wetness. She couldn't put her finger on it; it wasn't a scent Taryn was familiar with. It was deep, however, and not altogether unpleasant.

It wasn't the smell of death or the smell of decay, it was the smell of hope.

Somewhere, off in the distance maybe, a kitten mewed. It was such a tiny sound, not distraught but curious, and she relaxed. Nothing could go terribly wrong when there were kittens around, right? She thought about trying to find it but then the scent of blood was overtaken by the cold, sweet aroma of cold milk again.

Taryn shined her flashlight around the room, the yellow light flashing off the silver surfaces like a spotlight, but she saw nothing that gave her pause.

Milk and blood, Taryn thought as she left the room. *Again. What does it mean?*

Milk and blood. Someone was trying to tell her something. But what?

EIGHTEEN

NEW HAMPSHIRE, 2017

Nicki scrolled through the last website then closed the laptop in fatigue.

“Learning anything?”

Shawn sat across from her in the living room, his own computer open on his lap.

"I don't know," she signed. "Maybe. Maybe not."

"You should take a break. You've been at it all day."

She stood and stretched, her joints cracking and popping as she moved. "You finding out anything?"

He shrugged. "Some of the house's history is interesting. The house used to be bigger, for one thing. A fire took off a whole wing."

"You said you thought that there used to be a back section," Nicki reminded him, "when we were walking around a few weeks ago."

"Yeah, you can tell that something used to be there."

"So what happened with the fire?"

"Daughter of the couple who built the house died," Shawn said. "She was twelve."

"That's sad," Nicki frowned. "And the parents?"

"Doesn't say," Shawn replied. "I'm assuming they lived through it. I've only gone through one document on Google Books, though. There are more."

"She could be our ghost," Nicki pointed out. "An angry spirit who's unsettled?"

"Does it feel like a child to you?"

"No," Nicki shook her head. "Not at all."

"To me either."

"Anything else?"

"Julian Alderman had the house built. He and his wife, Nora. They were apparently wealthy for the time."

Nicki looked around at the high ceilings, thought of the many rooms and the expansive property. "Yeah, apparently."

"How about you?"

"The boarding school was built in the late nineteenth century," Nicki told him. "I can't find a single negative thing about it. No ghost stories at all. In fact, there is a Facebook page dedicated to it and the former students and alumni, even their kids, get on there and talk about how awesome it is. Nobody ever has anything bad to say. Ever."

"Sounds like a cult," Shawn said mildly.

"You're telling me."

"So maybe we're barking up the wrong tree. Whatever is here was already here."

Nicki walked over to the window and peered into the darkness. She caught her reflection gazing back at her. Her normally thick, brown hair was looking dull, her eyes had bags under them. She hardly recognized herself.

"That doesn't explain the girl in the window."

"You're right."

She stepped away from the glass and turned back around to face her husband. "Hey Shawn, there is something else that's weird, though."

"What's that?"

"Taryn was involved in a lot of crap. You know what I mean?"

He nodded.

"Almost everything she got into wound up with a ton of publicity. I mean, if you Google her name you see a lot."

"Yeah? So?"

"I'm finding nothing about Hazel Hill," she repeated. "Nothing."

A look of understanding crossed over his face. "So if something happened while she was there..."

"Nobody knows about it?"

"Or they sure did their best to keep it hushed," he added.

The footsteps that abruptly appeared on the staircase were heavy, the kind of sound that would be made by thick work boots.

Nicki froze where she stood and looked wildly over at Shawn. In a split second he'd jumped to his feet and was heading for the door. "Stay here," he hissed, "and call the police."

Each room in the house had its own door so that the rooms could be closed off to conserve heat and air. He closed the door behind him now, shushing Nicki with his finger as he slipped out.

She could still hear the footsteps as they climbed the master staircase, then listened as they reached the landing and began making their way across the landing to the bedroom across the hall from them.

With trembling fingers, Nicki dialed 911 and waited for what seemed like forever for an operator to answer.

"There's an intruder in the house," Nicki whispered as she looked wildly around the room for something to use as a weapon. Her eyes landed on a fireplace poker and she picked it up and held it in unsteady hands. "They're upstairs."

The operator rattled off a canned response about someone being on their way and Nicki slipped the phone back into her pocket.

Shawn's movements up the stairs were light and virtually undiscernible by comparison. The contrast between his steps, and the intruders, made her shake even harder.

Who broke into a house and tried to be *heard*?

She knew her husband carried a gun. It was something that she wasn't totally on board with, and something that they didn't discuss, but tonight she was glad. She knew he had it on him, knew he'd use it only if he had to.

The fact that she hadn't heard a gunshot yet was both heartening and frightening.

Nicki noiselessly made her way to the closed door and put her ear up against the wood. With all the curtains open, she felt exposed. If anyone else was outside, they could see her in the well-lit room, but she couldn't see them. Unsure as to whether she should remain, as she'd been ordered, or to leave, Nicki balanced from one foot to the other and considered her options. Her car keys were on the table by the television. Assuming nobody was waiting for her out there, she could make it to the car.

That wouldn't work. She'd die before she left Shawn.

Going up to help him didn't seem like an option. She'd be in the way. She'd never held a gun, much less used one. With her luck it would backfire, or whatever it did, in her face.

She'd wait.

Please be okay, please be okay, she silently prayed.

No way could she lose her husband. Taryn had lost her fiancé. It had nearly killed her. Nicki couldn't lose both her husband and her best friend–it would kill her.

The house was unnaturally still. She couldn't hear a thing, not even Shawn traipsing around upstairs.

Despite her promise not to leave, she soundlessly opened the door and peeked into the foyer. Shawn had turned the light on and half the staircase was illuminated. Nobody was on it.

Gingerly, she stepped into the foyer and made her way to the bottom of the stairs and listened. Nothing.

"Shawn," she hissed. Then, a little louder, "Shawn!"

His voice echoed down at the same time that the piano began to play. The sweet, gentle music flowed through the downstairs like a lullaby. Nicki turned in surprise and faced the direction from which the music soared. The walls vibrated from the long notes as the delicate tune swelled through the first floor.

"Nicki?"

He appeared at the top of the stairs, confusion written all over his face. He'd put the gun away.

"Get down here," she hissed.

He scrambled down the stairs and joined her. Together, they locked hands and looked towards the back of the house.

"Did you find anything?" she asked, not meeting his eyes.

"Nothing," he answered flatly.

"Huh."

Somehow, now, she wasn't surprised.

"Nicki?"

"Yes?" she whispered.

"Is that a piano?"

"Yes."

"Huh."

He paused, his palm growing sweaty in her own.

"Nicki?"

"Yes?"

"We don't have a piano."

She looked over at him, saw his mouth set in a grim line.

"I know," she said, giving his fingers a squeeze. "I know."

NINETEEN

Boys' dorm

HAZEL HILL, KENTUCKY 1963

Ellen could feel Miss Mollett's eyes burning into her back as she scurried down the stairs.

"You come right back now, you here? Or take away your recreation privileges!"

“Yes ma’am,” Ellen cried without looking behind her.

Gosh that woman is about as mean as they come, Ellen thought as she dashed outside.

Was it a sin to lie? Even if it’s a small, white lie that doesn’t hurt anyone? Ellen didn’t know, though her mama would probably say “yes.” Still, Ellen was yearning for a friend and Logan was the closest she’d come. The letter was burning a hole in her skirt pocket but she smiled as she raced across the lawn, paused and looked behind her, then dipped down over the side of the hill.

She’d told her dorm mother that she’d forgotten her library book and had to go back for it. In truth, her book was stuffed up under her blouse, just in case Miss Mollett made her show it when she came back inside. Instead of the library, she headed to a grove of pine trees at the bottom of the hill. There, under the big rock, she slid her letter and grinned. Logan would come for it tonight and he’d reply. They’d been doing that for weeks now, sometimes just chatting about their days and sometimes planning to meet on the baseball diamond or else by the river where he’d bring his fishing rods for the two of them.

It was nice having a friend, nice to have someone to talk to.

Ironically, having a friend had made her so happy that other people were starting to notice. Though they weren't down and out friendly with her in her dorm now, they did notice her and speak to her. That was a change. And she no longer had to eat by herself.

Tryouts for the school play were tomorrow and she was going to audition. She'd never been in a play before but Mrs. Lykins told her that it would be fun and that everyone would get some kind of role.

Things were looking up.

She was gone and back within ten minutes. She knew that because as soon as she made it back to her dorm room, Miss Mollett was shouted down the hall to her, "You were gone for ten minutes!"

Ellen rolled her eyes as she entered her room, but she wasn't perturbed. Se happily removed her book, a Cherrie Ames novel, from up under her shirt and flopped down on her bed. She had things to look forward to, a friend to talk to, and a good book to read.

Life wasn't bad.

* * *

"I thought you were coming on Sunday."

Ellen hated the whine in her voice, hated sounding like a baby on the phone in the parlor where the other girls could hear her.

"Well honey, we were planning on it but your aunt is sick and we have to go help with the kids," her mother explained. "We'll be back in a week. I'll call you next Sunday."

Ellen only spoke to her parents once a week. They called every Friday afternoon when her classes were over. They didn't have a phone, but her mother cleaned houses on the weekend and she used Mary McNeil's phone when she was there each week. Ellen was jealous of the other girls who were able to call home whenever they wanted.

"Well, okay then," Ellen sighed.

She'd had so much to tell them–like getting the part in the school play and meeting Logan and getting an "A" on her report about ancient Rome. Worse, on Sunday afternoon when the other girls were visiting with their parents and walking around campus with them, she'd be alone. Maybe the only one without anybody.

"You take care now, okay? And your daddy says hello."

Ellen muttered a goodbye and hung up the phone.

"You finished Ellen?" Patty Henderson, a Junior, was waiting impatiently behind her. She wasn't waiting to talk to her parents–she was waiting for her nightly call from her boyfriend who lived in Index.

"Yeah," Ellen mumbled. "Sure."

Head down and feeling melancholy, she made her way back up to her room. Now what was she going to do? What was she planning on doing if they were coming?

"I guess I'll start learning my part," Ellen sighed, bringing out her playbook.

She only had eleven lines (she'd counted) in the play but they were eleven good ones and she had two costume changes. Plus, she'd been placed in charge of making the posters to hang around the school.

With new resolve, Ellen stretched out on her bed with the little booklet in hand. She'd be fine. It was sad that she hadn't seen her parents last weekend and wouldn't see them this weekend either but at least she had things to do. She'd be fine.

TWENTY

NEW HAMPSHIRE, 2017

"You're back!"

Nicki smiled as she slid into the booth. Shawn filed in across from her and gazed quizzically at the server. "You have a friend?"

"I guess so," Nicki replied. "Aside from you, she's the only one who knows me here."

"I'm Lori," their sever offered. "We met last week."

After she'd taken their drink orders and walked away, Shawn opened the laptop he'd set on the table while Nicki pulled a notebook from her purse. "Okay, you go first," he prodded.

"Taryn noted that she'd started making a list of things that she wanted to know about the house," Nicki began. "So apparently she realized that something was 'off' rather early on."

"Which she would've done anyway, because of her photos," Shawn added.

"Right. Only we haven't found any of her pictures of Sarah's house, so we don't know what she saw."

"You have the notebook that she was writing in. What does it say?"

Nicki opened it and smoothed out the first page. "She started making a list here. We have 'history of the house', 'Sarah's thoughts', and 'ghost stories and legends.'"

"So when Taryn moved into the house, it doesn't sound like she knew a lot about it."

"But she apparently thought that her aunt did, and she was trying to figure out what Sarah knew," Nicki said.

Lori returned to their table at that moment and placed their drinks down in front of them. When she saw what Nicki held, she laughed.

"I remember that," Lori said. "She was in here the day she was working on it. Well, one of the days anyway. She came in at least once a week, usually on Thursdays."

"You saw this notebook?" Nicki asked.

"Uh huh," Lori nodded. "She was researching ghost stories and stuff. She asked me about them. She was very interested in any of the stories that might exist about the house she was living in."

Nicki and Shawn looked at one another with wide eyes.

"Well, can you fill us in on any of them?" Shawn asked.

"Will I get to be on your TV show?" Lori teased him.

"I don't know," he teased back. "Maybe so!"

"Let me take your food orders and I'll be right back!"

They were so impatient for Lori to return that it seemed to take forever. When at last she came back, Shawn scooted over and made room for her. “Sit,” he ordered, and she did.

“So, spill it,” Nicki pressed. “Tell us what you know.”

“Well, she was real nervous the first time she asked me about the house,” Nicki began, “and I don’t think she was feeling very well. She was very pale, had bags under her eyes. Like she hadn’t been sleeping well.”

Understandable, Nicki thought. *It’s hard to sleep in that house.*

“She asked me if I’d heard anything about haunted houses in the area and I told her that the only stories I knew were about the house on the other side of the lake.”

“Which was where she was living,” Shawn pressed.

“Right,” Lori agreed. “So I told her some of the stories that I’d grown up hearing.”

“Which were?”

“Well, for starters there are the caves,” Lori said. “Underwater caves that are meant to hold monsters and things. I don’t know, really. I’ve heard about them but always kind of thought they were fake. And then there’s the little girl in the cellar.”

"Girl?" Shawn asked at the same time as Nicki asked, "Cellar?"

Lori leaned forward and bent her head so that the other tables couldn't hear. "There was supposedly this kid killed in a fire back, I don't know, a hundred years ago or something. Before she died, her dad supposedly had her locked up in the cellar, on this little mound in the middle of the floor. She'd sit in a chair. When I was growing up, the kids would whisper, 'She sits in the chair and stares.'"

Nicki shivered in spite of herself.

"And you told this to Taryn?" Shawn asked.

Lori shrugged. "Yeah. But she didn't seem that surprised or freaked out or anything."

"No," Nicki replied, "she probably wouldn't have. Taryn saw a lot."

"Well, like I told her, it's not necessarily the ghost stories that are so weird about the place," Lori said. "It's the bad luck."

"What do you mean?" Shawn asked.

"People have a habit of dying there," Lori explained. "Or doing really bad things. It's like the people who are associated with the house either go crazy and kill someone or else they get killed themselves. Like my grandmother, for instance. She cleaned the house back in sixties. She worked there for a few weeks and started getting sicker and sicker. Came home and had a heart attack. She was only thirty at the time with *no* history of heart problems."

"That's odd for sure," Nicki said, hoping that she could encourage Lori to share more.

"Yeah, seriously," Lori agreed. "And the homeowner, Julian Alderman? He technically died in the fire, but town gossip has always said that Ben Warwick killed him. Ben that used to work for him. The whole town knew that he set the fire, but he wasn't ever put no trial."

"Wait, so the Alderman guy died in the fire too?" Shawn asked. Lori nodded. "That wasn't in the book I read."

"Oh yeah, he died too," Lori said.

"Why did this Ben fellow kill him?" Nicki asked.

"No idea. He'd apparently been totally fine for years and then just went crazy one day," Lori shrugged. "Nobody knows why. I'm telling you, that house does it to you."

"Anything else?"

"Well, as I told your friend, plants and stuff have a hard time growing there. We never fish on the lake because it never has any fish on that side and even the animals tend to stay away from that part of the woods. There have been a few boats that have capsized and killed people when they got close to the other side of the lake, too." Lori grinned sheepishly and ducked her head. "I guess it all sounds crazy."

"No, it really doesn't," Shawn assured her.

"I mean, nothing really bad's happened there in a long time." Lori suddenly paused upon realization of what she'd said. "Well, of course, except for what happened to your friend."

"Someone tried to hurt her while she lived there," Nicki pointed out.

Lori bit her lip. "Yeah, I heard about that too. She was up there, living by herself. I was worried about her. I mean, we do have some kooks around here but still...that house. I think it does make people crazy."

The signal for their food rang out then and Lori had to excuse herself. Once she was gone, Nicki and Shawn looked at one another.

"So what do you think?" Nicki asked.

"I'm not sure," Shawn said. "It could all just be urban legends. I mean, you've seen bears there. I've heard moose and I know I've seen fish in the water."

"Yet we also know that someone came in on Taryn and that she did die there suddenly," Nicki pointed out. "Not to mention Sarah."

"Sarah was sick," Shawn said, "like Taryn. That was inevitable."

"Well, you're the researcher. Your job is to research some of the bad things that went on. Make a timeline," Nicki ordered. "Let's see when this stuff started and if there's any pattern."

"And your job is to go through that flash drive," he ordered back. "See what's on there. She made a column called 'Sarah's thoughts' and I'm sure she found something. See what Taryn learned."

"I still don't feel good about Hazel Hill," Nicki murmured. "I still think it ties into this."

Lori returned with their plates balanced on her arms. "I hope you all are hungry. They were particularly generous with the stew today."

"Hey Lori?" Shawn asked as she was setting the plates on the table. "The last time you saw Taryn, what was she like?"

Lori paused with Nicki's bowl mid-air. "Well," she began, as though trying to remember, "it was odd actually."

"How so?" Nicki asked.

"She looked, I don't know, almost happy," Lori shrugged. "Content."

"So you weren't worried when you last saw her?" Nicki was confused. Surely, by that point, Taryn would have been very ill and very afraid of whatever was going on in her house.

"I wasn't, no," Lori replied. "It's probably the best I saw her look."

After she was gone, they turned and looked at each other again.

"Well that doesn't make any sense at all," Nicki muttered.

"You're telling me, sister."

But their stew was hot and the bread was soft so, for a while at least, they forgot about Taryn and her ghosts.

TWENTY-ONE

HAZEL HILL, KENTUCKY 2014

Armed with a flashlight, Miss Dixie, and her tablet, Taryn again stood in the kitchen's doorway. Before entering, she took in a big gulp of air and gave herself a little pep talk.

"You can do this," she told herself. "You'll be fine. Milk can't hurt you."

Miss Dixie's weight around her neck was comforting. Each time she took a step, her camera pounded against her skin and rather than being uncomfortable, Taryn was glad for it. In many ways, her camera was her friend. They'd been through a lot together, had seen a lot. Taryn took her everywhere she went.

Making sure the Audacity program on her tablet was up and running and microphone plugged in, Taryn entered the small room and set to work.

First, she placed the tablet on the work island in the middle of the floor. It was mostly empty, save for a few tattered boxes and fast food containers from others who had wandered down there for exploration or mischief. Taryn pressed "record" and angled the mic so that it could pick up as much sound as possible.

Then, after ensuring that her flashlight batteries were working, she turned on her camera and began taking pictures. Starting at the door, she worked her way around the room counterclockwise. First, she'd shine the light at the wall or corner, starting from the ceiling and working her way down. Then, after getting a feel for what she was looking at, she'd take her pictures.

This time, she studied the screen after each shot.

The first six were unextraordinary.

"Nothing but dust and garbage," she muttered. She decided that she'd ignore the mold and other things growing up the wall that were probably going to make her sick.

"I really should start traveling with a mask..."

She'd made it halfway around the room and had just gotten to the one small window when something remarkable *did* happen.

Taryn could feel a shift in the air. Something ever so slightly changed until she realized that she was no longer breathing in the damp, musty air of the present. It was cleaner somehow, and cold. Very cold. The cold air filled her nose and lungs, sending chills down deep inside of her. She shined the flashlight around the room, searching for an alteration, but saw nothing.

"Hello?" she whispered.

The air remained deathly still.

Hands trembling, she lifted Miss Dixie to her face and snapped. The white light momentarily blinded her; she was still seeing stars when she gently let her camera drop back down.

The window above the sink flashed, like a wink, and then grew dark again.

Taryn gulped and looked down at her camera. She knew she'd see something, knew that this would be the moment in which things changed for her on this job. She almost didn't want to look.

As she reached down and turned her camera over, her phone began to ring. She ignored Matt's ringtone, the "Ghostbusters'" theme song, because she was already studying the LCD screen.

"Well," she breathed heavily. "Well."

The room in the picture didn't look much different than the one in which she was standing. The long metal island in the middle of the floor was still standing, what appeared to be the same appliances (or at least similar ones) lined the walls. Although silverware and bowls were stacked on the side of the sink under the window, there didn't appear to be any food containers or goods visible anywhere. The kitchen was very neat and tidy.

The main difference, the only real difference in fact, were the bars on the window.

As Taryn brought the little screen closer to her face, the air shifted again. The same scent returned, that aroma of freshly mown hay and something fresh that she couldn't put her finger on. And blood. Always the blood. Taryn sniffed at the air, trying to wrap her brain around what she was smelling, but before she could process what was going on around her, the music began.

The voice was surprisingly strong. The female vocalist could've been just about any age–she had that unearthly soprano that could place her pre-puberty to elderly. Matt's call was abruptly cut off as the song swelled and echoed, bouncing off the walls and Miss Dixie, as though searching for a surface in which to land.

The song was an old one, an ethereal lullaby that Taryn herself had known as a child in her grandmother's bed. "All the Pretty Little Horses." Her nana, Stella, had sung it to her in the late hours of the night as Taryn had snuggled deep into her arm–an expanse of skin that smelled like baby powder and alcohol.

In the blackened room, the innocuous slow-paced tune's lyrics had never felt more haunting:

Hush-a-bye, don't you cry,

Go to sleep my little baby.

When you wake, you shall have,

All the pretty little horses.

Taryn wrapped her arms around her chest and closed her eyes, every cell in her body awake and alert. The voice swelled and swelled, growing stronger and stronger with each verse until the singer reached the end. Even then, the last word seemed to linger in the air for just a moment before dissipating, leaving nothing behind but a wisp of a note.

She knew that her visitor was gone before she opened her eyes. The room was back to its present state again; the air had returned to its customary dampness and smell of rotten decay.

Sniffing, Taryn reached up and wiped the tears from her eyes. Her nose was starting to run. She wasn't frightened. If anything, she felt curious.

But she also felt very, very sad.

Something awful happened in here, she thought to herself as she gave Miss Dixie a comforting pat. *Something terrible.*

She had to find out what it was. And help if she could.

* * *

Taryn was surprised to find Clark Reynolds getting into his car as she left the building. He raised his hand and motioned her over and she obliged.

"Enjoying this weather?" he asked, motioning to the day that had suddenly turned bright and cheerful.

Taryn nodded. The scent of spring abounded; the freshness of new flower blossoms and sprigs of greenery permeated the air. The dampness of the kitchen and lunchroom continued to cling to her clothing, however, and it was hard to shake them off.

"Turned into a nice day," se remarked as she neared his car, a black Mercury with a window covered in duct tape.

Clark was carrying a ratty box which he now balanced on the hood. His hands were dusty, his pants stained with something black. Taryn thought he might have cobwebs in his gray hair.

"You been caving?" she asked.

He laughed, a thin brittle sound with a smile that didn't quite reach his eyes. "Just trying to find some things for the church," he explained as he gestured towards the box.

"We've just about cleared everything out, but people keep remembering things they want me to root around for."

"I guess most things got cleared out a long time ago," Taryn prodded. After all, the school had been empty for more than forty years.

Clark nodded. "When the academy closed, we came in and got the perishables and some of the more sentimental items. The ladies wanted their old cheerleading uniforms and pomp oms, the boys wanted their basketballs and jerseys. You know the sorts of things that people desire, the things that remind them of their youth."

Taryn smiled in encouragement.

"What we mostly have left as records. Financial records for the most part. Nothing that would be of any importance or interest to anyone else," he added quickly.

"I'm surprise to find so much furniture inside," Taryn said. "It kind of looks like everyone just got up one day and left."

Clark sighed. "We tried to donate the beds and dressers to another school in southern Kentucky, but they didn't want them. Didn't want the band uniforms either. Too 'old fashioned', they said."

"Could you sell them now? Make some money for the church?"

Taryn hated to see waste.

"If you can talk the board members into doing it then be my guest," he said in a strangled voice. "Most of them don't want to see the items go. They still cling to the idea that the old school is going to re-open."

With demolition slated to start in a few months, Taryn didn't find that likely.

"Well, I just wanted to see how you were," Clark said, slapping his hands together. "Must get back to the missus."

"Good luck getting the rest of the stuff out," Taryn told him.

"Next time I might look for some of the costumes behind the stage," he grinned. "For personal reasons. I was in the drama club. Best time of my life."

She thought about that as he pulled away, about a teenage Clark reciting lines in front of an audience, bowing to applause.

Taryn could totally see that. There was something artificial about the man, something that made her think of a thick façade.

I guess everyone has a public face, she thought as she began loading her supplies into the back of her car. *I just wonder what his real one looks like.*

She was positive that she hadn't seen it.

TWENTY-TWO

NEW HAMPSHIRE, 2017

Nicki stood in the middle of the bedroom floor and waved the bundle of sage in the air. Thick, white smoke drifted from the little green leaves and drifted up to the ceiling. She immediately covered her mouth and stifled a cough. She hadn't expected there to be so much smoke involved.

The guy at the store in North Conway had told her to make sure that she got all the corners, but Nicki wasn't taking any chances; she was going to sage the heck out of everything in the house.

Now she moved over to the wardrobe where she pulled open the maple door and waved the bundle around until her clothes were covered in a smoky film.

"Couldn't hurt," she muttered behind her hand.

Outside, she could hear a chainsaw going. Shawn was cutting down some trees that had fallen in the storm they'd had a few nights ago. Said that he was going to cut them up for fireplace wood. Nicki wasn't sure about that. Did Shawn even know how to chop wood? Or use a chainsaw?

Oh well, she figured. *He hadn't cut off a limb yet. He'd probably be fine.*

She'd done two of the spare bedrooms upstairs, and the master, but there was one more left. It was the storage room across from her. Nicki stood at the closed door now and waited.

"I hate this room," she whispered aloud. "Can't I just ignore it?"

No, she couldn't. If any room needed to be cleansed, it was this one.

Taryn hadn't liked it either, even though it had been her mother's childhood bedroom.

"It gives me the creeps," she'd told Nicki on the phone. "Even Aunt Sarah kept the door shut all the time. I could sleep in there, but I didn't. I tried, but I couldn't."

With the sage still blowing smoke in her hand, Nicki finally took a deep breath and pushed her way inside.

Taryn's mother's old bedroom was a beautiful room or, at least, it had been before either Sarah or Taryn herself had started moving boxes in there and turning it into storage. From the gorgeous mahogany four-poster bed, Nicki could see the swell of the mountains and Shawn working away outside through the window. Porcelain-faced dolls sat in a tidy row, growing cobwebs, on the handmade bedspread. In one corner of the room, a rocking horse waited patiently for its rider while, in the other, a Victorian dollhouse still contained what looked to be all its little furniture. It stood almost as tall as Nicki.

On the opposite side of the room there was a wardrobe similar to the one in the master bedroom, and it was propped open. Nicki could see frilly dresses and slips. She wondered why they were so young. After all, Taryn's mother would have lived there as a teenager.

Perhaps Sarah had brought the children's things back out, thinking that Taryn as a child would enjoy them. When she'd been younger, Taryn had spent a lot of time in the house. That had only stopped when she'd grown older and the invitations had ceased. Taryn had never understood why that happened.

There was nothing scary about the room. With a fire roaring under the intricately-carved mantel and a good dusting and polishing of the wood, it would've been downright cheery.

Nicki couldn't understand the chills that ran up and down her spine.

This room doesn't want me in here, the thought suddenly ran through her head.

Then she laughed. "Oh, Nicki. Grow up. You're acting like a kook."

With determination, Nicki marched to the farthest corner and began waving the bundle of herbs around in the air.

"Protect and cleanse this house," she chanted, kind of making it up as she went along. "Only positive energy here!"

She couldn't be completely sure, but the air seemed to ripple slightly.

Nicki quickly turned around and looked behind her. There was nothing there.

Now, feeling a somewhat less confident, she walked to the other corner. "Cleanse this house," she repeated, her voice a little more subdued.

This time, she could almost see the waves in the air as the room swelled like water from the sea.

Swallowing hard, she quickly made her way to the third.

"Protect this house, cleanse this room."

There was a cracking sound, like the floor beneath her was giving way, and Nicki yelped as she jumped in the air and nearly lost her balance. When she looked down, however, the hardwood floor was solid.

One corner left, she gulped.

She could do it.

The white smoke billowing stronger than ever, Nicki marched to the last corner and waved the bundle around before her one last time.

"Cleanse–"

Before the words were out of her mouth, the bedroom door slammed shut with a *bang*. The pictures on the wall shook in their frames and one toppled to the floor, the glass shattering into a hundred pieces.

Overhead, the lights flickered once, then twice, then went out completely.

Nicki gasped and fell back against the bed. The bedspread under her fingers felt grimy and soiled from the accumulated dust and she imagined thousands of little ants crawling up her arms, could all but feel them scurrying under her sleeves and towards her neck.

She quickly scrambled back to her feet and clutched the sage even more tightly as she looked around, trying to find her bearings.

The room was vibrating. Or, more accurately, the air around her was vibrating. As a pungent odor of decay and moldy earth began to fill the air, Nicki struggled in the darkness to see the door and find her way out.

"Shit, shit, SHIT," she cried when she ran into the wardrobe and smacked her nose against the door.

There was another presence with her, but it wasn't the ghost of Julian Alderman or his daughter who had died in the fire. It wasn't Taryn or Sarah. Whatever slithered around her and poked at her legs now with icy cold tendrils of air was not human, of that Nicki was certain. She could feel it sliding up her body, moving through her hair, and caressing her face.

"Go away!" she screeched, frantically clawing at her face and shaking her head, as though she'd just walked into a spiderweb. "Get out of here!"

And just as quickly as it had started, it stopped. The room was suddenly flooded with light again as the bulb above flickered back on. The air once again smelled dusty and closed off; the coldness and decay were gone. And, as she watched in fascinated horror, the bedroom door slowly creaked open until it came to a full stop right before it hit the wall behind it.

Nicki stood rooted to the floor. Her instinct was to fly from the room, leave the house, and go straight to Shawn. Only, she couldn't move.

Something else had entered the room.

Where there had been a putrid stench and almost tangible hatred, there was now daffodils and sweetness. Heat flooded Nicki's body and the ends of her hair lifted not with intrusive cruelty but with teasing tenderness. She felt the pressure of something touching her cheeks and, a second later, realized that it was the gentle warmth of a hand.

Then, the smoke that had continued to puff from the sage all at once blustered upwards into a curling cloud that rose from where she stood and shot into the last corner where it circled the wall and ceiling before disappearing.

Nicki wasn't sure whether to laugh or cry. She'd contacted something or someone. And they wanted her there.

TWENTY-THREE

Administration building

HAZEL HILL, KENTUCKY 1963

Logan flopped down on the ground beside her and laughed. “I’m going to make a soccer player out of you yet!”

Ellen looked over at him and stuck out her tongue. “Maybe I don’t want to be a soccer player.”

"You *should*," he shrugged. "You're good with your feet."

"I don't know..." she looked down at her scuffed shoes. "I'm getting kinda beat up."

Logan poked her arm with a stick. "You getting all prissy now that you're a big time actress?"

Ellen couldn't help but preen. She *was* doing a good job in rehearsals.

"Are you gonna come see the play?"

Logan glanced down at his legs and shrugged. The big bruise he'd had that stretched from his knee almost to his angle was now a pale yellow. He'd said that he'd fallen on the ground at recess. He fell a lot. Was always hurting something. Ellen didn't understand that, because he was very good at sports.

Logan didn't go to Hazel Hill Academy, he went to the local school. Some of the students at the academy were locals, day students, and didn't spend the night there but there was still a public school in town that carried most of the locals. She wished that he went to the academy with her, even if he meant that he left every day.

"Don't know," he said at last. "Gotta find some money."

"I could probably get you a ticket," she said. "We get two."

"What about your mom and dad?"

Ellen sighed and leaned back into the grass. There was never anyone down at the sports' fields. It was always just the two of them. She liked it that way.

"They're not back from Tennessee yet," she said. "Might not make it back in time at all."

"Weren't they supposed to come back–"

"Two weeks ago," Ellen finished, "yeah."

"That's rough."

"I know," she agreed. And she missed her mama terribly. By the time she saw her again, it would have been two months or more.

"Well, I'll come if you can get the ticket," he promised shyly.

Ellen smiled happily at her young friend. "Good! Because you're gonna love it! It's super funny."

"I guess, uh, you've made a lot of friends in the theater too," he said shyly, his face turning pink.

"A few," Ellen answered honestly. "But none as good as you!"

Truthfully, she had made some friends with a few of the freshmen and sophomores (the older students still looked down their noses at her). She still considered Logan to be her best, though.

The distant sound of the dinner bell began to echo down the side of the mountain.

"Oh!" Ellen jumped to her feet and smoothed down her britches. "I gotta get back up there! I can't be late. I'm on floor duty tonight."

Logan didn't even bother hiding his disappointment. "Well, will I see you tomorrow?"

"If it looks like I can make it, I'll leave you a note at lunch," she promised.

She felt him watching her as she scurried up the mountain path, disappearing into the trees.

* * *

"Ellen!" The voice carried down the hall and found Ellen lying on her bed. "Telephone!"

"Coming!" she cried back in reply.

Ellen ran down the hallway as fast as she could.

Wonder who it is, she thought.

She wasn't expecting a call. It was only Wednesday.

"Don't run!" came the stern bark from inside her dorm mother's room. "Ladies don't run!"

"Sorry Miss Mollett," Ellen said as she slowed down her steps while still trying to move quickly.

Miss Mollett stepped from her room and considered Ellen with distaste. "You will go back to your room and try that again, this time acting as a lady."

"But I have a telephone call and–"

"Now!"

They'll hang up, Ellen thought miserably, but she returned to her room and tried it again, this time moving quickly without breaking into a run. When she hit the stairs, however, she took off.

"Ellen," her mother said on the other end of the line. She sounded very far away. "What took you so long?"

"Sorry Mama," Ellen said. "Is everything fine?"

"Oh, everything is good," her mother replied.

Ellen felt happy. This meant that her parents were home! They'd be able to see her play for sure now.

"Are you coming to see me on Sunday?"

She had so much to tell them, really tell them now. She hadn't even spoken to them in over a week.

When her mother hesitated, however, Ellen knew that the news was not good.

"Mama?"

"Well, your aunt is still not doing well and..." her mother paused, as though searching for the words. "Well, we've decided to stay."

What?

"Huh?" Ellen asked in surprise. "What does that mean?"

"We're going to live in Tennessee for a while," her mother answered, her voice small.

Ellen felt her heart drop. "For how long? Why?"

"Until we're able to return to Kentucky," she replied. "It probably won't be any longer than next summer."

Next summer?! But that meant...

"What about Christmas?" Ellen whispered, trying not to cry.

"Oh, you can visit your cousins and your aunt and uncle in Campton," her mother said, forcing cheeriness into her voice. "They'll love to have you!"

A few minutes later, Ellen hung up the telephone feeling defeated. Her parents had moved to another state and hadn't even told her that they were doing so. They'd miss Christmas with her, her birthday, Easter...

With her head hanging low and her feet dragging the ground on the way back to her room, Miss Mollett didn't even notice her this time.

TWENTY-FOUR

NEW HAMPSHIRE, 2017

Shawn shook his head and patted his wife on the shoulder. “A séance? Really?”

“Come on Shawny,” she pleaded. “You know

people. What's the point in having a husband with a paranormal show if you don't bring in his resources every now and then?"

"Yes, Nicki, but my show is..."

"Fake?" she offered.

"Scripted reality," he corrected her.

"So fake," she grinned. "But you still know people!"

"What, exactly, do you hope to accomplish with it?"

Nicki shrugged. "See what's in the house?"

"What if you don't like what you find?" Shawn, always the pragmatist.

"I'd still like to know what I'm living with..."

He sat down across from her on the bed and took her hand in his. "Are you sure you don't just want to do this because you want to try to talk to Taryn?"

Nicki blushed. "Well..."

"There's no shame in that, honey, but you really need to try to move on," he said gently. "I'm worried about you."

"I'm trying," she insisted.

For several seconds they locked eyes, a virtual stare off, until Shawn finally exhaled loudly and looked away. “Fine, fine! I’ll make some calls.”

“Thanks sweetie!” she called after him as he left the room.

Once he was gone, she returned to her computer screen. The research on Hazel Hill Academy was moving very slowly. She’d hoped to find online information that would give her some hints as to what may have happened there but, so far, there was nothing. She hadn’t yet made it all the way through Taryn’s notes, either. So far she’d said very little about the school. Most of her notes had been about the buildings, her general thoughts and reactions to their condition.

Taryn had been a big fan of the library, for instance. Nicki couldn’t blame her. It had apparently still contained almost all its original books–some first editions going back to the late nineteenth century.

“What’s going to happen to these?” Taryn had asked one of the board members, a Clark Reynolds that she spoke of often.

“We’ll probably toss them,” he’d told her. “Nobody has the room for them.”

So Nicki hadn't blamed Taryn, either, when she'd filled her trunk.

After reading that entry, Nicki had gone to the little library downstairs and searched the shelves until she'd pulled off all the volumes that Taryn had rescued–easily identifiable by the "Hazel Hill Academy" stamps in the back.

She'd also loved the music building, an airy, open-spaced building with what she termed "killer acoustics" and old instruments hanging on the walls for decoration. (She'd have taken those, too, if she could've reached them. Darn high ceilings.)

Taryn's notes about the house were mostly about its history. So far, Nicki had learned that Julian Alderman had built the home after he married a local woman, Nora Bennington. She'd died in childbirth, as many women had done during that time.

"The house's first casualty," Nicki had said aloud when she'd read that part.

Though she wasn't quite sure that she believed in that tale just yet.

Taryn had made a note about Nora's picture, but she didn't specify what was interesting about it and Nicki hadn't come across the image yet. She'd made her own note to find it.

Their daughter, Delilah, had indeed perished in the fire. Other than the urban legends about her father locking her in the basement (*she sits in the chair and stares*) Nicki couldn't find a single piece of evidence to support that. What she did discover was that Delilah had not attended public school and that few people had seen her. Indeed, the parties and balls that had been held at the house before Delilah's birth had all come to a screeching stop after she arrived.

But then, Nora was dead, Nicki reminded herself. *Her husband probably didn't feel like celebrating after that.*

'Child Missing from Academy.'

The headline had Nicki pausing and hitting the "back" button. How had she missed that?

The article was dated 1957. It had been scanned and uploaded to a blog entitled "Mysterious Kentucky." There were, unfortunately, only a dozen or so entries.

Nicki quickly began scanning the fuzzy words, hoping for information that might send her in a new direction.

"15-year-old Daisy Wellman of Frenchburg went missing from Hazel Hill Academy on October 11. She was seen in her Home Economics class but did not show up for dinner. When she did not appear for turn in, authorities were contacted," Nicki read. "Parents are deeply concerned."

The image below showed an additional article. '*Remains of missing Academy girl found in Morgan County.*'

"A missing student from Hazel Hill Academy was discovered on November 7th. Her partially nude body was found on Grassy Creek by Herrington Ford, a farmer. Cause of death has not yet been determined."

Nicki stopped reading and looked at the picture of the bright-eyed brunette. "Ouch," she whispered, "that sucks."

'*Parents Blame School for Missing Girl's Death*' and '*School Enrollment Continues to Drop for Academy*' were the next two headlines to follow.

By the time Nicki was finished reading, she'd read between the lines and drawn some of her own conclusions. Daisy had apparently had a history of running away, which was why she'd been sent to Hazel Hill to start with. Her parents had probably hoped that a stable school environment, with rules and a schedule, would help get her on the right track. It sounded as though she'd run away from the school as well and had simply taken a ride with the wrong person. Nobody was ever charged in her death.

Well, that's sad, Nicki thought, *but it wasn't exactly the school's fault.*

She'd played hooky from school as a teenager. If a kid wanted to get out, they'd find a way.

Evidently, though, the academy had a hard time bouncing back from that bad press. And that had been in the days before good PR people.

Still, it had her wondering. Was Daisy the girl in the window? She went back and looked at Taryn's picture. The image was so blurry that it was hard to see any features clearly. It *could* have been her, she guessed, but it was just as likely that it wasn't.

Nicki sighed and closed the laptop.

"Lunchtime!" Shawn called from downstairs.

"Coming!"

Before she left the room, however, she glanced back at Taryn's notebook. On the very first page, Taryn had written something very peculiar, something else that Nicki had yet to figure out.

"Believing in ghosts got us killed."

"Believing in ghosts brought me to life."

"What did you mean?" she whispered to the air. "What were you going on about?"

She knew that there was a chance she'd never know.

* * *

The woman sitting across from Nicki didn't wear a long, flowing skirt or have hoop earrings. She wore jeans, a flannel shirt, and had her hair pulled back in a ponytail. Nicki guessed her to be around forty or fifty. She brought two men along with her, one who looked young enough to be her son and the other who, with the same dark eyes and blackish hair, could've been her brother.

"Call me April," she'd said when Nicki had invited her in.

"April lives in Boston," Shawn had explained. "We used her in an episode that's airing in the fall. She's done a lot of work like this."

April had smiled and nodded. "It's not a career, talking to dead people, but I help out where I can."

She introduced the men as "Billy" and "Jordan" but didn't go into detail about who they were to her or what they did.

She'd had strict instructions on where the coffee table should be placed, however, how the lighting should be, and who should sit where. Now that they were all gathered around, candlelight flickering and sending shadows against the wall, Nicki found herself growing nervous. For his part, even her sceptic husband appeared ill at ease. Though April smiled a lot and looked normal enough, she had an air of seriousness about her. Nicki was already sold.

"It may not work," April said softly, directing her words at Nicki. "Sometimes it doesn't."

"It's okay," Nicki told her. "I'd still like to try."

April nodded. "I understand."

She did not make them hold hands or chant. Instead, once they'd all settled and were as relaxed as they could be, April bowed her head and began to pray. "Heavenly father, please protect us, your children, from any negative entities that might want to cause us harm. Amen."

"Amen," the others echoed.

When she looked back up, she had a look of serenity that Nicki envied. April appeared to be so confident in herself, so comfortable. Nicki wondered how that felt.

"Spirits of the past, you are welcome to move among us," April began to chant, her eyes closed. "Be guided by the light of this world and visit upon us."

Nicki looked around expectantly, certain that something would suddenly pop out and jump scare them, but nothing happened.

"Is anyone here with us at this moment in time?" April asked, her voice strong and sure. "If so, please make your presence known."

Even Shawn looked around expectantly, as though waiting for Casper or one of his friends to pop through the walls.

The house was quiet.

Too quiet, Nicki thought suddenly. Even the grandfather clock had stopped ticking.

"We welcome you to join us, to be here with us," April urged. "Please, make your presence known."

A low hum began filling the room. Nicki would've put it at an E flat, if she was remembering her scales correctly. It began faintly and unobtrusively, like the drone of a running refrigerator, but it slowly grew louder and louder until there was no mistaking that it wanted to be heard.

A smile spread across April's face. "Welcome," she said. "Could you make our candles flicker?"

The flame on the black candle nearest Nicki danced obediently and then straightened again, stilled by an invisible hand.

"Thank you," April murmured.

Bill and Jordan, in unison, did the same. "Thank you."

"Do you have a name?"

The humming came to an abrupt stop and, in its place, was a groan. It was loud enough to have Nicki jumping in response and even Jordan appeared startled which, to Nicki, wasn't a good sign.

April's brow creased. "May I ask your name?"

The groan came again, this time louder and more obtrusive. It was right behind her. Whatever was making it, she could feel its hot breath on the back of her neck. "Shawn?" she whispered.

He looked over at her, his face pale. "You're okay," he whispered back. Then, looking at April, "Right?"

“We only accept positive energy and goodness here tonight,” April said firmly. “If your intentions are not true then you must vacate the premises now.”

The laughter that permeated the room was not human, that was something that they’d all agree upon later. It couldn’t have been. It was too deep, too raw, too angry.

When the thick, dark cloud smoke began creeping in through the windows and sliding under the living room door, the room filled with their sounds of surprise and fear. Nicki began to rise to her feet, but April shushed her and motioned her to sit. “Down,” she ordered. “We haven’t closed the circle.”

The blackness was so thick that it was opaque. Nicki knew that it was alive, knew that it was part of something bigger. Anger, hurt, rage, maliciousness–every raw and horrible emotion she’d ever felt rose from it like steam and hung in the air like droplets of moisture clinging to a steel bar.

She closed her eyes and shuddered, envisioning a protective coat of light and goodness covering her.

It can’t hurt me, it can’t hurt me, she chanted to herself, imagining that the others were doing the same.

“Go away,” April ordered again, “leave this house!”

Her voice was still strong, still confident, but Nicki could hear the tinge of fear in it.

The blackness grew thicker, encircling them like a snake ready to pounce.

"Is there anyone you can call?" April asked, looking at Nicki. "Someone who can help?"

Confident that April wasn't referring to a plumber or Ghostbusters, she opened her mouth to answer but before she could say Taryn's name, or even Sarah's, the smoke surprisingly disappeared. It was replaced by the sound of music. And laughter.

"Someone's dancing," Jordan spoke lightly. "That's what they're doing."

April nodded, looking visibly relaxed. "Can you speak to us?" she asked.

Nicki wasn't sure that was such a good idea, considering what happened last time.

There was no direct answer, but the candle closest to her flickered again and a light blue smoke, this one sweet-smelling and misty, rose from the flame. It hung in the air parallel with Nicki's face for a moment and then dissolved, leaving behind a warm spot.

“It’s a man,” April whispered, “I can feel it. It’s a male presence.”

“And a female too,” Bill added. “She just got here.”

April smiled serenely and nodded. “I feel her now.”

They waited expectantly while April lifted her hands into the air and held them out, palms up. When she opened her eyes, she had a dreamy look on her face. “This is for you, Nicki,” she said. “You’re very much protected.”

Nicki was overcome with the urge to cry. The idea that someone was there with her, looking out for her when there was something so god-awful nearby...

The music soon came to a stop, the laughter slipping away without so much as an echo. Once again, the sound of the grandfather clock could be heard from the foyer.

“We’re alone again,” April assured them.

When the lights were back on, April sat down on the sofa next to Nicki and held her hand. It was cold and dry. “You must be very careful here,” she said, her tone serious and authoritative. “There’s something dark.”

“An angry spirit?” Nicki asked.

April shook her head. “I don’t think so.”

“A demon?”

April laughed. "I wouldn't put it like that. Sometimes these things don't have proper names to go by, so we give them terms that make us feel as though we have a handle on them. Demons, poltergeists, devils...they're all words for things we don't understand, things that go back before the beginning of time."

"So you think there's something here that's very old?"

April nodded. "Yes, I do. We, as a culture, have forgotten about these things. We ignore them. The Indians remembered. The ancient cultures knew them. Us, however, with out flat screens and Teslas and Netflix? We think we've moved beyond those barbaric ideas that were based on superstition and fear."

"But they're still here," Nicki said.

"They're still here," the other woman agreed.

"Does it want to hurt me?"

April sighed and tucked a loose lock of black hair behind her ear. "It wants everyone to hurt. It doesn't know joy or happiness. It's nothing but pain and misery. These kinds of things, they need something to keep them grounded, something to keep them hidden. Without that, they'll come loose and wreak havoc. A bit like Pandora's box, you could say."

"What can I do?"

April smiled and squeezed Nicki's fingers. "You're lucky, in a sense. You have someone here protecting you. Protecting this house."

"Who is it?" she asked hopefully.

"I wish I could tell you what you want to hear," April sighed. "But I don't know that it's your friend. In fact, it feels like more than one person. It's a gentle spirit, someone without any fear or hostility or anger. It's their goodness keeping this in the box. Without them, well..."

Once everyone had left, Shawn sat down on the sofa next to Nicki and began rubbing her feet. "So after all that, what's the verdict?"

"Cliff Notes version?" Nicki asked.

He nodded.

"There's something really bad here but something really good is keeping it from killing us all," she offered.

Shawn grinned and patted her toes. "Sweet!"

Nicki laughed and cuddled into him. He was teasing her, but he'd been scared as well. They all had.

What had she gotten herself into with this house?

TWENTY-FIVE

HAZEL HILL, KENTUCKY 2014

Taryn clutched her camera tightly as she entered the church. She wasn't a churchgoer, wasn't particularly religious, and she was glad to have Miss Dixie with her. Churches made her nervous. For some reason, just as everything grew quiet, she always had the strongest urge to just start singing out as loudly as she could. Thankfully, she'd restrained herself so far.

"Hi honey," Rosa cried as she made her way to the back of the sanctuary to here Taryn stood. "I'm so glad you made it!"

Rosa wore a loose, blue silk dress that hugged still visible curves. Taryn thought she looked nice. In fact, as she looked around the small sanctuary, she was surprised to see that every woman in the room wore a dress. The men wore either suits or sports coats. The last time she'd been to church in Nashville, people had entered in baseball caps and jeans. It was something she was trying to adjust to; as a child, the folks in her grandmother's church had dressed up like they were going to a formal tea every Sunday. Of course, that was more then twenty years ago so...

"I hope I'm dressed okay," Taryn said nervously, glancing down at her long peasant skirt and ruffled blouse.

"You look beautiful," Rosa assured her. "Here, come sit by me."

She took Taryn by the hand and led her down the aisle to the very first pew. An older woman in her eighties was already sitting there, waiting.

"Mother, this is Taryn," Rosa said.

The woman turned and smiled. She was a tiny woman, probably not even five feet. Taryn could see that even without her having to stand. She wore a soft gray suit that almost matched her slate-colored hair.

"I'm Millie," she said in a gentle voice. Taryn took the proffered hand. It felt soft and dry in her own.

"It's nice to meet you," Taryn said.

"Mother brought green bean casserole to dinner today," Rosa told her as she slid into the pew and patted the seat next to her. "You'll love it."

Taryn's belly rumbled in response. God, she was starved. She'd been working so hard on her paintings over the past few days, she'd barely stopped to eat. Yesterday, she'd finally remembered to run into IGA in West Liberty and pick up snacks. She'd basically been living off Chips Ahoy and Doritos.

The service was blessedly short, and Taryn was happy to see that they got programs (and that the preacher actually stuck to the schedule). She stood and sang from the hymnals when it was required of her, bowed her head and prayed when necessary, and sat with a polite expression while the preacher droned on about Babylon. Inside, though, her mind was going ninety-miles-an-hour as she thought about what was going on up on the campus.

Another photo had come through to her. She'd taken several in the auditorium since she'd been there and not a one of them had shown anything out of the ordinary. Until yesterday.

Taryn wasn't sure what had called her back to the admin building, what had drawn her to the stage, but she'd gone. Then, standing in front of all those empty chairs, she'd taken a picture. It was just one. She knew in that moment that she didn't need anymore.

She'd also known, even without looking, that something would be on it. And it was.

The church ran a secondhand store for the community. For the past year or so, they'd apparently been using the auditorium for storage for the donations they took in. The whole back section was full of boxes and bags of used clothing, shoes, and household goods. It looked like a Goodwill had exploded back there.

Those items were gone.

The moth-eaten, faded velvet curtains were gone as well and were returned to their rich royal blue. No plaster falling from the ceiling, no buckled floor. It all looked as new as the day that she was now looking at...

And, thanks to the poster that hung on the door to the auditorium, Taryn thought she could figure out what that day was. She couldn't wait until the service was over so that she could ask Rosa.

The dorm and the auditorium, Taryn thought now to herself. *Something about those rooms.*

But what?

She didn't feel any animosity, didn't feel frightened. Whatever was there didn't want to hurt her. She'd been startled, yes, but not scared.

My, how things had changed. She'd gone from being skeptical, from being nervous to even be on her own, to seeking these things out.

Who knew my calling was as a ghost chaser? She smiled wryly to herself.

Her "adventures" had been well documented online. She'd once worked at a former stagecoach inn in Indiana, Griffith Tavern, and the organization that had hired her had used her experiences for their Go Fund Me (or was it Kickstarter?) publicity. Things had exploded from there. She still occasionally Googled herself and read some of the subreddits and forum posts about herself.

Many people didn't believe in what she did, thought she was a fraud. That was okay.

It was interesting, though, that so many people knew about her, discussed her, and yet...

Why did she feel so alone?

*   *   *

"Are you sure you don't need anything else to eat?" Rosa pressed.

Taryn, whose stomach was already bloated and starting to hurt, groaned in protest. "I honestly don't think I can."

Millie pushed a small plate of chocolate cake across the table. "You need to eat more," she commanded, "get some meat on those bones."

Well, how could she resist that? Taryn obediently dug in to what amounted to her third desert.

"Mother, I've seen some of her work and she's very good," Rosa said. "I'll have to show you some online."

Taryn assumed she was referring to her paintings and not her ghost hunting. But you never knew.

"Her paintings of the academy are top notch," Clark agreed as he walked up to the table.

Taryn looked up and smiled. "Hello! Nice to see you when we're not scaring each other."

"Oh?" Rose asked quizzically, looking from one to the other.

"We've startled each other on campus a few times," Taryn explained, "when he's been there to pick up some things."

"What things?" Millie asked.

"Just some things people have asked for," Clark said vaguely. He wore no expression. "You ladies enjoying your dinner?"

Taryn nodded. "It's very good," she replied.

"Sit down Clark, take a load off," Rosa offered, pointing to an empty chair.

He took a step back and shook his head. “No, no, I must get back to the missus. We’re going to the cemetery today and have to leave soon.”

He said his goodbyes after that and wandered off.

“They lost a child back in the eighties,” Rosa explained once he was out of earshot. “It’s been hard on his wife.”

“That’s sad,” Taryn said.

Millie nodded and, without looking up, said, “People take children for granted. They don’t know how lonely it can be, how much you can grieve, if you’ve lost one or the good Lord didn’t bless you with one.”

“I’m sorry,” Taryn said. “Did you lose a child?”

She immediately wanted to kick herself. As if it were any of her business!

Millie didn’t look offended, though. “Just had trouble conceiving,” she replied quietly. “It happens.”

“We have a rose garden behind the house,” Rosa said softly. “Mother used to go out there and sit every day and pray that she’d have a child. Now she goes out there every day and thanks the Lord that he gave her one. She’s always been grateful.”

Millie looked up at her daughter and smiled sadly. "You've always been my miracle, dear. Always."

Taryn felt a pang of envy. She and her mother had never been like that. Her own mother had been wrapped up in too many other things to give much thought to Taryn. She was much closer to her grandmother, and to her aunt. Matt's parents had been the same towards him, which probably helped explain their bond even more.

"I hate to change the subject," Taryn said, "but I wanted to ask you about something."

"Sure," Rosa said.

"What year did the school put on the play 'Our Town?'"

Rosa chewed on her lip as she tried to remember. "I'm not really sure. Mother?"

"That would've been 1965," Millie replied without hesitation. "Spring of '65."

"You sure?" Rosa asked.

"Positive," Millie replied. "I know because I was two months pregnant with you at the time and still having morning sickness. I didn't think I'd make it through the play."

Something flashed across Rosa's face but before Taryn could ask if everything was okay, her stomach lurched and nausea overtook her. She quickly rose to her feet. "Bathroom?" she asked in a strangled voice.

She barely made it in time. She didn't throw up this time, but sometimes the other thing was just as bad–if not worse. The pain shooting through her stomach while she sat on the toilet was almost blinding. As she sat there, hunched over and crying with her arms wrapped around her waist, Taryn rued the day that she'd ever heard of her condition. When it was this bad, when she couldn't even enjoy getting out and eating, she sometimes wished that it would just go ahead and kill her.

Twenty minutes later, she was able to leave the tiny bathroom and go back to the basement room where everyone else was eating. On her way out of the bathroom, however, she happened to notice an older man sitting along at the bottom of the stairs.

"Hello," she said politely. Then, wondering if he'd been waiting for the bathroom, "I'm sorry I took so long. I got a little sick."

He waved his hand in the air and smiled, though the smile didn't reach his eyes. "It's okay," he replied. "I just needed some air. Sometimes being around so many people makes me a little claustrophobic."

"I know what you mean," Taryn said.

She couldn't put an age on him. Seventy, perhaps? He was short, stocky, and completely bald. Liver spots dotted his hands and right cheek, but he had a kindly smile and bright eyes. She liked him sight, though they'd only exchanged a few words.

"I'm Taryn," she said but before he could reply, Rosa came around the corner.

"There you are! I was starting to worry!"

Taryn allowed herself to be dragged away but before she disappeared around the corner, she saw the old man's shoulders hunch and his face drop into his hands.

There's sadness everywhere, Taryn thought as she entered the brightly-lit room with the chattering and laughter. *You never have to look very far.*

TWENTY-SIX

NEW HAMPSHIRE, 2017

Nicki was loving Wolfeboro. She enjoyed North Conway, because of the shopping and restaurants and views of the White Mountains, but Wolfeboro was slowly winning her heart. The little lakeside town was straight out of the *Gilmore Girls*.

She and Shawn had taken to driving over there every couple of days to eat at the Asian restaurant and to walk around the lake, eating ice cream. It was peaceful, and it was good to get out and be around people sometimes. They enjoyed each other's company but sometimes it felt good to a part of something bigger.

"There's a hardware store up here and I need some nails," Shawn told her, pointing to a place on up the sidewalk. "You want to meet me at the dock?"

They'd just had supper and were on their way to get milkshakes. Stores were going to start closing soon, though, so if he needed something then he had to go.

"Sure, I'll see you there. Want me to order?"

"Peanut butter chocolate," he replied as he leaned in to give her a kiss on the cheek.

The little ice cream stand was right there on the lake. It was an order-at-the-window kind of place, which Nicki loved, and it boasted a few picnic tables where you could sit and watch the sunset.

"Back again?" The middle-aged woman who greeted her at the window offered a smile.

One thing Nicki was learning was that the longer she was there, the more familiar she became, the more people seemed to warm up to her. In the beginning she'd thought that everyone in the area was so cold, so unfriendly. Turned out that they apparently just needed time to get to know her.

"It's becoming our routine," Nicki responded with a laugh. "I'm going to gain twenty pounds this month."

"I won't put any calories in it this time," the woman grinned. "How about that?"

"Sounds great!"

"Chocolate peanut butter for the mister and strawberry for you?"

Nicki nodded happily. "You got it!"

While she waited, she turned and faced the placid water. The sky was already turning a deep pink; purple streaks cross through the ivory clouds likes someone had taken a paintbrush to them. Man, it sure was pretty there. Nicki wished she were rich so that she could buy a house right there on the waterfront and drink milkshakes every day.

"You staying here?" The woman asked when she brought out the shakes. "On vacation?"

"Living here," Nicki replied. "For a while, anyway."

"Oh, where at?"

When Nicki told her, the woman's eyes softened. "I knew your friend a bit," she said. "She used to come here and get milkshakes as well."

Nicki looked down at her straw wrapper and sighed. Knowing that Taryn had gone there too made her feel close to her friend. "Peanut butter?"

"Same as your mister," the other woman replied.

"I want to ask you something, if it's okay," Nicki said, suddenly feeling bold.

"Sure, what is it?"

"The house I'm living in, have you heard any stories about it being bad luck? About people dying there and such?"

The woman took a deep breath, looked up at the reddening sky, and then sighed. "I've heard those tales, yes, but I don't know that I believe them. The truth of it is, all places have bad periods. Take Lewisboro, for instance. For several years we were having a bad time of it. Crime was up, tourism was down. Lost a lot of businesses. But then, around three years ago or so, things started looking up again. Now we have so many tourists that our inns and hotels are filled and I've had to take on another helper."

Nicki nodded. She had a fair understanding of the tourism industry. There were periods of feast and famine. "And the crime rate?"

The woman shrugged. "Hardly hear about bad things now. I mean, I know that your friend was attacked but that was a rare thing. Not something that happens a lot. She lived alone and..."

"It was different," Nicki agreed. "There were other things going on."

"Yes," she nodded. "Otherwise, things have been calm here lately. It's a good period. I don't think it has anything to do with a house."

Nicki thanked her and started to walk away but then paused. Spinning around on her feel, she called out again. "Before this last time, when was the last 'bad' period?"

The woman, who was starting to close her stand, stopped what she was doing while she appeared to mull it over. "Oh," she said at last, "I reckon it would be back in the seventies, early eighties perhaps. But like I said, it comes and goes."

Comes and goes, Nicki thought to herself as she slid onto a bench holding both milkshakes. *Comes and goes.*

There was something to that. She just needed to put her finger on it.

*   *   *

Shawn entered the library with a grin that stretched across his face.

"You're looking peachy," Nicki said.

She was going through the bookshelves again, pulling out the ones that Taryn had rescued from Hazel Hill. She'd decided that they needed their own special row so that she could locate them more easily.

"I have good news," Shawn said.

And he really did look happy.

"Do tell!"

"They've picked me up for another season," he began happily.

"And?"

"And they want *you* to join me as co-host!"

Nicki was shocked. "Me?"

Shawn nodded and grabbed her by the shoulders. "Do you know what that means?"

"Um, no?"

"Twice the salary."

And when he told her what that salary would be, she almost fainted. "Oh my Lord, Shawn, we wouldn't know what to do with that kind of money!"

"I *know*!" he yelped, stomping his foot on the ground. "Things are looking up!"

"But..." Feeling dizzy, she inched backwards and collapsed in the overstuffed chair behind her.

"But what?"

"I've never been on TV. I don't know how to host anything."

"Aw, babe, you'll be fine," he assured her. "They just want us to talk to each other like we always do. Play off each other. Be natural."

"I don't know..."

"We'd travel all over the world," he said, his voice dripping with enthusiasm. "You should hear the places they want to send us for future episodes. Glastonbury, Sedona, Salem, New Orleans, Sarajevo..."

Now she was really getting dizzy. Traveling to exotic locations with her husband, for free! Eating at nice restaurants, not having to worry about the bills...It did all sound very good.

"But who would take care of the house?" she asked at last.

Shawn looked around at the small room they were in and sighed. "Another reason why I think we should sell."

"But I don't want to sell," Nicki protested.

And she didn't. As crazy as things had been there, she was finally starting to feel at home. All her routines, the cleaning she did every day, the plants she wanted to put in the ground, the work she wanted to do upstairs...Maybe she'd stay away from the cellar and Taryn's mother's old room, but the rest of the house would look great! And she'd even been thinking about having children lately. You know, if they could get rid of the ancient demon or whatever was living in their home...

"With all that extra money, can't we just hire someone to keep it up while we're gone?"

"Nicki," Shawn said patiently, "this isn't our house. This wasn't even Taryn's. It's not our responsibility. She'd be okay if we sold it. You can keep anything you want out of it. But this wasn't *our* dream."

And the television show wasn't hers and yet, there they were!

"It's starting to feel like it's mine, though," she whispered.

"What?"

"Nothing."

"Just think about it," Shawn pushed. "Okay?"

He looked so darn happy, so excited, that Nicki could do nothing but agree.

Marriage was much harder than she'd anticipated.

TWENTY-SEVEN

HAZEL HILL, KENTUCKY 1965

Ellen bounced off the stage with a grin. She was the only ninth grader with a leading role and she couldn't have been happier.

Take that Cindy Becker, she thought smugly. *Ha*!

Cindy was a senior and she'd been reduced from lead in the last production to assistant stage manager.

"Good job short stack!"

Johnson was a Junior and one of the dreamiest boys Ellen had ever seen. He was tall with thick blonde hair and big blue eyes and looked like he could've been on the cover of just about any magazine. Ellen had secretly liked him since the eighth grade, but he didn't know she was alive.

"Thank you," she replied with a grin.

"You may have to help me with my lines," he said, throwing her a wink.

"Oh my God!" Her roommate, Jenny, all but squealed in Ellen's ear when Johnson was out of earshot. "Did you hear that?"

Ellen squeezed her friend's hand back in happiness and began to jump up and down. "He knows who I am!"

Together, the two girls hugged and giggled all the way out the door.

"Are you going to Beta Club now?" Jenny asked.

Ellen thought long and hard about it, but then shook her head. "I'm really tired," she said. "I was up half the night trying to learn these lines. Can you tell them that I don't feel well? I think I'm just going to go lie down."

"Ha ha," Jenny snickered. "You're going to go lie down and daydream about Johnson!"

"Maybe," Ellen smiled back. "And maybe tonight he'll dream about me!"

She was still smiling when she entered the dorm and raced up the stairs. Once she landed on her floor, however, she slowed down and tried to remain as obtrusive as possible. She didn't want to get in trouble with Miss Mollett again. She'd already gained two demerits this month. One more and she'd lose ice cream social privileges.

She really was tired. So sure that she wasn't going to get a part in the play, she'd put off learning the monologue until the last minute and really had stayed up half the night before learning it.

Now, alone in her room, she stretched out under her covers and closed her eyes. In her arms she clutched her white poodle–a stuffed animal her daddy had brought her when he'd visited her back in February. He'd come without her mother that time because he'd already been in the area, or so he said. Ellen knew that wasn't true, though. Her mother had told her the truth when they'd spoken on the phone that weekend.

The stage manager for 'Our Town', Ellen thought with pleasure as she began to drift off to sleep. The whole school would get to see her shine. And Logan would come, too. She'd make sure of what.

It was the clattering of footsteps outside her door that awoke her. When she heard Miss Mollett's voice, however, she kept her eyes closed and pretended to remain asleep. Whatever that woman wanted, it couldn't be good.

She knocked on the door once but didn't give Ellen the chance to open it. A few seconds later, she entered the room with Mr. Moody, the director.

"This is one of our scholarship students," Ellen heard the dour-voiced woman say.

Under her covers, Ellen' lips tightened. There was no need to announce it to the world like that...

But then...

"Look at that," Miss Mollett spat with disgust. "Her family can't afford to pay her tuition, makes us cover her supplies, yet they'll spend money on frivolous toys for her."

Ellen's eyes stung hot with tears. Before she could announce that she was awake, her dorm mother and the director were already leaving her room.

After they were gone, Ellen let the tears fall freely as she clutched her poodle to her chest.

The little dog had cost $10 in West Liberty. It was an exorbitant amount for her family–an amount that they rarely even had to buy groceries with. When they'd moved back from Tennessee over Christmas, however, she and her daddy had been in a store and she'd seen it and wanted it to bad that she could taste it. She knew he couldn't get it for her, knew that for Christmas she'd be getting candy and hand-me-downs from her cousins.

But she thought about that dog for a month.

And then, in February, he'd brought it.

Had found some extra money, he'd claimed. They'd marked it down, put the toy on sale.

Not true, her mother later told her on the phone. He'd sold some of his own tools and had driven all the way back to West Liberty to buy that little dog for her.

It was the first time she'd ever had a new toy.

* * *

"I'm not trying to make you mad," Logan told her, "but I think you need to be careful. I know Johnson's family and I know him. He's bad news."

"He is not," Ellen pouted. "He's a nice guy."

"Look, just because he's handsome doesn't mean that he's good," Logan said. "I've known him and his brothers all my life. I'm just saying to be careful."

"Everyone likes him," Ellen protested.

"It's because they don't know him," Logan muttered under his breath.

"What?"

"Never mind," he said. "Here, let's go over your lines again."

They were sitting by the river, watching the muddy water roll past. It had rained the night before, so the Red River was swollen and high. Ellen liked it when it was like this. It somehow made it look bigger, more exotic. Like the Mighty Mississippi.

"Don't you ever want to get out?" she asked. "Go someplace else?"

"I reckon I like it here well enough," he said. "It's a good place."

"Yeah but..."

"But what?"

"Don't you want to see places like Paris and New York and Wyoming?"

The thought of being on a train, of flying on an airplane even, gave Ellen chills. Maybe she'd be a stewardess when she grew up. Wear those beautiful outfits and fly all over the world. Or maybe she'd be a newspaper reporter. Or a movie star! She changed her mind daily.

"I don't know about big cities," Logan said. "I've been to Lexington and there were just too many people for me."

"I've never been to Lexington," Ellen confessed, "but I've been to Morehead. I liked it well enough."

"I was thinking that, when I get older, I wouldn't mind settling down right here," he said.

"On the river?" Ellen teased him.

Logan laughed. "On a farm, maybe over on Pigeon Ridge. It's nice there. Lots of flat land."

"You gonna have a wife and a bunch of kids?" Ellen grinned.

To her surprise, Logan's face turned pink. "I don't know," he mumbled. "I'd like to, I guess."

"I'd better like her," Ellen said. "She'll have to get along with me first."

Logan looked like he wanted to say something but then closed his mouth and looked away.

He's acting so weird lately, Ellen thought. *I wonder what's wrong with him?*

"Well, we'd better start going over them lines or else you're not gonna know what to say on your big night," he said when he finally faced her again.

Ellen opened her play booklet and handed it to him. "Here, you read the other parts."

For the next hour, they practiced by the riverside together. It was about as peaceful of a time as Ellen had known.

TWENTY-EIGHT

CHEERLEADERS

Patty Landrum Rita Brewer Brenda Patrick Julie Morris

NEW HAMPSHIRE, 2017

Nicki had no idea how old the woman was who sat across from her at the table. She could've been in her forties or in her sixties.

"My housekeeper is timeless," Taryn had told her, and she was right.

Taryn had also confessed that her housekeeper scared the living daylights out of her and Nicki could see that, too.

"I've been waiting for you to call," Charaty told her. "Nobody can keep up this house on their own."

"Sorry," Nicki apologized. "It was a budget thing."

"I understand being poor," Charaty nodded. "It's why I work. If not for money, I'd do nothing all day long."

Nicki didn't think that was true. Charaty had barely stayed still the moment she'd sat down. The woman was a ball of energy. She was also "handsy." As soon as she'd walked through the door, she'd touched the furniture she'd passed, had straightened some books on the shelf, and had even returned Nicki's cereal bowl to the kitchen. It was kind of unnerving.

"I was hoping that you could start coming back out once a week," Nicki said.

"You come into sudden money?"

It was so funny, her bluntness, that Nicki didn't waste time on being offended. "Sort of. My husband's television series got renewed."

"Don't watch TV anymore," Charaty said. "Not since MASH is gone. Now that was a good show."

As far as Nicki knew, MASH had been off the air for a very long time.

"If you'll pay, I'll come," Charaty shrugged. "I can come on Thursdays."

"That works for me."

Though their business was technically over, Charaty did not move to get up. "And now you'll tell me why you really wanted to see me."

She detected some kind of accent there. Russian? German? Nicki couldn't tell. She liked it, though, liked that the other woman was as straightforward as she was. Nicki thought she might be damn near psychic, too.

"It's about my friend, the one who lived here?"

Charaty nodded. "I didn't expect it to be about anyone else. What would you like to know?"

There was one question, only one that really mattered to Nicki, and she'd been holding onto it for a long time. She'd considered not asking it at all, mostly because she didn't want to know the answer. But now...

Nicki cleared her throat. "At the end, before she, uh, passed away, was she sick? Was she okay? Was she..."

Charaty's stiff demeanor underwent a noticeable difference and Nicki saw her soften in an instant. "I know what you're asking," she said, "I know what you want to know."

"You do?"

Charaty nodded and smoothed back her hair. "I can tell you this much, this much that I know. She was not in more pain. She was not miserable. I knew that she was sick, because we talked, but she was not in agony. In fact, in those last few days, I had not seen her happier."

Nicki felt as though a weight had been lifted.

"Really?"

Charaty smiled gently. "Truly. I saw a change come over her in the last few weeks of her life. She appeared to be content. I assumed that she had accepted what was to come and had made peace with it."

Nicki wasn't sure about that. Taryn was a fighter. No way would she have gone softly into that good night.

"It was almost as if..."

"As if what?"

Charaty blushed, which made her look much younger. "I've been around for a long time now. Been around many young ladies. I can usually recognize it when it happens but with your friend, with Taryn, it was confusing."

"What was it?"

"If I didn't know better, I would have been convinced that she was in love, that she'd found a beau."

Nicki frowned. "But she rarely left the house."

Charaty sighed and then offered a secretive smile. "I know," she said. "But there are some things in this life that defy explanation. The older I get, the more I realize how little I know and understand about the world."

"Have you ever heard or seen anything in this house? Anything that might make you think that..."

Now that Nicki was asking, she felt foolish. Surely this no-nonsense woman sitting in front of her did not believe in ghosts.

"We don't know everything about this world. I've accepted that. If there is more to life than what we have here, and I believe that there is, then this house knows those secrets," Charaty said kindly. "Some places are special, they are doorways. There are no reasons for such things, they just exist. I have accepted that."

When she was gone, Nicki stood in the foyer and looked around.

A doorway. Was this house a doorway? Did it have a special purpose, one that nobody could understand or explain?

And if Taryn had been in love, then who was it with? She was dying and a virtual recluse, only leaving to eat at the tavern and get milkshakes.

Maybe Nicki hadn't known her at all.

*   *   *

Nicki was surprised by how happy she was to hear Matt's voice on the other end of the line. It had been months since they'd last spoken.

"How are you doing?" she cried. "I thought you'd fallen off the face of the earth!"

"I've been living, mostly," he replied. His voice was faint, as though he struggled to speak. "Working a lot. You?"

"Just keeping busy," Nicki answered.

"How's the house?"

Nicki felt a wave of guilt. The house should have been Matt's. She didn't know why that hadn't occurred to her before. It should have been his. He and Taryn had known each other since they were children; he was the closest thing she had to family. They were soulmates. Maybe not the kind that married and had children and lived happily ever after, but there were different kinds of soulmates. There was no doubt they were meant to meet.

"Hard without her," Nicki said. "I know I never saw her in it, but I feel her everywhere I go."

"So do I," Matt said sadly. "Everywhere."

"Are you still with NASA?"

"I actually took a sabbatical of sorts," Matt said. "I'm working on a research project and they're letting me telecommute."

"That sounds kind of fun," Nicki said encouragingly.

"It was either that or let me go," he explained. "It was difficult getting up in the morning."

"I understand."

"I still can't believe that we didn't know. That it was that bad and..."

"I know," Nicki agreed. "We knew she was sick, but her death was still a shock. That's what makes it so hard."

"It's almost like she got killed in an accident."

"I know!" Nicki was glad that someone else understood. "I feel the same way."

"I don't mean to be so depressing," Matt laughed at last. "I guess I was just feeling a little down and wanted to talk to someone who understood."

"I get it," Nicki assured her. "I want to ask you something, though. I was talking to Charaty, Taryn's housekeeper, today and she said something that made me think of you. Did you speak to Taryn much in those last few weeks?"

"Only once in that last month," Matt said. "And it wasn't for very long. In hindsight I just assume that she was sick. At the time, I thought she was blowing me off. That she didn't have a use for me anymore."

Nicki sighed. As close as Taryn and Matt had been, as much as they'd loved each other, communication had always been a problem for them. They assumed that they knew what the other was thinking so much that sometimes they put too *much* stock in their individual psychic abilities.

Still, if they didn't speak in those last weeks then *that* answered that question,

They spoke for a few more minutes and then Matt excused himself. He was never much for talking on the phone. Even his relationship with Taryn had been mostly through letters, emails, and texts.

Before she hung up, though, Nicki had one last thing to ask.

"The blanket," she prompted.

"What?"

"The one that Taryn had left behind?"

"Oh, I mailed it back," he said. "It should be there."

"Yes, it's here," Nicki told him. "But don't you think you should have kept it?"

"But she liked it." Matt sounded as confused as he'd probably felt the first time he'd had that conversation.

Nicki hung up feeling frustrated and a bit vindicated. When Taryn had called off that part of their relationship, the blanket had been the final straw. She'd told Nicki what had happened and Nicki had told her, in return, that Matt was probably not aware of the implications of what he'd done.

She was right. He had no clue.

Would things have worked out differently if they'd talked? *Really* talked?

"Would Taryn have wanted them to?"

TWENTY-NINE

Stairs to gym

HAZEL HILL, KENTUCKY 2014

Matt's feelings were hurt. She's been doing that a lot lately. She didn't mean to, it just seemed to keep happening.

"I was worried about you," he complained.

"I know," she sighed. "I'm sorry. I've just been so caught up in this job. There are a lot of buildings to paint and I feel like I'm spread thin. I've basically been going home and crashing every night."

"You need anything?"

Taryn rubbed more cream on her legs then stretched them out in front of her on the bed. "I'll be okay."

"We used to talk every day.," Matt said sadly.

"I know," she frowned.

But then, he hadn't been calling her either. It wasn't all on her.

"Well, so tell me more about this job."

And so she did. When she was finished, he whistled. "This one sounds...weird. I guess 'weird' is the best word for it?"

"I guess so," Taryn said. "It's not like my other ones. There isn't even a lot going on. It's been very subtle. And yet..."

"And yet you still feel like you need to do something about it," he said.

"I do."

"Maybe you don't."

"I do," she repeated stubbornly. "I wouldn't be seeing or hearing things if I wasn't meant to do something about them."

"So you know the date, right?"

He knew better than to argue with her.

"I think it's 1965. That's when they did that play, anyway."

"I can look some things up for you," he offered. "See if anything happened."

"I've actually already been down that road," Taryn said. "The only thing I found was a runaway that ended in murder, but that was in the fifties. It was too soon. I don't think it's related."

"Nothing else?"

"Not a thing."

"Anything you can send me?"

Taryn looked over at her laptop. “A couple of pictures and a sound file, but prepare yourself for that one.”

“Why?”

“Because, this time, I picked up more than a picture. For your listening entertainment, you can now sit back and enjoy the music of the dead.”

“You serious?” Matt sounded shocked.

“Yep,” Taryn told him. “I used my tablet to record.”

“Huh,” Matt said, “we should’ve been doing that all along.”

“I know, right?”

“Well, send them on and I’ll see if I can’t come up with something else.”

“Thanks.”

He was quiet for a moment before he spoke again. “Is anyone bothering you this time?”

“Nobody,” Taryn replied. “I hardly ever see anyone. I’ve run into the board president a few times, nearly scared the hell out of me, but he was just taking stuff out. Other than that, it’s been fine. Not even any lookie loos up there.”

"What was he taking out?" Matt asked. "Just out of curiosity."

"Not real sure," Taryn said. "Basketball trophies? The first time anyway. Then I think he said something about financial records."

"Seems like they should've already had all of that out."

"Ha," Taryn laughed. "You should see their library. It hasn't been touched in thirty something years."

"No kidding?"

"Nope," Taryn said. "It's like these people just closed the doors, walked away, and didn't look back."

"And yet the alumni and staff act like it's Heaven on Earth?"

"I know," Taryn sighed. "It doesn't make sense. Or maybe it does. Maybe they don't want to look at it now, don't want to see what it's become. They wanted to leave it as it was."

"I get that," Matt said. "I'm not big on change myself."

Neither was she.

*   *   *

Taryn hadn't slept a wink. Matt's words had replayed over and over in her head all night. Something he'd said, something he'd asked. It had been bugging her and it wasn't until two in the morning that she realized what it was and why.

Now, at 8:00 am, she was driving to Hazel Hill in the morning sunlight. The fog was still on the mountains, the light still soft and dreamy.

When she reached the academy, she quickly parked and then hopped out of her car.

"Now, which way?" she asked, hands on hips.

It was what Matt had asked her about Clark. It wasn't just that he'd been looking for something, it was that he hadn't wanted to talk about it at dinner. And that Rosa, the historian, had had no clue that he'd been there looking at all.

He was up to something.

"What are you looking for, Clark?"

If any of the buildings around her knew, they weren't talking.

At least, not yet...

"I realize that this never works when I want it to," Taryn began as she lifted her camera to her face, "but it would be very helpful if you'd give me a clue."

She might have been imagining it, but it felt like Miss Dixie might have grown a little warmer in her hands.

Taryn started in the east and began diligently snapping photos, pausing each time in between to study the LCD screen.

The boys' dorm, that long gray building with little character but surprising breadth for the time, came out fine.

"Nothing to see here," Taryn murmured.

The music building, the last one built on the campus, was unremarkable.

"Well, it was built in the seventies, so I didn't think I'd see anything there, but you never know..."

God, she had to stop talking to herself. That was just sad.

She tried the barns and greenhouse– even the tennis court with the jaunty little tree growing in the middle of no man's land.

"I mean, seriously," she laughed a little. "Did I really think I'd get anything from there?"

The gym and library remained equally unimpressive, which was too bad really because she would've liked to have seen the gym in full swing.

Once she turned back around and faced the girls' dorm and the administration building, Taryn paused and took a deep breath. She'd known all along that if there was anything on the campus, anything she was meant to see, it was going to be found in one of those. She'd just wanted to be sure she tried it all and left no stone unturned.

"Your turn first," she said to the admin building.

The long, narrow building actually didn't look too bad from the outside so, at first, it was hard to tell whether or not there was anything different about the picture. When she zoomed in on it, however, she saw the missing window from the second to the last classroom.

Nope, this wasn't it either.

"Last but last not least..."

The moment the shutter clicked, Taryn knew she had something. She didn't have to look at her screen, but she did anyway because she was excited.

Once again, the girls' dorm was restored to its former structurally sound self. No holes in the roof, no broken windows, and a little bench by the stairs.

Oh great, she thought to herself. *Does this mean I have to go back to the kitchen again?*

She wasn't afraid but that didn't mean that she enjoyed being down there.

Upon closer inspection, however, she saw something in her photo that she hadn't seen the first time. There were curtains in the attic window. Green gingham curtains that she was certain hadn't been there before. She would've remembered them, she was sure. All the other curtains were white; these would've stood out.

"Well, why not start there?" Taryn asked her camera.

Sure, why not? She imagined it saying in return. Miss Dixie had always been a go-with-the-flow kind of entity.

The stairs to the top were steep and Taryn was tired. She hadn't gotten much sleep the night before and she was already dragging, which was a bad sign since it wasn't yet noon. Her legs wobbled with each step and she relied on the bannister to pull herself up once she got to the last set of stairs. Because she'd been unable to eat much lately, and had barely kept down what she did eat, she was already weak.

Gonna have to go back to the doctor when I get home, she thought. She'd had a blood transfusion two months ago. She'd been severely anemic at that time and they weren't sure why. Maybe she was again.

When she reached the attic, she paused in the doorway and considered her predicament. The tree that had been thrown into the roof cut the room in half so that she couldn't see the other side. Portions of the floor had caved in, too, which concerned her. The last thing she needed was to fall through the floor and break a leg. Or worse.

There were two sets of stairs going up, however, and she could go as far as she could get on this side and then walk up the other and do the same over there.

Great, more stairs...

The room wasn't entirely empty. For starters, there was the tree, but there were also some boxes and crates. A few of them were close to the door. To be on the safe side, and to more evenly distribute her weight, Taryn got down on her hands and knees and began crawling Grabbing ahold of the first wooden crate, she gently slid it towards the door and then nudged it aside with her shoe. She did the same for the second and third. There wasn't a way for her to grab onto the box and it was situated just a few inches from one of the biggest holes. She studied the quandary and assessed the situation but eventually gave up on it. It wasn't worth it.

"Hope whatever I'm looking for wasn't in that box," she mumbled.

Back in the safety of the doorway, Taryn began opening crates. She was astounded by what she found in the first one, though she didn't think it had anything to do with what she was looking for. (Though, to be fair, she had no idea what she might be looking for.)

Packed away in that crate, gathering dust and just inches from the intruding tree branches, were at least a dozen handmade quilts. Taryn knew the difference between hand sewn and machine sewn, her grandmother was a big quilter, and these were definitely by hand. She saw log cabin patterns, Dutch girl, tree of life...

"What a pity," Taryn said with regret as she gingerly refolded them and placed them back into the crate. Seemed like someone should've wanted them.

The second crate contained nothing but doorknobs.

"Well, that's random anyway." Especially since none of the doors in the dorm were missing knobs.

The third had books. They appeared to be old readers, perhaps middle school level, and most were ruined by mildew.

"Keeping them in an attic with a hole in the roof will do that to books, you know."

Even though they were damaged, she carefully packed them back away and slid the crate inside the room. She was a big believer in leaving things if not better than you found them then at least the same.

She'd gone through all three crates and though she loved the quilts, even liked the doorknobs, she hadn't found anything that might be useful.

"On the other side," Taryn grumbled.

To get there, she went back down to the second floor, walked the length of the hallway, and then climbed the other set of stairs on the opposite side of the building. By the time she reached the top, Taryn was panting and sweat was running down her face. She'd barely even exerted herself, but her heart raced like she'd just set a record for a mile.

To her luck, there was only one crate on that side of the attic. It was pushed far into the corner of the room and she wouldn't have even seen it except just as she was deciding that there wasn't anything there to be found, a ray of sunlight had burst through the whole in the roof and shined down upon it, illuminating the crate like a spotlight.

"I'll take that as a sign, I guess," she laughed.

There weren't any holes on this side of the attic, but she wasn't going to take any chances. Once again, Taryn got down on her hands and knees and crawled to the corner. The old floorboards creaked beneath her, complaining and groaning with her every move.

"You're okay," she told them, "just hang on a little bit longer."

Once she'd pushed the crate back to the doorway, Taryn paused and took another long look at the room. There were three twin beds up there and nightstands to match.

I bet it got hot up here in the summer and cold in the winter, she thought.

But still, it must have been cool to share that space with some girlfriends.

Knowing Taryn's luck, she would've been put up there with two girls she hated.

As soon as she opened the crate, she knew she'd hit pay dirt. She wasn't sure what she was looking at, but she knew that it was something. In addition to a dirty white stuffed poodle and a playbook, there was stack of letters at least six inches high tied together with an old, faded satin ribbon.

Taryn pulled the first one free and held it in the sunlight. “Ellen Rose,” she read.

The floorboard creaked in response.

“Well Ellen, let’s see what you have to say,” Taryn said and though nothing responded, deep inside she felt that she was on the right track.

THIRTY

NEW HAMPSHIRE, 2017

Nicki paced the porch, her bare feet making soft thuds on the wood.

"Maybe you're looking at this all wrong," Shawn suggested.

"How else should I look at it?" Nicki asked. "April said that there's something dark here, something ancient. Even Charaty said that there's something here that can't be explained. I don't just think that it's a ghost, Shawn. I think it's something bad."

Shawn had been digging up a tree root the day before when, to his surprise, he'd hit something with the shovel. "Nicki, come out here and see this," he'd called out to her.

There, buried in the ground close to where the tree had once stood, was a large pile of what looked like black, shiny stones. They'd clearly been put there on purpose.

"What are they?" Nicki had asked.

"Beats the hell out of me."

She'd gone straight for the old Google and, within minutes, had an answer. Black Tourmaline.

"So what does it do?" Shawn had asked.

Nicki read aloud. "Black Tourmaline repels negativity energy and is often used in times of crisis and stress. It is a protector and good for those who are sensitive to supernatural forces."

"Huh," Shawn had read over her shoulder. "Says it's also good for vampire protection, grounding, and Crohn's Disease. Very versatile."

"So it was planted there on purpose," Nicki said. "Taryn must have done it."

"Maybe Sarah?"

"Looks newer than that."

They'd found three more piles and, all in all, four had been buried at the four corners of the yard.

"Taryn was afraid," Nicki said now. "She was scared. That's why she planted those stones."

"She was living up here by herself and weird things were happening," Shawn said. "Yes, she was afraid."

"She must have been worried, too, to have done something like that. What did she think was going on?"

"I don't know, Nicki. Have you thought more about the show?"

Nicki shrugged. "I'm still thinking."

"We need a decision soon."

She stopped pacing and looked down over the lake. Were there truly underwater caves down there? Was it haunted too? Was something wrong with the whole property? The air was so fresh and crisp, the mountains about as beautiful as any she'd seen. Why did it have to be so...scary?

"Remember the place in Wales?" Shawn asked at last.

"Yes. I recall it."

"Some places are stopover points between this world and the next. They help people pass on, like train stations. They protect both sides," Shawn said. "Perhaps this property is something like that."

"Or the opposite," Nicki added. "What if this place is something evil? What if it's a catalyst for terrible things and it needs a stabilizing force to keep it grounded?"

Shawn looked at her in surprise. "You really think that, don't you?"

She shrugged. "I don't know. I'm still thinking."

She also had another phone call to make.

* * *

"Okay," Matt said, "I've got that information you asked for."

"Were you able to find anything?"

"Yes and no," he replied. "The good news is that there were some archaeologists there back in the late seventies and they did quite a bit of research. The bad news is that I don't have anything concrete about the land directly surrounding the property."

"What do you have?"

"Well," he began, "there's definitely a lot of Native American activity. The Ossipee made their home in the area and the whole region was used as a general trade route. The

Algonquins even fought the Mohawks over it at one point, but nobody ever lived there. The nearest village or settlement, however, was fifteen miles away."

"Is that odd?" she asked.

"Considering the proximity to so many bodies of water? Yes," he said. "It's odd."

"So maybe they didn't want to settle here? Why?"

"I don't know. In fact, the only thing I did find was what they wouldn't do–like bury their dead there," Matt told her.

"'There' as in here?" Nicki asked.

"That's right. Your township? Your little hamlet? Even the Native Americans steered clear of it."

"Great," Nicki groaned. "If the Indians were afraid of it then what chance do I have? No wonder Taryn went nuts and buried stones."

"The Tourmaline?" Matt asked. "I encouraged her to do that."

Yeah, that sounded like a Matt thing to do.

"Hey, do you know the story about the lake?" Matt asked suddenly.

"About the underwater caves?"

"Well, them too, but I meant the man who murdered his whole family and then hung himself..."

"Charming," Nicki said drily. "Anything else?"

"Oh, I can give you a whole list of weird stuff that's gone on around your lake and property," Matt assured her. "People dying unexpectedly, people snapping and killing other people. What do you want to know?"

"I think I've heard enough."

"Well, if you need anything else..."

Nicki, still processing what she'd told him, remained silent, deep in her own thoughts.

"Hey Nicki?"

"Hmm?"

"I would've taken care of her," Matt said sadly. "Even if she didn't want me there as, well, you know."

"I know."

"I would've done it anyway. She was my best friend. I loved her. Still do."

Nicki felt her heart patter just a little harder. "I know, Matt."

"I hate that she died alone."

Maybe she didn't, Nicki thought to herself, but she wasn't going to say that out loud.

"I even thought, there at the end, that she'd met someone else," Matt confessed. "She seemed so different. But when I spoke to people at the funeral they talked about how she'd barely left the house at the end. I just...I don't know. I can't stop thinking about it."

"How's the research going Matt?"

He sighed. "It's going. I don't know where I want to be anymore. This doesn't feel like home but I'm certainly not returning to Tennessee. There's nothing for me there."

"I understand what you mean," Nicki said, thinking of her own situation.

"It's funny," he laughed, "but I spent so much time helping Taryn with her job and the things that went on that now that she'd gone, I kind of don't know what to do with my time. So thanks for giving me something to look up."

After she'd hung up the phone, Nicki went back out to the porch where Shawn still sat in the swing. She walked over to him and, without a word, climbed into his lap.

"What's this for?" he asked, giving her a peck on the top of her head.

"For being here," she said, "and for being you."

They stayed like that until the sun went down.

THIRTY-ONE

Wolfe County, Kentucky

HAZEL HILL, KENTUCKY 1964

Ellen spun around in front of the mirror one last time, admiring her new dress.

"You look beautiful!" Jenny squealed. "Are you excited?"

"Yes!"

And she was, too. She couldn't believe that Johnson had invited her to the drive-in. She was only thirteen years old, but he'd chosen her over all the other girls in the play. She knew that they were teeming with jealousy, the same way that her roommate probably was but was hiding it.

"Have you seen his car? It's sooo nice."

No, Ellen hadn't seen his car. He didn't live on campus but other students had seen him driving around town with his older brother in a Buick Riviera.

"So what does your mother think about you going on your first date?"

Ellen bit her lip and looked down at her shoes. "Well, I haven't exactly told her yet."

"Ellen!" Jenny looked genuinely shocked.

"She'd just worry," Ellen said flippantly. "I'll tell her when it's done and over with. Then she won't have to be so concerned about it."

Her parents had missed another weekend. It was looking as if they weren't coming this weekend either. It was almost as if they'd forgotten about her.

"What about Miss Mollett?"

That was another problem. Ellen had fixed that, however. She'd waited for a weekend when her dorm mother was away visiting her ailing mother in Morehead before she'd said "yes" to Johnson's proposition. Miss Phelps, the fill-in dorm mother who was blinder than a bat and fell asleep at six every night, wouldn't even know she was gone.

"You're so lucky," Jenny sighed and said for what had to be the hundredth time.

"Yeah," Ellen replied happily.

Logan had not been happy, of course. He'd been downright sullen about it.

"I don't like him," he'd said. There had even been what looked like panic in his eyes, but Ellen was sure she'd misunderstood. "His family is bad news."

"He's nice, Logan!"

Logan had kicked at the dirt and swore. "Just wait a year and I'll have the money and the car to take you to the drive-in," he'd promised.

But she didn't want to wait a year. And she didn't want to go to the drive-in with Logan. She wanted to go right now, with Johnson.

“Oh Ellen,” Jenny said suddenly, pointing to her watch. “It’s time!”

The two girls squealed one last time and then Ellen grabbed her purse and ran down the stairs.

It was going to be the best night ever.

*   *   *

“Jenny,” Ellen hissed in the darkness.

She carried her shoes in her hands, so as not to make any noise on the wood floors, and gently closed the door behind her.

“Jenny!”

Her roommate didn’t budge. She was as dead to the world as a log.

Ellen sighed and carefully lowered herself to her bed. Her mouth still tasted like buttery popcorn and cola, her skin still slick from sweat.

The room was dark but not so dark that she couldn’t see her legs in the moonlight. They were bare, devoid of her stockings. She wasn’t sure what had happened to them. Her dress, once so nicely washed and pressed, was wrinkled and creased. Her hair was disheveled, her lipstick gone.

She was a mess.

Without getting undressed, Ellen slid under her covers and clutched her toy poodle to her chest. She continued to replay the night's events over and over in her mind: the things she'd said, the things he'd said, the choices she'd made...

Oh, she'd have given anyone to talk to. For a brief moment she considered Mrs. Lykins but then quickly discounted that idea. She'd get in trouble for sneaking out for sure.

Logan? No, he wouldn't understand at all.

Ellen was horribly confused. She'd thought that she would feel womanly, in control of her destiny. Instead, she felt scared and cold.

I'll go to sleep and wake up and everything will be better, she promised herself as she closed her eyes.

Lord, she hoped that was true.

THIRTY-TWO

NEW HAMPSHIRE, 2017

Nicki didn't spend a lot of time down at the lake. That was more of Shawn's place. Taryn had installed a bench, but Shawn had taken it a step further and set up a little picnic table and grill so that he could sit down there with his fishing pole and eat and drink. He hadn't caught anything yet, but he enjoyed the pretense.

Today, however, Nicki decided to branch out and go for a walk. She had a lot on her mind that she needed to mull over, lots of decisions to make.

Although you could see the lake from the porch, the distance was deceiving. At a brisk pace, it still took Nicki a solid ten minutes to get there and a little longer coming back, since it was uphill. It was steep going both ways and Nicki wondered how Taryn had been able to manage it, especially with her hips and knees that frequently dislocated on their own. For someone as sick as Taryn, and for someone who was easily injured, she'd gotten around surprisingly well. Taryn had never let her condition hold her back, though she'd known how to take breaks and relax when she needed to.

Nicki slipped in the mud a few times going down, so she took to holding onto the saplings to steady herself. The whole hillside needed to be cleaned out. Maybe that was something Shawn could do.

If they stayed.

At the bottom, the metallic lake was unruffled and as slick as glass before her. It was so gray that it barely looked like water at all; it appeared to be a solid surface. She'd heard that during the summer months she'd hear the sounds of children playing at the summer camp on the other side of the lake. She was looking forward to that. Nicki enjoyed children and the sound of their laughter.

What if the house was haunted by Delilah? Nicki thought. *Would that be okay?*

She decided that yes, it would. And it would've been okay with Taryn, too. Taryn had wanted a child, had wanted a daughter. It was something that she'd spoken about with Nicki at length. She knew that, with her EDS, carrying to term would be difficult. When she learned that there was a chance she'd pass it on, she'd decided not to ever try. It didn't matter anyway. Her uterus ruptured later and had to be removed.

Nicki sat down at the picnic table and looked out over the water. She'd almost had a baby once. It had ended in a miscarriage. It wasn't Shawn's, they'd only been friends at the time, but he'd been there for her. Looking over at him asleep in the chair next to her hospital bed might have been when she fell in love with him.

Maybe they'd try some day. With that show money, they could. They could do just about anything they wanted.

Nicki had never been so isolated. Taryn had spoken of how far removed from civilization she'd felt–miles from the closest town with only a small gas station in their tiny township. They truly were in the wilderness.

If she screamed, would anyone hear her?

Sarah hadn't waited to find out; she'd bought herself a gun for protection. Now Nicki wondered if, like Shawn, she should learn how to use it.

Ugh, she groaned inwardly, *so many decisions to make!*

Should I stay, or should I go...

Feeling somewhat relaxed as she gazed at the peaceful lake, Nicki pulled out her iPod and turned on Josh Kelley.

“Everybody Wants You” soon filled her ears with its joyful, rollicking tune and she leaned back and closed her eyes.

When first the droplet of water hit her hand, she thought it was raining. When the second smacked her in the face, she absently raised her hand and wiped it away.

Guess I have to go back up, she sighed. And she’d just gotten comfortable.

But then there was another. And another. And then the splash–a sound much louder than what the jumping of a fish or falling or a limb could’ve made.

Nicki opened her eyes with a start and gasped. The thick, black smoke from the night of séance hovered over the lake, not more than five feet from her. As it delicately lowered it’s into the gray surface, sprays of water flew out and dampened her. Nicki quickly rose to her feet and took a step back.

The thing, whatever it was, actually seemed to *shift* when she moved. When she edged her way to the path, refusing to turn her back on what she was seeing, it moved slightly to the left, as though mimicking her.

Holy hell, Nicki thought, *it’s watching me and following me!*

She didn't toss around the word "evil" lightly but it was the only term that Nicki felt adequately described what hung before her. Although it was black, when you stared at it long enough you started seeing the swirls of blue and green and red deep inside of it. They churned in a rhythmic motion that made Nicki want to keep looking so she forced herself to look away. That awful stench rose from it and, even in the fresh air, overtook its surroundings and filled the atmosphere with the rancid decay she'd come to expect from it. The feelings she got from looking at it was almost indescribable: grief, fury, jealousy, resentment, fear, sorrow, disgust...all the emotions that she usually tried to hide and smother within herself.

It's like it knew her, she'd later tell Shawn. Like it could see inside of her and pull out the very things she hated about herself.

Now, backing up the path, it flattened and branched out from side to side until it was at least five-feet long.

Nicki wasn't sure why it wasn't leaving the water and trying to go up the hill with her or even what it was doing, but she didn't want to hang around long enough to find out. Now that she'd found her footing and had a grasp of her fear, she turned and began to run.

As she raced up the side of the hill, she could feel it hot on her heels. The hot breath of whatever kept it alive pushed against her back, burning her skin. The song's bouncy tune was almost comically out of place with the fear and panic that threatened to consume her. If she weren't so scared, she'd laugh.

At the top of the hill she didn't pause and look behind her–she headed straight to the house. Technically she knew that it could follow her, had been inside before, but she didn't care. She ran inside and slammed the door behind her and locked it, as though keeping out a serial killer instead of a filmy mist.

Now, feeling irrationally safe, she peeped back through the window in the foyer.

Whatever had been there was gone. She could hear Shawn upstairs, moving around furniture and cursing to himself. It was a familiar sound it comforted her.

Still panting, Nicki slid down the door and crouched on the floor. She couldn't keep doing this, couldn't keep fighting whatever was here.

She wasn't strong enough, couldn't keep it up. Whoever the keeper of this thing was, it almost certainly wasn't meant to be her.

THIRTY-THREE

HAZEL HILL, KENTUCKY 2014

Taryn had been vomiting all morning. The ache in her stomach was at war with the pain in her legs and hips and so far neither side seemed to be running out of ammo.

Unable to drive, much less stand up all day and paint, Taryn was stretched out in her cheap motel room, eating pizza. It was the only thing that anyone delivered.

"We used to have a nice restaurant that delivered subs and salads," the front desk clerk had told her when she'd called down and asked, "but it got blown away in the storm."

She'd heard that a lot while she'd been in the area. "The storm," which to her was sounding more and more like a tornado, had apparently caused all kinds of trouble. It had demolished the town's one and only cinema and their Frosty Freeze (she drove to a neighboring county to eat at theirs), as well as what looked like half of Main Street (including their court house).

Not to mention the girls' dorm.

There were signs up on damaged buildings all over town: Closed for Renovation, Open Soon, etc. But Taryn saw no visible signs of rebuilding.

She loved these small towns but, like many rural communities, Taryn felt like the county seat was dying. Although there was a prison nearby, the only major place of employment was the school system. Unemployment was far above the national average, as were the number of people on disability. Even without the closings caused by the storm damage, there were more vacant storefronts than active ones.

It was sad, really. The little town was attractive. You could see the mountains from almost anywhere you stood and the people couldn't be any friendlier. In a different state, it would've been considered "quaint" and tourism would've been strong. Craft shops, farm-to-table restaurants, antique store, and microbreweries would've opened and hipsters and families alike would've flocked.

In Eastern Kentucky, though, it was just one more ghost town to add to the list. There were more Dollar Generals than there were restaurants. As a side job, a hobby really, she'd taken to photographing these communities that she stayed in. Taryn feared that one day they'd all be gone for good–razed to the ground to make way for subdivisions full of cookie cutter houses and shopping centers all in the name of "progress."

It made Taryn sad, but at least her pizza was good.

Once she'd eaten and was reasonably sure that it was going to stay down, she turned to the letters in her lap. A Lifetime movie played inaudibly in the background, despite the pleasant spring temperature, she'd turned her heat up. She wore her fuzzy socks and her old lady flannel nightgown. Taryn was comfortable, if not feeling *well.*

"Okey dokey Miss Ellen," she said as she carefully removed the faded ribbon from the brittle stack. "Let's see what we've got here."

She gently flipped through the envelopes and loose sheets of paper and quickly realized that they were all from the same two people–Ellen's mother and a boy named Logan. The ones from her mother were stuffed neatly back into their envelopes while Logan's letters were folded into little triangles.

Love notes maybe? Taryn wondered. She'd soon find out.

Dearest Love,

I hope you're doing real good in school and listening to your teachers. Make sure you study hard and get good grades. Daddy and I miss you and Elsie does too. We love you,

Mommy and Daddy

Taryn smiled. The letter might have been, what, fifty years old? But some things never changed.

The next was a little longer.

Dear Ellen,

We meant to come down last weekend but your Daddy come down with a sickness and we couldn't leave. He took to coughing on Wednesday and it didn't let up until Monday. He's doing a bit better now but still has aching in his chest from the cold. We hope to come and see you this Sunday.

Thank you for sending the story you wrote in your school. It was real nice. Granny liked it too. We are putting it in the Bible to show everyone when they come visit.

Love,

Mommy and Daddy

Dear Ellen,

We are very proud of you and how good you're doing in school. I bet you're making a lot of friends too so I don't know why you want to come home so bad. It's been cold here and Daddy's been cutting wood all week. He's got to clean out the stove before we make a fire in it but he might do that this weekend so he might not come with me. It's best that you stay there and not come here. Our old truck just isn't making it up and down the road every day with all this mud we are having and I don't want you missing school anymore. You will be glad you stayed.

Love,

Mommy and Daddy

Maybe Ellen was homesick, Taryn thought. She wondered how old the girl was.

Dear Ellen,

We are living here in Tennessee now and we like it good enough. Daddy is trying to get on at the factory and he thinks he has a good chance. I am working at a restaurant as the cook and I like it real well. I don't know how long we will be here. Your granny is going to send for you at Christmas if you want and you can stay with her or Aunt Ruth. I'll try to send something up if I can.

Love,

Mommy and Daddy

So while she was in boarding school, her parents just upped and moved to Tennessee?

"That's harsh," Taryn thought.

The next few letters were more of the same. Asking how Ellen was, telling her about her family down around Knoxville, talking about her father's health, etc. There wasn't anything unusual in them. They sounded like correpsondance between any young girl from any time period with her parents.

Dear Ellen,

We're real proud of you for getting the part in your school play. We hope to bring granny and come see it.

Love,

Mommy and Daddy

Dear Ellen,

Happy Birthday. It doesn't seem like you should be twelve. You're getting so big! I wish we could come spend it with you but your daddy's laid up sick again. We're staying with granny and she's called for a doctor. Don't worry none, though, he has probably just caught a chest cold. I hope you have a fun day.

Love,

Mommy

Good Lord, Taryn thought, reevaluating her original assessment. She'd only been eleven when they sent her there? Dang...

It sounded as though Ellen had been involved heavily in school activities. The letters referenced several productions she'd had parts in, as well as cheerleading trouts (she didn't make the squad), a folkdancing club, Beta Club, and even a Poetry Club. Ellen sounded as though she'd been busy. Her grades had apparently been good, too.

None of her school friends were mentioned, although there was the occasional reference to two of the staff members.

Dear Ellen,

I'm sorry to hear about your dorm mother. I am sure that Miss Molley is only trying to do what she thinks is best for you. She has many girls to take care of and look out for and it must be hard for her. Please try to be a good girl and not get in trouble.

Love,

Mommy and Daddy

Another one mentioned "Miss Molley" and her temper.

Dear Ellen,

I am sorry to hear that you got in trouble. I hope that you aren't breaking any rules. I know that you think you are too old for a whipping but sometimes it's the best way to learn not to do something again. I am sure that Miss Molley likes you but do please try to be a good girl and not get in trouble.

Love,

Mommy and Daddy

Ah, Taryn sighed inwardly. *A different time period. Back when teachers could actually swat you with a paddle.*

She tried to imagine a mortified twelve-year-old Ellen (or was she thirteen by then?) enduring such a humiliation. She wondered what the poor girl had done.

Although those particular letters were interesting, and Taryn would eeventually finish them, she put them aside and picked up the other set to rifle through then.

The handwriting in these was much different. It was blocky and uneven and sometimes hard to read. The paper on most of them was stained and, in some places, the pencil had gone all the way through. It looked as though they'd been written by someone who wasn't used to writing much.

Dear Elen,

I hope you come today. I am bringing you a glove too so that you don't hurt your hand.

Logan

Taryn smiled. What kind of glove? Were they gardening together? The next letter answered that.

Der Elen,

You hit real good. For a girl, ha ha. Next time don't swing so high and you might do better. When you com back do you think you can bring more of that good milk?

Logan

Der Elen,

If you can sneek out today then you should com down to the field. I have a baseball card to show you. You will lik it.

Logan

How sweet, Taryn smiled. This wasn't a teenage girl sneaking out of her dorm room to fool around with a boy–this was a little girl sneaking out to play baseball. Just two innocent kids, having fun together. She wondered who Logan was, assumed that he must have been one of the local boys that didn't attend Hazel Hill. Or maybe he did. They kept the sexes separated outside of classes and clubs so maybe this was the only way they could meet and play together.

Der Ellen,

I am sory that I will not be there today. I got hurt on the play ground at skool and it is bad on my leg to walk. I will try tomorrow or the other day. I hope you are having a good day.

Logan

As she sifted through the notes, Taryn detected a theme. On most days they met, talked about their days, and played together. Some days it was baseball, some days soccer, some days they raced back and forth across the field. On some days, however, one of them couldn't make it. Sometimes Ellen had play practice or folkdancing. Other days she had a lot of homework or a project to work on. His excuses were always the same–he'd gotten hurt at recess or fallen off the ladder in the barn. Or kicked by the cow.

Dear Ellen,

I wanted to see you today to help you with your lines but I was working on our fence and hit my hand with the hammer. It just hurts too bad to anything much with it. I will see you on Thursday and we will practice then.

Logan

"Uh oh," Taryn mumbled, reading between the lines. She wondered if Ellen herself had picked up on what was going on. She was only a child, so probably not.

Taryn's heart broke a little for the little boy.

Aside from that, it was obvious that he had a crush on her.

The letters carried on for what appeared to be at least two years. Nothing changed much, aside from his spelling and syntax improvement, but towards the end of the stack they began taking on a different tone.

Dear Ellen,

I know you got mad at me at the river the other day but I really am just trying to help. I know you think that Johnson is a swell but I am worried about him. I know his brother and know what he is like. I know Johnson too. Please try to stay away from him if you can.

Logan

Dear Ellen,

Thank you for the thermos and the soup you brung. It was real good. I know you think you are not a good singer but I think you are. You singing me that song about them horses and rubbing my head is the best I've felt since getting sick. My mama used to do that for me when she was alive too and it made me think of her. I think I am getting better now so can you come tomorrow?

Logan

Dear Ellen,

I waited for you to come today so that we could run lines and you could help me with that book report. Where are you? I will be okay because it is not due until Monday but I was hoping you'd help me because you read the book too. I promise that I will be at your play. Even if your mama can come this time I will pay to go. I made some money taking bags to the store and I will buy my ticket if I have to.

Logan

Taryn smiled. Sounded like Ellen had been getting him in for free. But had that meant that her parents didn't show up? It was starting to sound like Ellen was at the school, all the time.

Dear Ellen,

I'm afraid that putting these under the tree is a bad idea. What if it rains? How about we start hiding them there under the stairs behind the library? There is a little whole with concrete and they will stay dry. I am sory they moved our rock, ha ha.

Logan

So that's what they had been doing then. They'd been hiding letters to each other under a rock, and later under the stairs. Smart. Kind of like a secret mailbox.

Dear Ellen,

I am sorry you think I am mad. I am not mad that you went to the drive in with Johnson. Maybe I was wrong and he is an okay guy. If you like him and say that he is nice then I guess it has to be okay. I hope you still meet me too and we are still friends.

Logan

Dear Ellen,

I wanted to tell you that you looked great and did a good job in the play. You remembered all your lines and you were a star! I am very happy to tell everybody that you are my friend. I am sorry your mama didn't get to see this one. I hope she does the next.

Logan

Dear Ellen,

Are you feeling better? How is your chest cold? I had one too. It's okay that you can't bring me the milk and the peanut butter and bread anymore. I know you will be glad not to work in the kitchen anymore. I know you will like being in the libery.

Logan

So had she been bringing him food when she visited him? Taryn frowned. Poor Logan. What kind of life had he had? It sounded like, though Ellen was starting to become a social butterfly, she was pretty much all Logan had.

Dear Ellen,

I don't want you to think I am a doofus but I miss seeing you. You are my best frend. Are you still mad at me for saying you should not like Johnson? Are you sick again? Please write or see me.

Logan

Dear Ellen,

I have some money left. What do you want for Chrissmas? Is your mama and daddy going to be back from Tenesee by then or are you staying with your granny? You don't have to get me nothing, it's okay.

Logan

Dear Ellen,

After what you told me I have to tell you what I know. I should have told you sooner. Johnson and his brother did bad thing a long time ago. It was mostly his brother but Johnson helped. I want to tell you when I see you. I will bring your Christmas present then.

Logan

That was the last of Logan's. She looked through the other set, seeing if she'd missed one, but she hadn't. The rest of the letters from her mother didn't revel much more information either. What little Taryn got was that they'd gone back to Tennessee a couple of years after the first time and Ellen was meant to stay with her grandmother for Christmas. The letters abruptly stopped after that.

The pain medication that Taryn had taken earlier was finally kicking in. As she felt the warmth flooding through her and the awful pains start simmering down, Taryn placed the letters on the nightstand and leaned back against the bed.

She'd need to think about what she had just read, process everything. She was confident now that it was Ellen that she'd seen in the kitchen, Ellen whose voice she'd recorded on her tablet. Even the song was the same.

So what had happened to her?

Whatever it was, Taryn had a bad feeling about it.

THIRTY-FOUR

NEW HAMPSHIRE, 2017

Whenever Nicki was feeling low, there was nothing quite like a little retail therapy to cheer her up. Luckily, the outlet stores in North Conway offered plenty of options for that.

Three big shopping bags in hand, Nicki marched across the parking lock and hit the keypad for her trunk. She'd found several pairs of jeans and even a lightweight jacket for the chilly morning. And some tops. Maybe some socks. It had been a profitable afternoon, all in all.

On days like this, with the smell of spring in the air and the sky a crisp blue, it was hard to remember that she'd been feeling so mixed up lately.

"Face it Nicki," she scolded herself as she slid into her front seat and buckled up, "it's not just the ghosts that are bothering you."

Had she been using them as a scapegoat? Focusing on whatever was going on in the house so that she didn't have put any energy into thinking about what next steps she wanted to take?

Had she been using Taryn's death in the same way? Wallowing in her grief, obsessing over the loss of her friend so that she didn't have to live in the moment?

"Taryn wouldn't like that," Nicki muttered.

She pulled out onto the highway and began the long drive back. Shawn was in Portsmouth for the day, visiting a couple of vintage stores and eating lobster (she didn't do seafood and sometimes they needed some alone time) so she was a free agent as she flew down the scenic byway.

Nicki had not had many friends growing up. She'd kept to herself a lot, been somewhat of a loner. She'd preferred to have her nose in a book, or to go for long walks, over partying or gossiping with other girls.

Meeting Taryn had been a relief. For the first time in her life, she'd felt a kinship another female. They'd gotten along so well, had bonded almost instantly. With Taryn, it was almost hard to believe that she'd ever had trouble forming close relationships with other girls.

And, for the fist time in years, Nicki's mental health had even improved. Prone to depression and anxiety, she'd suddenly found herself feeling hopeful again. Even though Taryn had her bad days, and even claimed that she liked to throw herself pity parties now and then, she'd oozed a positive energy that was difficult to explain. It wasn't that she was abnormally happy or annoyingly cheerful (in fact, Taryn was often quite serious and retrospective) but people generally just felt good around her. Shawn had said so as well.

"She's an old soul," he'd said on many occasions. "This isn't her first time around."

After she died, Nicki had felt herself falling back into that pit again, wallowing in self-pity and losing herself. She'd stopped looking for work, stopped making an effort to keep up with what few acquaintances she did have. Stopped caring.

And then they'd moved to Sarah's house.

She didn't want to admit it, felt guilty to even think it, but she was feeling better again. As scared and overwhelmed with whatever was going on there as she felt, most of the time she was actually feeling *good*.

"Maybe it's because Taryn's spirit really *is* there," she said aloud.

The idea made her grin.

Josh Rouse's "Sparrows Over Birmingham" was playing on the radio so Nicki reached down and turned up the volume. With her windows rolled down, the wind in her hair, and her voice rising over the radio, Nicki sped down the road, enjoying herself.

Maybe I will take that job, she thought as she hummed along with the gospel choir in the background. *Maybe it's time for a brand new start.*

Suddenly, anything sounded possible.

*   *   *

She'd only visited the little cemetery twice before–once when Taryn was buried and once on Christmas Eve. Taryn had loved Christmas so Nicki'd had this idea of decorating her grave with a homemade wreath and fairy lights.

Being there had absolutely freaked her out; all she could think about was her friend lying underground in the dark. Taryn had been afraid of the dark.

Nicki hadn't returned since.

Now, however, she rectified that.

"Sorry chick," she whispered as she knelt on the cold, damp earth. "Should've been here sooner."

Behind her, the wind rustled in the trees and a crow squawked its discord.

Matt had picked out her casket. It was an ornate pink one, with rose-colored satin lining inside. He'd chosen a hot pink Betsey Johnson dress to bury her in. Taryn would've approved but she'd have also complained about burying a perfectly nice (expensive) dress underground.

Matt had made most all the arrangements. Nicki hadn't been able to, had barely been able to look at her during the visitation, though she'd sat in a chair by Matt and received visitors by the coffin.

They'd played Dolly Parton, Emmylou Harris, and Merle Haggard at her funeral. Matt had put together a video of Taryn, pictures of her as a child and as an adult, and set them to "My Favorite Memory of All" and it had played during the service. There hadn't been a dry eye in the house. People had come from all over the country–former clients, people she'd helped through her work, even a country music singer she'd once been hired by. She'd been better liked than she'd probably thought. Taryn had always felt alone.

"I know you're probably busy hanging out with Elvis and flirting with Hank Williams," Nicki began, "but I need to talk to you about something."

The crow squawked again then flew off its branch, the flapping of its wings filling the air with a rhythmic shuffling.

"I'm not real sure what to," Nicki sighed. "I know you left me the house, and I do love it, but Shawn wants me to work with him. And I don't know which choice is the best. Should we hire someone to watch over the house and return to it during breaks? Seems a shame to just let it sit here empty all that time, unused. Should we sell it and make a clean break? Should I stay here and dig in? I just don't know..."

A pregnant cloud passed over the sun at that moment and long shadows fell across the tiny family graveyard. Nicki shivered inside her newly-purchased Banana Republic jacket.

"Was that an answer?" she asked nervously.

To her left, the heavy wrought iron gate leisurely creaked open, moving deliberately on its hinges until it came to an abrupt stop just before hitting the fence behind it.

Nicki rose to her feet and turned.

"You want me to leave?" she whispered.

The gate fell back the rest of the way, making a ringing sound when it made impact with the fence.

Before walking away, she glanced back down at Taryn's grave and offered a watery smile. "I'll be back," she promised. "I will."

On her way out, she passed the graves of Julian and Nora Alderman. "Wife and Mother" her headstone read, though Nora had not lived long enough to enjoy the fruits of her literal labor. She'd apparently died shortly after giving birth.

How much truth was there to what she'd read and heard about Delilah, Nicki wondered. *Was there something odd about that child? Or had she simply fallen victim to country gossip and slander?*

It was hard to know.

Nicki traveled leisurely across the gently sloping lawn, moving past the tree stumps that Shawn had been clearing out and the spot where Taryn's aunt had kept her garden. When she reached the house, she stopped and looked up.

It really was an imposing structure and architecturally interesting, especially considering how far out it was built.

At one time, it really must have been grand, she thought.

Looking at the back of the house, where the other wing had once been, she could imagine how impressed people would've been when they came out here for parties and balls.

She and Taryn had talked about that during one of their calls. Had also spoken of the original owner, Julian, and the fire though Nicki had almost completely forgotten that conversation until recently. Taryn hadn't believed that Julian had killed his daughter before the fire or, as the other version went, that he'd set the fire on purpose. She'd believed that Benjamin Warwick was responsible.

"Taryn was researching the heck about this place," Nicki sighed. "Maybe she found something out."

But, if she had, she hadn't told Nicki. And she hadn't put it in her notes. The only thing she had to go on was on the third to last page where Taryn had written, in block caps, "BEN WARWICK GUILTY."

"What did you find out about this place anyway? And does it even matter?"

When Nicki had first arrived, right before Taryn's funeral, she'd felt good about the house. Even now, with everything that was going on, she still felt good for the most part. Maybe it wasn't the ghosts at all...maybe it was *her*.

She wasn't sure what made her glance up. It could have been instinct or she might have caught movement from the corner of her eye. Just as another fat, heavy cloud passed over the sun again, however, something in the storage room's window had her catching her breath.

The little girl had long, dark hair and it hung in curls around her shoulders. Her dress was yellow, Nicki could see that even from where she stood.

As Nicki watched, the child lifted both hands and placed her palms flat on the glass. Then, looking straight at Nicki, she threw her head back and laughed a long, silent laugh that continued until the cloud passed on and the bright sunshine flooded the window again with light.

Nicki decided that she might wait a while before going back in.

THIRTY-FIVE

HAZEL HILL, KENTUCKY 1965

Ellen was moping. That's what her mother called it anyway–moping. Jenny thought that she was just being a spaz.

"I'm going for a walk," Ellen sighed. "I might go get a book from the library."

"Okay," Jenny said with a wave of her hand. She didn't even look up from her textbook. Ellen thought she was probably glad to see her go.

Ellen had thought that things would be better once she came back to school from summer break, but they didn't seem to be. Johnson would barely look at her, much less talk to her. He'd moved on to a senior, a girl with big breasts and tight sweaters named Julia. The only time she gave Ellen the time of day was when she'd look at one of her friends, whisper something, then glance at Ellen and giggle.

Other people were doing that too, but Ellen wasn't sure why.

"Our Town" had gone just swell. Ellen thought she'd done a terrific job as the Stage Manager and she'd had two ovations. Logan had been in the audience, though her parents had not been able to make it, and he'd clapped so hard his hands turned red. She was hoping that Johnson would want to attend the reception with her at the church and walk her back to her dorm afterwards, but he'd run off back to his dorm with his friends and hadn't looked her way. Logan had gone with her instead and they'd had punch and cookies in the church's basement.

It was nice being home for the summer, because she'd missed her family, but it was also strange. She was so used to having a set schedule and routine–someone telling her when to wake up, when to eat, when to clean, when to study, when she could have free time, etc. At home, she wasn't expected to do much of anything except to help her mother with the chores and to help fix dinner. She'd taken to carrying a book around in her pocket and, after the table was cleared and the clothes on the line, she'd go out to the apple orchard and read. On rare occasions when their truck was running right, they'd go into Frenchburg and while her daddy met with people, she'd walk up and down the streets and go in and out of shops. Just looking, of course. She never had any money to buy.

She'd never really thought about how shabby her farm was before, either. She missed her dorm's thick, white walls and clean floors that were always kept mopped and waxed. The kitchen's scrubbed floors and the cool, fresh scent of cleaning soap and cold milk that was always there. Ellen had never had cold milk until she got to Hazel Hill Academy. Back home, her milk was always warm, straight from the cow, and sometimes had things floating in it.

Now that she was back on her farm again she was noticing the paper thin walls, the tattered curtains that blew against the windows with their broken screens. The peeling brick façade that never looked like real bricks. The mud that was tracked into the house and ground into the floor so much that no matter how hard you scrubbed it, you could never get it out.

She'd missed her school.

She thought that, with so much time apart, once she returned to school that Johnson would see her and be happy. She'd thought that he would miss her. After all, absence made the heart grow fonder. Right?

Not so with him

Logan had missed her, however. He'd grown taller over the summer, too, and was as tan as a berry by the time she saw him in late August. He was going to be very big and muscular. She teased him that he'd have lots of girlfriends one day.

"Don't want lots of 'em," he'd grunted, his face turning beet red.

He was thinking of dropping out of school. His daddy needed help on the farm and since Logan had graduated from eighth grade that May, he didn't see the need to continue on. Ellen was hoping he'd change his mind. He'd be the first to graduate from high school if he stayed, just like she'd be the first in her family as well.

It's why she was sent to Hazel Hill.

"Are you okay there Ellen?"

Beautiful Mrs. Lykins stood over the bench where Ellen sat with her book in hand. She looked down at her in concern. She was having a baby, everyone was talking about it, and it was true that she looked a little bigger. Her face was rounder, for one thing, and Ellen noticed that her teacher sometimes struggled to walk.

"I'm fine," Ellen smiled thinly. "Just came here to the library to check one out and thought I'd sit here and read."

"Well," Mrs. Lykins said, shielding her eyes from the sun as she looked around the lawn, "it is a nice autumn day. What are you reading?"

Ellen held her book up and showed her teacher the cover. "Nancy Drew," she replied shyly.

"Oh, excellent choice," Mrs. Lykins beamed. "If you enjoy them, you should also look for Agatha Christie. I think you'd like her as well."

"I will," Ellen said.

"We'll start reading her books when you're a junior, so you can get a head start now."

Ellen nodded and smiled politely.

Mrs. Lykins looked as though she might be about to say something else but then she grimaced and clutched her back, as though something had just kicked her hard. She didn't complain, though, or mention it.

It was strange to think of them as having outside lives. Some of her teachers lived on the campus and she would see them walking around with their spouses, or their dogs, and they'd be dressed in "normal" attire. She once saw her math teacher scratching the inside of his nose and, for a moment, she'd thought he was picking it. It was disconcerting. Mrs. Lykins, however, never changed. She was the same pretty, polite woman and teacher both inside and outside of the classroom. At least, Ellen thought she was. She didn't live on campus, so Ellen didn't see her much outside of school.

"Are you sure you're feeling okay?" Mrs. Lykins asked, narrowing her eyes. "You're looking pale."

"I've been very tired lately," Ellen admitted. "It's difficult being back on this schedule after being home all summer. I slept a lot at home and I had a summer cold. It is finally clearing up."

"Are you eating okay?"

That was always the first questions that adults asked children.

"Yes ma'am. I'm starting to. The cold made it difficult to eat but I'm fine now."

"You *do* look as if you've lost some weight."

Ellen knew she had. Her skirts and britches were loose on her. Over the summer she'd not had much of an appetite. She was hungry all the time now, though.

"Are your parents coming for the fall festival?"

Ellen shook her head. "No ma'am. They had to move back down to Tennessee again to be with my aunt. They will be back after Christmas. My friend Logan will be here, though. He's local," she explained.

"I know his family," Mrs. Lykins said with a smile. "He attends our church. He's a nice boy."

The dinner bell rang just then, signifying the time in which they were meant to line up and say their evening prayers. Ellen slipped her book into her skirt pocket. "I'll see you tomorrow," she told her teacher.

Even as she walked over to the bell and found her place in line, she could still feel Mrs. Lykins' worried eyes on her back.

THIRTY-SIX

HAZEL HILL, KENTUCKY 2014

Taryn thought she'd have felt better, but she didn't. If anything, she was a little worse. The inability to get out of bed and work was sending her into panic mode, too, so on top of her physical ailments she was suffering from anxiety.

"I am falling apart," Taryn groaned.

She'd called Matt, had stayed on the phone with him for nearly two hours the night before.

"I'm thinking of taking some time off," he'd told her. "I thought I might even come to Nashville..."

Taryn knew it wasn't for him to see his family.

"Oh Matt," she'd sighed. "Are you *sure* you want to quit?"

"I have a lot of reading to do," he'd teased her. "And I thought I might take up canning."

"*Matt...*"

"I'm not happy with my job," he'd told her.

"Is anyone?" Well, she was happy with hers but that was different. Self-employed people always looked a little happier to her, though they seemed to stress more than others about other things–like money.

"I'm afraid that if I don't get out now, I'll just stay..."

"But you work for NASA!"

"I know," he'd heaved a sigh of frustration.

Matt had wanted to be an astronaut for as long as Taryn had known him. When other boys in her class were talking about the army or pretending to be policeman, he'd made toy rockets that actually worked and fretted over the best way to explore other solar systems. And he'd almost done it, too! He'd gone to school to become an aeronautical engineer and had worked for the company of his dreams for more than six years. So why the change?

"It's not because of me, is it?"

"You don't want to come to Florida," he'd said. "And I can't blame you there. So maybe I can come to *you*."

"Look Matt," she'd said anxiously, "I can't be the one responsible for you giving up your dream to go to space. I don't want that pressure. It's not fair."

"With the way things are going, the space program's going to be disbanded and *nobody's* going to go to space," he'd snorted.

Still...he might joke about it, but she knew that Matt hadn't changed his mind about what he wanted to do. He was merely in a "funk." Taryn was sure of it. He'd leave, come to stay with her, and then he'd eventually regret his decision. Or was it *she* who would regret his decision?

What was it that was making her hope he did decide to come and fervently wish that he wouldn't in equal measure? What was it about her relationship with Matt that was so damn complicated? It hadn't been complicated when they'd been children, riding their bikes around the subdivision and watching for aliens in the night sky after watching "Close Encounters of the Third Kind." Or as a teenager when she'd kept his school picture in her backpack and had taken it out every time she went to the bathroom at school, to look at it and sigh over his shock of black hair.

She'd tried to analyze her feelings, tried to mull them over and over in her head to get a grip on them. But she always changed her mind, always changed the subject on herself.

If I tell him no, she'd thought on more than one occasion, *then I'll lose the closest person in the world to me. There will be no way to recover our former friendship.*

So she held on.

"You're mine Taryn," he'd told her while lying in bed the last time they were together. She'd been just about to fall asleep and his words had sounded as though they were coming from a dream, so much so that in the morning she hadn't been totally if sure if she hadn't dreamed them. "I don't see how you could *ever* belong to anyone else. You've always been mine."

The idea was chilling and relieving.

Under everything else, in the back of her mind, something tugged at her. Something she didn't understand. Another purpose, another love, another *life*...

Eh, maybe she'd spent too much time around ghosts and old buildings.

"I don't want to be your excuse," she'd objected on the phone. "If you're unhappy and want a change, well, that's one thing. If you're using *me* to make that change, to talk yourself out of something for whatever reason, then that's something else entirely."

He hadn't said much after that.

When they'd hung up the phone, he'd texted her the song lyrics to Rodney Crowell's "What Kind of Love" and she'd smiled. Sometimes when they didn't know what to say to each other, they spoke in lyrics. He'd been asking her who else but him would drive out in the pouring rain to be with her, who else but *him* would give her everything he had?

She had no doubt that it was him. Nobody loved her like Matt, not even Nicki. Not even Andrew.

"Yoo hoo!" The knock on her door had Taryn sitting up in bed and muting the volume. "Anyone in there?"

She immediately recognized Rosa's voice and wondered how she'd known where to find her. Then again, it *was* the only motel in the county so...

When she opened the door, she saw the spunky blonde standing there in pink overalls, holding a steaming crockpot in her arms. "Hi there!" she cried cheerfully. "A little birdie told me that you were sick so I brought you over some of my homemade vegetable soup and sourdough bread!"

Tarn could already smell it and it smelled like Heaven in a box.

"You'll have to overlook the mess," Taryn apologized as Rosa let herself into the room and began searching for an outlet. "Let to my own devices, I can turn a room upside down in no time."

"Oh, don't you worry," Rosa laughed. She plugged in the crockpot then began removing Styrofoam bowels and plastic utensils from a canvas bag she'd slung over her shoulder. "When Mother and I go on our tours, I always manage to make a mess of things."

Taryn caught her own reflection in the mirror just then and cringed. She hadn't washed her hair in at least four days and now, with its natural curls, it stood out from her head in a knotted mess. Her face was pale, her mascara from two days ago ran down her cheeks, and she was almost certain she smelled.

"Just let me go change," she began as she headed for the bathroom.

"Don't you dare," Rosa ordered her. Taryn stopped in her tracks. "You go right back to bed."

Taryn did as she was told.

After she'd dished out the soup and brought Taryn a bowl, Rosa smoothed out the blanket on the empty bed and sat. "Your paintings are beautiful," she murmured as she looked around the room. "I feel like I could walk right into them. They look exactly as I remember the campus. The way it was."

"Thank you," Taryn replied bashfully. "It's been a fun job."

"How much do you have left to do?"

"Not much," Taryn said. Hence another reason for the push to find answers as quickly as she could. "I just have to finish the music building and tennis courts."

"Mother is going to be so tickled," Rosa smiled. "She's very excited."

"Your mom went to the academy, right?"

Rosa nodded. "And worked there."

"Would she know a girl named Ellen? Ellen Rose?"

Rosa cocked her head to the side and appeared to mull it over. "Name sounds familiar but I'm not sure I know her. She's not an alumni, I can tell you that. I have all of those records."

"There's another name," Taryn said, "but he didn't go there. First name is Logan. This would've been in the sixties."

"Oh, I know Logan," Rosa laughed. "I've known him all my life! He's older than me, of course, but his farm is just down the road from ours."

Taryn felt herself growing excited. "Is there anything you can tell me about him?"

She knew it was a longshot, but part of her had hoped that Ellen had dropped out of the academy, gone back to her home, and eventually married the little boy who'd loved baseball.

"Well," Rosa said, "he never married..."

Damn, killed that angle.

"He keeps to himself the most part. Raised tobacco for years and then took the buyout when they offered it, just like a lot of people around here. He wound up putting his towards livestock so he raises cattle now."

Taryn had sat there debating on whether or not she should tell Rosa about the letters. They were so personal and had remained unread for so long. It felt intrusive to share them. But then again, Taryn herself had read them and she was a complete stranger.

"I found these letters," she said at last, pointing towards the stack on the nightstand. "They're from an Ellen

Rose to Logan. They apparently used to meet down at the baseball diamond and played together for a long time."

"Oh, how neat!" Rosa slapped her hands together. "It certainly is hard to think of him as having ever been a child. I bet he'd like to have those."

"I was hoping that he was still alive," Taryn said, "so that I could give them to him."

"Oh he's still alive," Rosa assured her. "He goes to my church."

Taryn suddenly felt better. All she had to do was go back to the little country church again and she could hand them over herself. And then maybe *he* could answer some questions about Ellen.

"Oh, that's great," Taryn sighed with relief. "If I'm feeling better, I'll try to go on Sunday."

"He'll be there," Rosa said. "He is there every Sunday."

Taryn was about to change the subject, ask her about the books in the library again, when Rosa's face alit with pleasure.

"But wait, you kind of met him when you were there a couple of weeks ago!"

"I *did*?"

Rosa nodded. "You spoke to him while he sat on the steps by the bathroom. That's our Logan, alright. He's not much on being around people. Has always preferred to be alone."

THIRTY-SEVEN

HAZEL HILL, KENTUCKY 1965

Logan was disappointed; Ellen could see it all over his face.

"I just don't think I can walk that far," she said again.

"But you love to fish!"

"I know," she sighed, "but my stomach really hurts. And I'm very tired."

"You're always sick these days," he complained. Still, he tossed the fishing rods on the ground and gave up. He knew better than to push her.

"I know," she said again. "Ever since that cold I had this summer. I just haven't been able to shake it."

"What feels bad?" he asked.

"I'm just exhausted," she said and, as if by emphasis, she sank to the ground and laid back on the grass. "I can't get enough sleep. And I am hungry all the time. All the time! If I don't eat, my stomach hurts."

"I can tell," he laughed. "You're getting big."

"Yeah," she grumbled, "I had to let my skirt out around my waist today. It's embarrassing."

"My mom got sick like that," Logan said quietly, the laughter stopping. He gingerly sat down beside her and studied her face. "Before she passed. She was tired all the time. First she was eating a lot and then she couldn't eat at all."

"I don't think I have your mama's sickness," Ellen assured him. "Some days I feel just fine."

"Are you going home for Thanksgiving this week?" he asked, changing the subject.

"My granny is meant to send for me on Wednesday," she replied. "You doing anything?"

He shook his head. "Don't know. Might go to my uncle's. Sometimes we do."

"Well, I'll miss you," Ellen said lightly, giving him a little punch in the arm. "You're my best friend."

Logan's eyes lit up with pleasure. "Really? Nah! You don't want a boy as your best friend."

"And why wouldn't I?"

"Because boys and girls can't be friends forever."

"Why not?" Ellen demanded, rising to her elbows.

"Cause one of them always winds up getting married," he teased her.

"Well, that's true," she said, flopping back down to the cold ground.

"Unless..." He looked about as bashful as she'd seen him.

"Unless what?"

"Maybe me and you could get married one day," he said, not meeting her eyes.

"Well maybe we can," she retorted. "Then we can be friends forever."

Suddenly her stomach gave a lurch. It wasn't painful, exactly, but the sensation was something unlike anything she'd ever felt.

"Are you okay?" Ellen could see the worry on Logan's face.

"It's my belly," she said.

"Does it hurt?"

"It's moving!"

"Like you gotta go to be private?" he asked. "Sometimes mine does that before I go."

"Sort of like that," she said, then she winced as she felt it again. It was a fluttering, a slight movement, as though there were little mice running around inside.

"Here," she demanded, grabbing his hand. "Feel."

When she placed it on her stomach, he brought it back like he'd touched something hot.

"It's nothing bad," Ellen told him, "just feel."

Logan delicately placed his hand just below her breasts and waited. Within seconds, his eyes grew big. "There's something in your belly Ellen!"

"I know!"

"Maybe you really are sick like my mama," he said, his voice almost breaking.

The realization of what was going on dawned on her almost at once, however. She'd grown up on a farm. There'd been lots of animals. It couldn't be that much different.

What in the world was she going to do?

THIRTY-EIGHT

NEW HAMPSHIRE, 2017

Shawn took another look at Taryn's notes and furrowed his brows. "So Taryn found out that this, what, thirteen-year-old girl was pregnant?"

Nicki nodded.

"And you think that had something to do with whatever went on down there?"

"It must," Nicki said. "Look, she wrote it out right there: Ellen, 13, pregnant. She wouldn't have written it if it didn't mean something."

"Okay, I'll buy that," Shawn admitted. "But that's all she wrote?"

"Literally," Nicki pointed again. "It ends there. Although she did mention the girl that was found dead, Daisy. That's the one that I told you about. She only mentioned her once and that was early on. I don't think she thought it was relevant."

"Have you Googled this Ellen, along with the academy?"

"I did," Nicki nodded. "Zilch."

"Hmm..." Shawn got up and placed another log on the fire in their bedroom. It was a chilly night and the fire had made the room nice and toasty in minutes. Nicki loved having a working fireplace in their bedroom. It was one of her favorite things about the house.

"Did anyone from Hazel Hill come to the funeral?"

She shook her head. "Not that I can remember."

"And are there *any* other names on there?"

Nicki flipped back to the beginning of the document. "Rosa Hinkle, who she lists as the historian, and Clark Reynolds. I can't find Clark on the internet, except to see that he lives in Hazel Hill. Rosa has a Facebook page. Says she lives in Nashville, which is kind of interesting, but the rest of it is private."

"Send her a friend request," Shawn suggested. "See if she can tell you anything."

Nicki went ahead and did that now.

"Shawn, I think that–"

Before she could finish her sentence, there was a knock at their bedroom door. Shawn was halfway across the floor, poker in hand, when the door flew open as though propelled by a heavy gust of wind. The flames in the fireplace flickered and then shot upwards, making the room brighter with their intensity.

"Shawn!" Nicki whimpered.

They could both see that the doorway was empty and that no one was there. Still, Shawn ran out onto the landing and flipped on the light.

"It was just the wind," he said, but his voice shook.

Just then, the room filled with the sound of dainty feminine laughter. It was a child's laughter, a voice full of mischief and playfulness. Though they saw nothing, both Nicki and Shawn heard the pattering of little footsteps as they raced across the bedroom floor, stopping at the window. Then, to Nicki's dismay, tiny handprints materialized in the fog on the windowpane. They continued to appear the glass, first two and then three until the entire window was covered.

The masculine sound of a man clearing his throat came then and the handprints stopped. As the little footsteps scurried across the floor once more and disappeared onto the landing, their bedroom door was again pulled shut with a force that neither Nicki nor Shawn could explain.

"Well," Nicki said weakly.

"Well," Shawn echoed.

"I guess we have more than one ghost?"

THIRTY-NINE

Library and girls' dorm

HAZEL HILL, KENTUCKY 2014

Taryn still felt delicate but she managed to hobble into church on Sunday where she sat in the pew with Rosa and her mother, Millie.

"How was the soup?" Rosa whispered.

"Best soup I ever had in my life," Taryn answered truthfully.

"My darling's a wonderful cook," Millie said, patting Rosa on the hand. She looked over at her daughter with adoring eyes and Taryn's heart melted just a little.

"Logan's here today," Rosa said. "He's four rows behind us. I told him to wait around after the service."

Unfortunately for Taryn, potluck was only the first Sunday of every month.

Because she was anxious and excited to talk to Logan, the service could not have gone any slower. She tried to listen, tried to pay attention, but the preacher's voice was one of those even-toned monotonous ones. She had to fight to stay awake.

Finally, however, noon came around. The congregation stood and said their final prayer, the organ music played, and they were dismissed.

"Come with me," Rosa said, taking Taryn by the arm. "Mother, you stay right there. I'll be back."

"Mother doesn't walk well on her own," Rosa explained. "I'd like to see her in an assisted living community. We have a nice one in Lexington, but she won't go. Won't leave Hazel Hill. I guess that's how all of us feel."

"Logan," Rosa called as they neared the back of the sanctuary, "this young lady here wants to talk to you."

"He's got a hearing aid," Rosa whispered in Taryn's ear, "but you'll still need to speak up."

It was hard to imagine that the elderly man in front of her had ever been a little boy with bruised legs, shocking red hair, and a missing tooth. He didn't have a hair on his head now and his face was covered in liver spots. He had a big grin, though, and even though he stood over six feet tall (even now) he looked as gentle as a giant.

"How about we sit right here," he said, gesturing to the pew behind him. "They keep the padded ones in the back for us old folks."

Taryn laughed and sat down beside him.

"You don't look old to me," she said.

"Well, looks can be deceiving," he said with a smile. "I have a lot of miles on this old body."

Now that she was closer to him, he looked younger than the seventysomething she'd originally pegged him for. He was also good looking in an aged Robert Redford kind of way. (More "An Unfinished Life" than "The Way We Were" or even "The Horse Whisperer.")

"Rosa says you have something to talk to me about," he said shyly.

"I do," Taryn replied. "I, uh, found some things that belong to you. I was wondering if you wanted them back."

"To me?" He laughed. "I think you must have the wrong person."

People were filing out the door, moving past them, and many paused and then took second looks as they tried to determine what Taryn might have wanted with one of their most inobtrusive members.

"I'm sure they're yours," she insisted. She reached out, patted his hand, and watched as he smiled again. "Did you know an Ellen Rose?"

The smile remained on Logan's lips, but the color drained from his face. For a brief moment, Taryn was afraid that she'd just caused him to have a heart attack.

Oh no, she thought, *not on my watch!*

But then he regained his composure and straightened his back.

"A long time ago," he murmured. "A very long time ago."

"You two used to write letters, hide them on campus," she said. "I found them."

His eyes grew wide at her revelation. "My letters?" he sputtered. "You found them?"

"Packed away in a box, up in the girls' dorm attic," she replied.

"I'd, uh, certainly like to see those," he said, clearing his throat.

"If you tell me where to meet, I'll bring them with me," Taryn said. "They're in my motel room right now."

He nodded and wet his lips. "I didn't know she'd kept them."

Taryn grinned. "Looks like she kept them all."

"Little Ellen..." Logan shook his head, as though he couldn't believe it. "Haven't spoken of her in years."

"What happened to Ellen?" Taryn asked.

She couldn't tell him about the photo, couldn't show him the picture.

"Oh, I don't know," he said sadly. "She left the academy. Went back home, I think. Went home for winter break and never came back."

"And she never wrote to you? Never said goodbye?"

But he didn't have to tell her; the answer was obvious.

"She was a sweet girl," he said. "A sweet girl. My best friend."

"I read the letters," Taryn said, her face flushing with embarrassment. "I didn't mean to invade your privacy but I didn't know what they were at the time."

"Oh, that's fine," he laughed thinly. "Just little ramblings from a kid. Nothing important."

"There was one thing you mentioned, one thing that stuck out," Taryn pressed. She wasn't going to ask him about the bruises, the injuries. The food Ellen brought. But she would ask him about Johnson. "There was a boy that it sounded like Ellen was seeing. You weren't too keen on him. Johnson?"

Logan lifted his head and peered into the sanctuary. They were alone now. Still, he lowered his voice. "A bad seed, that one," he whispered. "His whole family. I tried to warn her. She didn't listen."

"What did they do?"

"It was a long time ago," Logan said at last. "Nobody remembers anymore. Didn't care too much at the time. They were only concerned with the money."

Taryn wanted to ask him more, but Rosa entered the room and approached them at that moment. Clark Reynolds was right on her heels. "You two having a nice talk?" she asked.

Taryn nodded.

"How are you feeling?" Clark asked, looking concerned.

"Better," Taryn replied. "I'm going up to the academy after this to work some more. Probably be doing some evening hours from here on out."

"Oh, did she tell you about the letters?" Rosa asked Logan.

He nodded and glanced over at Taryn. "She did."

Rosa turned to Clark. "Taryn here found some letters that Logan wrote to a friend back when he was a kid. They were up in the attic. Isn't that nice?"

Clark beamed. "That's wonderful! Nothing like taking a walk through the past, eh Logan?"

Logan nodded his head and smiled. "Nothing like it."

"Would you like to see him back when he had hair?" Rosa asked Taryn. "There's a picture in the hallway."

"Oh now, she doesn't want to see that," Logan protested.

"No," Taryn teased him, "I really do."

They all filed out behind Rosa, walking behind her like obedient little ducks. When they reached the hall, she pointed up a large black and white photo montage hanging on the wall. "There," she said.

Logan looked to be around fourteen years old. Even in the grayscale, you could tell that his hair had been a distinct color. He wore dungarees that were just a little too short and a shirt buttoned the wrong way. Beside him was a tall, attractive woman She held a baby in her arms.

"That was taken at the Christmas madrigal," Rosa explained. "The baby there? That's me."

"Oh, is that your mom?" Taryn asked. The woman who held Rose had soft blonde hair and a sweet smile. She looked so proud holding onto her newborn.

"That's her," Rosa said. "I was her miracle baby. Born early. We had a bad snow that year, too. Madrigal had to pushed back to January because everyone got snowed in."

"It was cold that year," Logan agreed.

Millie came in from around the corner, moving at a snail's pace, and joined them. "Wasn't he a handsome boy?" she asked, patting Logan on the arm. "Always was one of my favorites. Wished I could've taught him."

"That's right," Taryn said, turning to face Rosa's mother. "You worked at the school. Were you a teacher?"

"English for twenty-three years," Ros answered. "Until the school closed."

Millie nodded.

Logan regarded her with genuine affection. "She was Ellen's favorite teacher," he told Taryn. "She spoke of her all the time."

"So you knew Ellen Rose?" Taryn asked in surprise. She'd never thought to ask Millie.

"Oh yes. She was there for, what, two years?"

Rosa looked at Taryn and shrugged. "I didn't know that."

"Mrs. Lykins was everyone's favorite teacher," Logan said with a smile.

"I did my best," Millicent "Millie" Lykins replied.

FORTY

HAZEL HILL, KENTUCKY 1965

Jenny regarded her roommate with scrutiny. "You're always so cold," she said.

Ellen pulled the cardigan tighter around her and crossed her arms over her chest. "I can't help it," she laughed thinly. "I'm cold blooded."

"Yeah, well, you're burning me up with all those layers you wear," Jenny laughed.

Ellen shivered inside, hoping that Jenny couldn't see the real truth. So far, nobody else had.

"So are you going to your granny's for Christmas tomorrow?"

Ellen nodded. "They're meant to come and get me at noon."

She was on the verge of panic; her grandmother would take one look at her and know the truth. Ellen knew she would. And then what? Her mother was going to be so disappointed. Her daddy probably wouldn't even look at her. Would they make her give it up? She'd have to drop out of school for sure.

Johnson knew. In a moment of weakness, she'd told him.

Oh, in her childish heart she thought he might care, that he might tell her that everything was okay and that he would take care of her.

He hadn't.

Instead, he'd laughed in her face and told her that it wasn't his problem.

She hadn't told another single soul. She'd considered telling Mrs. Lykins, because she'd always been so nice to her, but she couldn't. She was too ashamed of what her teacher might think of her. And, besides, Mrs. Lykins had left months ago. She was having her own baby and hadn't been able to teach this semester, might not even return in the spring. She had her own trouble.

And Logan? She couldn't possibly tell him, couldn't stand to have him look at her the same way that Johnson had.

Ellen just wanted to bury her head in her pillow and cry. Indeed, she'd already done that more times than she could count.

Realizing that Jenny was watching her closely, Ellen put on a fake smile and tried to make herself appear cheerful. "Are you looking forward to Christmas?" she asked.

Jenny nodded. "Looking forward to the food," she said and both girls laughed.

The urge to urinate suddenly came on strong. She'd been doing that a lot lately, had barely been able to hold it in.

"Be right back," Ellen cried before jumping to her feet and scampering out the door.

She'd just made it to the toilet in time when there was a knock on the door. "Just a minute," she called.

"Hurry up please."

"Ugh," Ellen groaned. It was her dorm mother.

Her stomach had been so weird lately. Everything was uncomfortable. She was hungry but couldn't eat and her belly was rumbly and sick all the time. It was the worst case of indigestion she'd ever had.

When she'd washed her hands and opened the door, she was surprised to see Miss Mollett still standing there, waiting. All it took was for her form mother to look pointedly down at Ellen's stomach for her to realize that she'd been found out.

"Come inside," Miss Mollett ordered, ushering Ellen into her own room.

Ellen obliged and Miss Mollett closed the door behind her.

She'd been in that room before but she was never not taken aback. She'd never seen anything so...religious. There were crosses on every wall. Over her bed, a bed that contained nothing but a plain white spread and flat pillow, hung a humongous painting of the Sermon on the Mount.

There were no other decorations, nothing personal to reflect a family or friends. No color.

"What are your plans?" Miss Mollett demanded. She didn't invite Ellen to sit in one of the tiny room's two chairs so she stood.

"I don't know," Ellen whispered.

"You won't get married," Miss Mollett informed her. "Not now, not ever, so you might as well wipe that idea from your mind."

Ellen hung her head, trying not to cry.

"You should have been sent away and if I'd realized your condition before this week, we would have seen to that."

Ellen nodded. She'd done something wrong; she might as well take the punishment.

"The last thing we need is another scandal like the last one."

Ellen knew that by the "last one" she was referring to Daisy–the runaway who'd been found murdered on the side of the road.

"Who did this to you?"

"Johnson," Ellen whispered.

She didn't have to give a last name, everyone knew him. He was their star basketball player, had the lead in all the school plays. Everybody liked him.

Miss Mollett pursed her lips, but also managed to look troubled. "He comes from a good family. He might help."

"He won't," Ellen assured her. "I asked."

She sighed. "We obviously need to keep you young girls on a tighter leash. You, not even fourteen years old, and he almost an adult. I don't know that we could survive that."

"I'm sorry," Ellen said.

"When your grandmother comes to collect you tomorrow, we will have a talk with her, decide what to do then."

Ellen knew that, by the tone of her voice, the conversation was over. She let herself out with resignation but as she walked down the hallway back to her room, the panic rose. She wasn't ready to tell her granny! There had to be a way to stop that, to keep everything from happening so fast.

Her belly lurched again, and she almost doubled over in pain.

She needed to come up with something.

FORTY-ONE

HAZEL HILL, KENTUCKY 2014

The room was pitch black and cold. So cold. She shivered and drew herself smaller inside the plastic that encased her. Why wasn't someone coming for her?

Each time she moved, the pain grew worse. She could no longer feel her extremities. She'd known cold, or thought she had, but this was far beyond anything she'd experienced. This was a pain so deep, a chill that reached into her soul.

She tried to move, tried to shift, but couldn't. Her body was stiff, frozen to the floor. The only warmth she felt was when the sticky plastic touched her skin.

In pain and exhaustion, she closed her eyes and began to sing.

Just as suddenly as it had begun, the pain was gone. The frigid air was replaced by a warm, balmy breeze. She could feel her muscles loosening up and relaxing, could feel the life course back through her veins as her blood ran hot.

When she opened her eyes, she was standing by a window. The sky was a deep blue and the shone down over the expansive lawn, casting a pearly glow on the bright green grass.

The room around her had a fresh-smelling scent–roses and pipe smoke. It was a comforting scent, one that made her feel safe and secure.

She reached out and touched the glass and was surprised to find that she could feel the hardness, the cool windowpane beneath her fingers.

Tinkling laughter suddenly filled the air. As she stood there in the window and watched, a little girl with long, black hair darted across the lawn, her locks flowing behind her like streamers. A tall, thin man was right behind her, a grin spread across his face.

She felt herself begin to smile, felt the love and happiness swell within her heart.

When she opened her mouth to call out to them, however, brought back her hand to rap at the window, she couldn't. Nothing came out but a low whimper, no matter how loudly she tried to scream. Her hand was suddenly frozen in space, unable to move.

Suddenly, the room began to spin. Dirty dark smoke began to fill the room, began to claw at her feet and long skirt. The smell was pungent–the stench of meat that had rotted in the sun. She gagged, clawed at her throat as the nastiness threatened to crawl inside and choke her.

Fight, *she urged herself,* fight to beat this back. You *can* beat this, you can beat this!

Taryn woke up screaming into her pillow.

*   *   *

"I was in my aunt Sarah's house," she told Nicki. "I knew that I was, because it was so familiar, but I wasn't myself."

"And in the first part of the dream?"

"I don't know," Taryn shrugged. "I didn't recognize it. I just felt so cold."

When Nicki called (ringtone: Emmylou Harris' "Boy from Tupelo" because of her fascination with Elvis.), Taryn had pulled over into a tiny church's parking lot. She didn't normally drive and talk on the phone, not when the roads were so curvy.

"Are you scared at the school? I mean, do you feel like something evil is there?"

"No," Taryn shrugged. "Not at all. In fact, I feel kind of the opposite. People have been very nice and it looks like kind of a utopia. I mean, we're talking about a dreamlife here in the mountains–get educated, folkdance on the weekends, high school basketball games, school plays, girls in pretty dresses, ice cream socials, nice looking buildings..."

"Yeah, so, I want to go there now..."

"I know, right?" Taryn laughed. "Me too!"

"And you're not even picking things up from the rest of campus?"

"Nothing," Taryn replied. "Not a thing."

"So this is a different kind of haunting," Nicki murmured.

"You're telling me."

"What's the rest of the area like?"

Taryn spent the next few minutes telling Nicki about West Liberty, about the abundance of farmland and presence of a few rare tobacco farms, of the tiny gas stations and country stores, of the little red-bricked church with its potluck Sunday dinners...

"That's settled it," Nicki swore, "Shawn and I are totally moving there!"

"There's a town on the other side of the hill," Taryn said, "and it's called Helechawa. Some of the people at the church told me that it's because it was so deep in the mountains that settlers said it was 'hell each way.' You know, if that changes your mind..."

"Sounds like Reading."

The two women giggled over that for several minutes.

"Oh!" Nicki suddenly burst out. "Did I tell you that the Ceredigion House is having their open house soon? They sent me an email, probably sent you one as well. They want us to come. It's not until August so I thought you might be able to make it."

Taryn had met Nicki and Shawn at the Ceregidion House, a stately old mansion on the moors of western Wales. The three of them had worked there together for several months as the owners attempted to restore the house to its former glory. It had been one of the best times of Taryn's life. She still wished that she was there, sitting in the dark little pub with Nicki, drinking wine and talking about their futures in front of the fireplace. Eating tortes and apple pancakes. Going for long walks around the countryside. It had been a good time.

"I'd like to go," Taryn said. "We'll have to see how I feel."

"Yeah, that's what I told them when I wrote them back," Nicki said. "Oh, but it would be so much fun! You should really try."

And Taryn would try. She desperately wanted to go. But she was feeling a little worse each day.

She was scared.

FORTY-TWO

NEW HAMPSHIRE, 2017

Charaty stood before Nicki with her purse slung over her shoulder. "I'm finished now. You can pay me if you're ready."

"Yeah, sure," Nicki said, looking up from her laptop. "Just hold on a sec."

"She was always like that too," Charaty said, glancing at the screen. "Always looking at her pictures, always researching. Her head was either in a book or on her computer."

"That was Taryn," Nicki agreed.

"Things got better with her here," Charaty said as she stood in the doorway and waited for Nicki to go through her wallet. "I don't want you to think that everything was bad. People will talk, will say bad things. Like that poor little girl."

"What little girl?"

Charaty snorted. “I know you’ve heard the story about the ghost in the cellar? There’s nothing to back that up. Nothing. Back then, people had nothing better to do than to talk. This place is so small that a whisper can be heard a mile away. If there’s nothing else to say, they will gossip.”

“So you don’t think the rumors about the child are true?” Nicki asked.

“If there is something here, it’s not a child,” Charaty murmured, “and it never was.”

Nicki was silent, considering.

“What do you mean ‘better’?” she asked at last.

“When her aunt passed away, we had a surge of crime, lots of drug problems. Businesses started to close. Then your friend moved into the house and things began improving. Fewer arrests, new businesses coming in…” Charaty offered a genuine smile. “I told her that she’d come here at a good time.”

Nicki paused and turned around. “Can you hold on for a minute?”

Charaty nodded. “I have no place to be.”

Nicki went into the library and pulled off a sheet of notebook paper from Taryn’s binder. When she re-entered the living room, Charaty was sitting in one of the winged back chairs. “Can you answer some questions for me?”

“Maybe,” Charaty shrugged.

“When did the man on the pond kill his wife?”

For the next half hour, Charaty gave her a rudimentary timeline for the biggest tragedies and crimes that the area had seen. Nicki sorted them by decade, making a list under each one, starting back from the eighteen hundreds. When she was finished, she saw that there were obvious gaps.

“Okay,” she said, chewing on her fingers. “Right here is a gap or something, from like the eighties until fairly recently. What was that like?”

Charaty looked over at the paper. “Good times. Nothing too bad. Those were some of the best years for us.”

“Okay,” Nicki nodded. “And this gap here, in the eighteen hundreds?”

“That’s when the town was settled, when it was beginning,” Charaty explained. “Again, it was a good time.”

“And things started getting bad *here*...” Well, it was obvious when things started getting bad. Around the turn of the century and it seemed to last until the eighties.

"Does it mean something?" Charaty had a keen look of interest on her face. She was no head to head with Nicki, peering at the sheet of paper.

"Maybe." Nicki sat back in her chair. "Charaty, do you believe that people can shield a place? That can be appointed to do something like that? That their presence can protect something or somewhere, keep the bad out?"

"If plants and rocks can do it then why not people?" Charaty asked.

"Do you believe that this place is special?"

Charaty nodded. "Yes, I do. There is something here. It draws people. They come and either they find what they are looking for and stay or they hurry on out. The power is strong. It is polarizing. The Indians knew it. The early settlers knew it."

"And you feel pulled to this place?"

Charaty nodded. "It is in my blood."

"But what is it? What is making it like this?"

Charaty smiled gently and shook her head. "I think you are searching for an explanation that you're not going to find. There are no answers in your computer or on your paper. Some places defy our reasoning and logic. They just exist. Something exists within them, something both good and evil. It is pure. It's as ancient as the gods. Maybe it is simply nature."

When Charaty left, Nicki sat in her living room, looking at that piece of paper for a very long time. She knew why Taryn had gone there, knew why she'd stayed.

And knew why she and Shawn could not.

* * *

"Are you positive?"

Nicki nodded her head.

"The little girl, the thirteen-year-old?"

She raised her arms and gave him a helpless look. "I don't know what else to tell you."

Shawn plopped down onto the sofa and studied Nicki's face. "You're sure she's dead and you're positive that was her in the window in Taryn's picture of Hazel Hill."

"I'm sure." Nicki had spent all day reading. And looking. And thinking. She'd reached several realizations.

"Because of the pictures..."

"She kept them in another file," Nicki explained. "They were hidden, which makes sense because what happened was covered up. It's something that *nobody* wants getting out. Taryn did her best to protect Ellen, too."

And now Nicki was sorry that she'd ever opened Taryn's laptop and went rooting around through the folders that she'd had no business opening–because it was clear that Taryn had wanted some tings to remain hidden.

"And this other decision that you've made, the one about the job and the house," Shawn pressed her. "You're sure about that as well?"

She bit her lip and looked at the floor. "Yes."

"Darlin, you'd better start talking because it seems to me you've come to a lot of conclusions and my curiosity is at an all-time high now..."

Nicki walked over to the sofa and settled herself on the floor next to Shawn's head. "She took pictures of most of what happened. You can see for yourself. And then I can explain the rest."

"Let's hear it."

FORTY-THREE

HAZEL HILL, KENTUCKY 2014

She still wasn't feeling well but Taryn was still hellbent to work on her painting. She didn't like getting more than a couple of days behind. Plus, it would be nice if she finished early. She'd get the remainder of her lodging stipend from the church even if she didn't stay the entire month. While her financial situation was vastly superior and more stable than it had been several years ago, she still worried about money.

Caroline Herring sang "Song for Fay", a tune written about the Larry Brown novel *Fay*, on her iPod while she used the rest of the daylight hours to finish some shading. When the song switched and turned into "Paper Gown", Taryn smiled and rolled her eyes.

"Caroline, *honey*," she muttered. "You know I love you but sometimes you just gotta lighten up."

Of course, Caroline was kind of like Emmylou Harris. Even their "happy" songs sounded sad. It had taken Taryn forever to convince Matt that "Love and Happiness" was an optimistic song about wishing the best for your loved ones. Just from the melody he'd assumed someone was dying.

"You listen to the most depressing music," he was fond of telling her. "And you're a negative person at all."

"Well..." she smiled now to herself. "Sometimes I am." If people could see what was inside her head, they'd probably steer clear of her.

It was one of Taryn's greatest regrets that, although she could see the past through her camera, it was never her past. Of all the people she'd lost, she'd never been able to make real contact with them. Had never been able to "see" them through her lens. She'd give just about anything to return to her nana's farmhouse in Franklin and see her rocking on the front porch. Or to hold up Miss Dixie and see Sarah out there weeding her herb garden. Walk back into her old house and see Andrew, her fiancé, napping on the couch.

The problem with a gift like this is that you couldn't control it, could never really predict what it was going to do next.

"Good for other people that I have it, hard on me," she mumbled now, just thinking of the jobs she'd done in the past and the various ways she'd used her "talent."

It was weird being on this side of campus. She was used to being on the side closest to the road–over there by the girls' dorm and admin building. Here, at the music building, she was surrounded by dilapidated barns, storage buildings, and a greenhouse that looked downright scary. (She was sure that if she went inside, she'd be taken right to that apartment where Jim Hensons' Muppets were living in "Troll.")

When her phone rang and she saw that it was Matt, she answered.

"Hello my little love," he sang.

"You sound chipper this evening."

"I'm in a good mood," he said. "I fixed a most excellent supper. Goulasch over mashed potatoes with homemade ciabatta bread."

"Sounds good," Taryn told him. "I had some Pringles."

"If you'd come down here, or invite me up there, I'd cook for you."

"I *can* cook you know," she said. Taryn paused after speaking, realizing how rude she'd sounded.

"You're a good cook," Matt agreed, ignoring her tone and moving on along. "So what are you doing right now?"

"Finishing up for the day, actually." She began putting away her brushes and paints. Due to the condition of the road, she hadn't been able to drive all the way to the music building so her car was back on the other side of campus. She'd had to lug all of her supplies with her. "What are you up to?"

"I rented a movie, 'The War of the Worlds', and I'm getting ready to watch it," he said.

"You sure you wanna watch that?" she teased him. "The last time you watched an apocalyptic film you had nightmares for week."

It was true; Taryn was the horror movie geek. Matt couldn't stand them. It had taken her a while to convince him to watch "Stand By Me" and "The Shawshank Redemption" because he'd seen Stephen King's name and refused to even read the blurbs. Taryn, on the other hand, watched them all: big budget, low budget, no budget–she'd yet to meet a horror movie she wouldn't try.

"Well, maybe you'll have to come down here and hold my hand," he said.

"Maybe I will," she teased him back.

"Seriously? When you coming?"

"Maybe next week," she said. She'd already started walking across campus, her plastic tote rolling along behind her on the wheels she'd installed. "I have to go back home and rewind first."

"Hey, have you thought anymore about you and I moving to your aunt's house together?"

Taryn stopped walking. The rundown tennis court was beside her. For some reason, it freaked her out. Maybe it was due to the mini jungle that was currently growing inside. She'd taken pictures of it, hoping to see a past in which it actually looked like a game could be played on it, but not even Miss Dixie had been that good.

"I thought you were joking," she said.

"I really do need a change," Matt said. "I think that might be it."

"Might doesn't really cut it, Matt," Taryn sighed as she began walking again. The wheels against the pavement were so loud that she could barely hear her own voice. "You have to be sure. A change is cutting your hair, buying a new wardrobe, taking up yoga. Not quitting your dream job to move to the wilderness and figure out life."

"Why not?"

"Because you'll regret it," she said, raising her voice over the racket. "And then you'll be upset with me."

"I could never be upset with you," he laughed.

But that wasn't true; he'd been upset with her plenty. He got upset when she'd had her first kiss with Bobby Haney behind the school. He got upset when she'd lost her virginity to the religious nut in college (who later told her that God told him they couldn't date but that she could still keep paying for his stuff when they went out "as friends"). He got upset when, after Andrew died, she didn't grieve in the way that he felt she should.

Heck, he got upset when she got engaged to Andrew. Matt had never liked him.

And she grew upset with him plenty–like the way he sometimes carried on about his ex-girlfriend, Clarissa. Or the way he was so self-involved that he could ramble on for hours about minutia, never once stopping to see if the other person had anything to add to the conversation. Or the way that he thought he was the best at everything he did.

But he had good points as well–no, *great* points. His empathy for people knew no bounds. He could hardly stand to watch the news because his heart hurt for everyone in trouble. And he was super creative; you should see the detailed drawings that he created in his coffee foam. And smart? The boy had been far and above every teacher he'd had in elementary and middle school. An imagination that knew no parallel. And nobody alive loved her the way that he did.

"Hey Matt?"

He'd been chattering on about something, vegan ice cream or something, when she came to a complete stop in the middle of the road and interrupted him.

"And then I learned that if you–"

"MATT!"

"Wait, what?"

"My car door's open," she said, dumfounded.

Matt snapped right to business. "Call the police. No, wait, you stay on the line and I'll use the landline to call. Are you at the school?"

"No, I mean yes I'm at the school but no, don't call," Taryn said. Leaving the plastic tub behind, she made her way to her car. It wasn't just one door, but both of her backdoors. They weren't standing wide open, but someone had definitely been in them and not closed them all the way.

"Is anything missing?"

Taryn poked her head inside and looked around. "Doesn't look like it," she said, "but someone definitely went through some things. My notes and sketches are scattered all over the seat."

Just get in the car and drive away," he ordered her. "Don't stick around to find out."

"Yeah, good idea." She wasn't going to argue with him. It might have just been some curious kids, but in the off chance that it wasn't, she didn't want to find herself in a bad situation.

"Are you in the car?"

"Inside, doors locked," Taryn replied. "I think I'm going to go to the Frosty Freeze and give the police a call, just in case."

It was almost completely dark and she was getting nervous. Whoever was there might still be around.

"Give me a call when you get there," Matt said. "Or else I'll worry."

"I will."

She was halfway down the road, almost to the Frosty Freeze, when she remembered that she'd left her supplies in the middle of the road.

* * *

She knew that returning for her tote was probably a bad idea but it contained all of her paint supplies, as well as the canvas she'd just been working on. If someone had really been in her car then her stuff probably wasn't safe sitting out in the open.

Taryn was damned if she was going to start that painting over from scratch.

The campus was deathly still when she pulled up to the parking lot. With only one streetlamp by the library, it took on an almost unearthly ambience. The buildings were all hulking shadows, some of them nothing more than dark outlines against the black sky.

Taryn shivered and clenched her fists.

In and out, she told herself as she put her car in park. And she was going to leave it running.

The good news was, her tote was still there. The hot pink Rubbermaid container was still waiting for her in the middle of the road, just before the dip that would take her to the other side of campus.

After taking a good, long look around to make sure nobody was nearby, Taryn jumped from the car and marched towards the container.

Almost there, almost there, she chanted to herself in time with her steps. Miss Dixie swung back and forth across her chest, keeping her own little rhythm.

The grating sound of the wheels on the pavement again interrupted the tranquil night like a slap in the face.

"Well, if anyone is still here then they know I'm here too," she mumbled. No use trying to hide now.

She couldn't hear a single thing other than the clanging and clattering of the wheels. If anyone was creeping up behind her, she'd have been blind sighted. For that reason, she didn't walk so much as skip as she made her way back to the car. When she reached her car, she popped her trunk and lifted the tote. As soon as it was in the air, she froze, tote parallel with her chest.

"What the..."

She'd heard it once before and had mistaken it for a kitten. Now she was very, very certain that she'd been wrong. It wasn't a kitten, it was a baby. A little baby. A newborn. Taryn had never been around newborns, but she watched a lot of television. She knew their cries from the MTV and TLC shows.

And then there was the scream–the long, blood-curdling scream that raised every hair on her arms.

Taryn quickly dumped the tote into her trunk and slammed the lid, then looked around wildly for the direction in which the cries had come.

The kitchen, of course.

Forgetting her idling car and the promises she'd made to Matt and herself, she quickly began moving towards the girls' dorm her heart racing and her breath coming in uneven bursts.

Two things happened then and they occurred so closely together that, for the next little bit, the two would become one event: the gunshot rang out and the woman began to sing.

At first, in her confusion, Taryn thought that the gunshot was in the past. After all, the baby and woman were. When it happened again, however, and she felt the bullet whiz by her ear, she knew that she was wrong.

When she turned around and looked behind her in surprise, a dark figure stood mere feet from her car. Though the streetlamp shined down on them at such an angle that it was impossible to determine if they were male or female, the pistol they held before them was real enough. Taryn could see the glint of it in the moonlight.

She began to run.

Zigzag when you run, she panted, *the police say not to run in the straight line.*

Good Lord, was she being shot at?

The next bullet that went by her head was the answer.

Taryn turned at the admin building and went straight for the front door. To her dismay, it was locked. It had *never* been locked before.

"Shit!" she cried.

When she turned and looked behind her again, the figure was still coming at her.

She needed the cover of darkness, to be in a place that they couldn't see her. Where she was, the streetlamp and her headlights casted such a glow that she may as well have had a spotlight on her.

Run, run, she could almost hear Nicki screaming in her ear.

I'm running, Nicki! I'm running!

At the back of the admin building she paused and caught her breath. They were still coming after her, she knew it even if she couldn't see it. If she could just get to a place where she could call the police...

The kitchen was just steps away. That door at the bottom of the stairs was heavy. She could block it.

Now, soundlessly but quickly, Taryn slipped down the stairs. She was ecstatic to find it unlocked. Once inside, she locked the door. Then, being as discreet as she could, she lifted one of the round folding tables and brought it to the door. After wedging it up against the door, she finally stopped and rested. She couldn't hear him or her coming down the stairs or even walking around outside. Luckily, the basement only had a couple of windows and they weren't big enough for a person to fit through.

The singing.

"All the pretty little horses..."

Taryn gulped. She'd wandered right into the very place in which the baby's cry and the woman's scream had originated.

The ethereal singing swallowed the air around her, leaving Taryn breathless.

As though she were moving through molasses, little by little Taryn tiptoed into the kitchen, holding her breath and not even daring to breathe.

The room was dark and empty, but Taryn knew she wasn't alone. Momentarily distracted by what was going on around her, she lifted Miss Dixie and began to snap.

FORTY-FOUR

West Liberty tornado damage

HAZEL HILL, 1965

Once Jenny had said goodbye and left, Ellen quickly pushed her packed suitcase under her bed. Now, if someone looked into their room, they'd think that she was gone as well.

Miss Mollett was waiting for Ellen's granny to arrive but she also knew that her dorm mother's own ride would be there to get her at 5:00 pm. Everyone had to be out of the dorms by then. If she could just make herself scarce until then, she'd be fine. Miss Mollett would simply think that Ellen had slipped off with her family before anyone could see her.

"Are you sure you don't want to come here?" her granny has asked her on the telephone.

"Jenny's family has a big Christmas. They want me to come to their house," Ellen had lied.

She felt terrible fibbing to her granny like that but she just wasn't ready to let everyone know. She needed time alone, time to think. If she just had more time...

Ellen shrugged on her winter coat and eased herself from her room. Nobody was in the hallway so she tiptoed to the stairs then quickly moved down them, quiet as a little mouse. When she got outside, she looked both ways then slipped around the corner.

Before Ellen started working in the library, she'd worked in the kitchen doing the grunt work. She knew it inside and out. She also knew that there was a little closet that was never used. She could hide out there until everyone left and then she could let herself out and go back to her room.

Then maybe she'd have time to think about what she could do to get out of this mess.

Her belly and back were hurting something awful, but she tried to ignore them.

Before she started down the stairs, she stopped and looked behind her. She had the queerest sensation that someone was watching her, but she didn't see a single soul. Most everyone else had already left for their winter break. There weren't that many people left on campus.

The closet was tiny, not bigger than three feet long and three feet wide. It was cozy, though, and soon Ellen had stuffed herself inside and had settled amongst the boxes of extra dishes.

Now all she had to do was wait...

* * *

Ellen was cold. She wished she had a watch because she had no idea how long she'd been in there waiting. It would be dark soon, or maybe it was already dark, and she could leave. She'd dozed a little and that had helped pass the time.

She wondered about Mrs. Lykins and how she was. She hadn't seen her since the start of the semester. She'd only stayed for a week and then she'd taken leave. There were rumors about her, rumors about her having a baby. Stories about her being sick. Ellen hoped she was okay.

When her legs started cramping and the pain in her back worsened, Ellen finally stood up and stretched. It was pitch black in that closet and she was ready to leave.

Even though she knew that it was likely that everyone had gone, Ellen was still cautious when she opened the door and stepped out into the kitchen. She could barely see her hand in front of her face.

She crept to the tiny window and peered through the bars, looking for any cars that might be in the parking lot. There weren't any.

When she took another step, the pain that shot through her stomach was almost unbearable.

"Oh!" Ellen yelped as she doubled over and clutched her belly. And then, "Oooohhh" as the warm liquid trickled down her legs and puddled at her feet.

She'd delivered two litters of puppies. She knew the glazed looks that the dogs got in their eyes when they were about to give birth, she had heard them make that low, whimpering sound before one came out. She'd seen them howl with the pain, had seen the slimy little things that slid out of them like waste.

Ellen had never thought about the fact that the same things were going to happen to her.

Panicked now, and still doubled over, Ellen painfully worked her way to the basement door. There was one little window in it, just big enough for her to fit a hand through. Through it, she could see that the campus was dark and deserted.

"Ooohhh," Ellen groaned again, this time louder.

She reached down for the handle and turned.

And then she turned again.

It wouldn't open.

Straightening as best she could, Ellen used all her strength and both hands to turn the knob and tug on the door, but it was no use. It was locked, and the heavy oak wasn't budging.

"Help me!" Ellen screamed at the top of her lungs. "Help me!"

A figure appeared in the window just then, a familiar face just inches away. "Please," Ellen begged, "find something to open the door with. I'm having a baby!"

But Johnson just stood there and listened. And then he walked away without even turning back.

When another searing hot pain coursed through her lower body, Ellen collapsed onto the floor, the whole room going black.

* * *

Ellen might not have known what to do, but her body did. She wasn't sure how long she'd been unconscious but when she awoke, something inside of her had changed. Things were moving down there and there was a lot of pressure in her lower abdomen. She felt as though she were having a bowel movement, like she needed to strain as hard as she could.

On her hands and knees, she crawled back into the kitchen until she was under a light switch and then she slowly climbed up the wall and flicked it with her finger before dropping back to the ground in exhaustion.

With a little bit of light now, she could see that her skirt was covered in blood and fluid. Ellen reached down and tugged off her bloomers, they were stained beyond redemption now, and laid back against the wall.

And when she just could take the feeling of pressure anymore, she began to push.

* * *

The baby was the tiniest thing she'd ever seen, almost as cute as the little puppies she'd delivered out in the barn. It had known just what to do, too, when she'd removed her cardigan and lifted her blouse.

There wasn't any comfortable place in the kitchen or dining hall for them to go but she'd tried to make them a little bed in the corner by the stove. Now, exhausted yet somehow pleased with herself, she looked around and tried to assess her situation.

The windows wouldn't work. Even if she could fit through them, and she thought she might be too big with her belly, they all had those bars. She could probably use some knives or something to pry open the door. She'd try that next.

If not, well then, surely someone would come by. The campus wouldn't be deserted all winter break. Right?

She dozed off and on throughout the rest of the night but she tried to keep herself awake as best she could. The baby, a little girl, she wrapped up in her skirt, feeling bad about how stained it was, and held her close. Whenever it was hungry it would root around and mewl like a little kitten. Sometimes she wasn't sure if it was getting anything out of her. It sure didn't act like it was satisfied. Once, after suckling on her so hard that she cried out in pain, it let out the biggest squawk she'd ever heard.

After that, she tried shifting her in different positions, rocking her back and forth, and holding her head in her hands to give her a better angle. She wanted to get up and walk around with her, pace the floor and stretch her legs, but she was just too weak.

Ellen was famished, too. They'd cleaned out the refrigerator and cabinets before everyone went home because they hadn't wanted the food to spoil. Now Ellen was hoping that there was some scrap left behind, a block of cheese or can of beans that someone had forgotten.

Hours passed, and the sun came up. Her baby was restless, and Ellen was exhausted. She thought babies were supposed to spend most of their time sleeping but hers never stayed gone for more than half an hour at most. Just as soon as she got good and asleep herself, her baby would wake her up with a piercing scream as it rooted and snorted just like a little piglet, trying to find her.

"Shhhh," she tried to pacify it. "It's okay."

That just seemed to make her angrier.

Ellen knew that she needed to clean her baby off, needed to clean herself off, but it was so cold in the kitchen that she was afraid of getting them wet. Any moisture would surely freeze them to death. She did the best she could with dishtowels and damp sponges that were drying on the sink.

When the sun started setting again, Ellen attempted to get up. "We have to try to get out of here little one," she said. Her baby looked up at her with big, wide eyes and she could have sworn that she nodded.

"You just stay right here in your little nest and I'll be right back."

She'd managed to reach behind her and pull out some trash bags from a drawer. She'd plucked one apart and stuffed the other bags inside. This she put on the floor and then covered with her coat. It was nicer than putting her baby on the hard, concrete ground anyway.

As soon as she got to her feet, her baby began to whimper.

"Shhhh," she hissed down. "I'll be right back."

The baby wasn't having any of that, though. The longer she stood there, the louder she screamed.

"Oh okay," Ellen sighed. Still feeling shaky and a little off balance, she bent over and gently lifted the crying, red bundle from the floor. "Come with me."

Her baby was not to be pacified, however. On and on she cried. Finally, as though by instinct, Ellen raised her shirt, opened the coat, and pressed the baby against her. The skin on skin contact seemed to work.

"Hush a bye, don't you cry,

Do to sleep you little baby..."

The baby whimpered but didn't try to do anything else.

On legs she hoped wouldn't fail her, around and around the room Ellen walked, looking inside cupboards and doors as she tried to find something to eat.

"Close your eyes..."

The only thing she found was milk still dripping from the machine in the corner. They had not empties it. Ellen lifted the top and looked inside. There was enough for her. Enough to keep her from starving.

When she was convinced that her baby was truly asleep, she carefully laid her back on the garbage bags. After finding a clean glass on the counter, she silently poured herself a glass. The cool liquid felt good against her throat and the smell of dairy comforted her.

Funny how both of us are soothed by milk, she laughed to herself.

For the next hour she worked up a sweat as she tried using knives, forks, and even a hammer to get the door open. It was no use. It wouldn't budge.

"And of course there's no way to get from down here to upstairs without going outside," Ellen thought sadly.

Until someone came to find them, they were stuck.

She'd no sooner sat back down then her baby was awake again, searching for food.

* * *

It was the cold, and not her baby, that woke Ellen up. She thought she was dreaming at first, dreaming that her toes had turned into icicles and that she was standing in the middle of an icy pond.

When she woke up, she couldn't feel her fingers and her lips wouldn't work properly.

Frantically, Ellen looked down at her baby to check on her. She was fine. The garbage bags were acting as insulation and though she twitched a little in her sleep, her skin felt as warm as it could.

Teeth chattering and shivering, Ellen wrapped her cardigan tightly around her. When she stood and looked outside, the sky was turning dark again and the trees were bent from the wind.

While her baby continued to sleep, Ellen searched for more insulation. All she found were more garbage bags. Getting to work, with one she cut holes for her legs then slipped it on like a pair of pants. The others she unfolded and stuffed into her "pants" and then used the tape to tie it together at the top like a makeshift belt. The bloody dishtowels she bound around her bare legs.

It helped for a while but as the night wore on, she may as well have not even tried. The cold was seeping into her skin, cutting right down to the bone. She didn't think she'd ever felt anything like it. She tried to feel grateful that she at least wasn't outside in the wind, but it was hard to look on the bright side when your lungs were turning into blocks of ice.

"It will get better in the morning," she promised her baby.

* * *

By daylight the temperature had taken a turn for the worse.

Ellen was no longer breathing properly and she'd ceased having feeling in her legs. In the beginning, she'd been able to get up and walk around–had forced herself to do so for the circulation. Now, however, she couldn't even stand. Her fingers had turned blue several hours before. Her teeth had chattered for the longest time but now they were strangely silent.

"Someone will come for us," she whispered to her baby.

She looked up at her mother and blinked. Ellen reached down and brushed a speck of dust from the baby's cheek. In doing so, her fingers touched cold skin. It was the last thing she'd feel.

"Oh no," Ellen cried.

With great difficulty, she removed her last outer layer, her cardigan, and wrapped it snugly around the little one. She then laid it back on the garbage bags and covered it with the coat and skirt.

They fell back asleep.

When Ellen awoke, she was surprised to find that she wasn't even cold. In fact, she felt blissfully comfortable.

"See?" she whispered to the tiny little human that was snuggled in next to her. "I told you it would get better."

She tried to pick her baby up to nurse her, but she couldn't. Her arms were no longer functioning the way they should. Instead, she opened her blouse and leaned over. While her baby suckled, she sang.

"Close your eyes, you will see

All the pretty little horses..."

The baby gurgled in what, to Ellen, sounded like happiness.

"I'm going to take a nap now, okay?" she said sleepily. "Just for a few minutes."

Then Ellen leaned back against the stove and closed her eyes.

FORTY-FIVE

Hazel Green Christian Church

HAZEL HILL, KENTUCKY 2014

Dumfounded, Taryn scrolled back through the pictures on her screen. They were all there: the little girl lying on the floor in a pool of blood and fluid, the little baby wrapped in a stained skirt, the pile of garbage bags, the hammer by the door, the man looking through the window, the little mother and baby huddled together by the stove, the girl leaning back with her eyes closed...and Millie standing over the frozen body of Ellen, holding the tiny infant in her arms while a dour, middle-aged woman looked on.

"Oh, poor Ellen," Taryn cried, forgetting all about her current situation. "Poor little thing. She froze to death!"

Literally.

Had the baby lived? When had it been found? And where was Ellen?

"Is that what you wanted, Ellen?" Taryn spoke softly in the hushed room. "You wanted someone to know about you? To know what happened? Is that what you've been trying to tell us?"

Taryn's phone did not have a signal in the basement. She'd tried it several times, to no avail.

How long had she been down there? An hour? Half an hour? She wasn't sure.

What she did know, however, was that she wasn't going to hide out in the kitchen and suffer the same fate poor Ellen had. She was going to fight.

The only thing that she could see to use as a weapon was a baseball bat leaning against the stove. She didn't know how it got there or where it came from, didn't care, and it wouldn't protect her against a bullet, but it was all she had.

After carefully moving the table away from the door, Taryn eased it open and cautiously slipped outside. She didn't see anyone.

From where she stood, she could see her car. Oddly enough, it was still idling.

Perhaps whoever had been trying to hurt her left. She might be okay.

Taryn didn't stick around to find out if anyone was lurking in the shadows. When she saw the coast was clear, she took off at a run across the lawn and through the small parking lot.

When she reached the car, she heaved a sigh of relief. "Yes!"

She heard the gun cock before she saw it or the man who held it.

"Just tell me where they are," he pleaded. "That's all. Tell me where those letters are, and you can leave here and never come back."

Taryn didn't have to turn around to know who was standing behind her. She'd instantly recognized Clark's voice.

FORTY-SIX

West Liberty tornado damage

NEW HAMPSHIRE, 2017

It didn't make any sense. Matt had said it and Charaty had even alluded to it, but Nicki had remained unconvinced. And then there, in her virtual notebook, Taryn had confessed it herself.

She'd been at peace.

Something had happened within those walls, on that property, that had convinced Taryn that she was right where she needed to be.

"Believing in ghosts brought me to life."

Had she fallen in love? And, if so, then with whom? She'd been alone...right?

In the last few days of her life, Taryn had written only of happiness and peace. Not contentment, she hadn't accepted her fate and was ready to die, she'd been *happy*. Maybe even deliriously so.

"Home," she'd written. "I am home."

For the first time since Taryn's death, Nicki was starting to feel serenity herself. Taryn hadn't suffered, hadn't been in agony at the end. Had even found some measure of happiness that perhaps nobody could comprehend. She'd reached an understanding about something in her life and it had exulted her.

"Finally, I am where I belong."

"You were meant to be here Taryn," Nicki said aloud, looking out over the lake off in the distance. "How much of that had you figured out for yourself? How much did you know?"

Maybe all of it.

And because of what Taryn had done, because of the choices she'd made, Nicki now knew the ones that were best for her.

FORTY-SEVEN

HAZEL HILL, KENTUCKY 2014

Taryn put her hands up in the air and backed towards the driver's side door. "I don't have them here, Clark," she said slowly. "They're back in my room."

Clark looked wildly around as if trying to decide what to do next. His eyes were bloodshot, like he hadn't slept for a very long time. His hair stuck straight up from his head in tufts. From the way he was waving the gun around in the air, Taryn feared that he'd kill them both by accident if nothing else.

"I can get them for you," she said, trying to make her voice calm. "You can go with me."

"Yeah, yeah," he bobbed his head up and down like a yo-yo. "Let's do that. Let's go."

But when Taryn turned around to get inside the car, he shouted at her. "No!"

"What's the matter?" she asked. "Don't you want to ride with me?"

"You won't get them," he sneered. "You'll trick me."

"I won't," she promised. Then she pointed to the ignition. "You can drive if you'd like."

Oh, please say no.

"It's too late," he snapped. "You've told everyone. Told them all."

"Told who what?" Taryn was genuinely confused. She'd learned a lot over the last few days.

"About the girl, about her death."

"Ellen's death was an accident," Taryn said, wondering how he knew about it and why it scared him.

"Ellen? No," he spat. "Who cares about her? Daisy!"

"Daisy?" Then Taryn remembered–the girl who'd ran away and was murdered. But that had been years before Ellen.

"I honestly don't know what you're talking about," she said sincerely.

"The letters," he said. "He told her in the letters."

"Logan?" Taryn thought back to what Logan had written, trying to remember his words. "No, he didn't tell her. He said he had something to say but he never said what it was. She died before he could."

Clark reached inside his coat pocket and produced a hand full of papers. "These, I got these," he shouted. "He told her in them, he did!"

Taryn stood there, dumbfounded, as they fell to the ground like confetti. "I followed her to see if she'd talked to anyone, saw her getting them out of the steps." Now Clark was rambling like a lunatic but as long as he was talking, he wasn't shooting. "I found these, these I kept. But the others, I could never find them. They did something with them. *You* have them! And I need them!"

"You can have them!" Taryn swore again. "I promise!"

But the look in his eyes was total madness. Whatever deep end he'd been treading water in had just gone over his head.

He started at her, gun raised high in the air, and Taryn clenched her eyes and braced for impact.

And then, to her surprise, there was another sound.

"Clark Johnson Reynolds." Taryn opened her eyes and saw Rose, in blue jeans and a sweatshirt, standing just inches from Clark, a gun pointed at his head. "You put that down right now. Mother's already called the cops."

Millie stood off to the side, her silver cane propping her up. She nodded.

"Mother knew you were up to something," Rosa said, directing her words to Clark. "When Taryn said that you were here, taking stuff out. How you kept showing up. You were watching her, hoping she wouldn't find what you were sure was still here."

"I knew she was snooping around," he barked.

"I was taking pictures," Taryn said pointedly

"They wouldn't have thrown her things out, would've kept them," he said. "But I couldn't find them."

How had it been so easy for me to find the crate, Taryn wondered. *Had Ellen herself had a hand in that?*

"And when I saw the look on Logan's face when we were talking about Ellen," Rosa said. "The way *you* looked..."

"I never did care none for you," she said stiffly. "I knew you got that girl in trouble, knew it was you all along."

Clark lowered his weapon and looked from one woman's face to the other. "It was an accident," he said, his face dropping. "I didn't know. I didn't know she'd die or I would've opened the door, I swear. Who could've known?"

Millie's face contorted into something wretched.

"You left her in there," she said quietly. "She could've lived."

"What do *you* care?" he spat. "You got something out of it, too."

Millie turned white and then red when Rosa looked over at her. "Mother?"

"You were my miracle child," she whispered. "I always told you so."

Taryn could hear the siren before the cruiser raced onto the campus. She could see the flashing blue lights lighting up the night sky. Relief settled over her. As it grew closer and closer, however, Clark dropped to his knees. "Make it stop," he cried, covering his ears with his hands. "It's so loud."

"Oh stop it," Rosa snapped. She continued to hold the gun on him. "Just stop it."

"Make it stop!"

"Make what stop, Johnson?" Millie asked.

"The *baby*!" he wailed as he rocked back and forth on the ground. "Can't you hear it? Can't you hear the baby crying?"

FORTY-EIGHT

NEW HAMPSHIRE, 2017

Shawn shook his head sadly then passed Nicki a teacup. “It’s hot,” he warned her.

“You make better tea than I do,” she smiled.

Shawn shrugged. "One of my many admirable qualities."

"I saw it all, Shawny," she sighed.

Shawn pulled out a chair across from her at the table and sat. Silently, they both began adding sugar and milk.

"I know sweetie," he said. "Those pictures were horrible. No wonder Taryn wanted them hidden away."

A tremor ran through Nicki and she tried to shake it off like an insect. The thought of that poor little girl trapped alone in that cold room...

"I looked it up," she said, "it was a freak temperature drop. They said that it hit almost twenty below zero with the windchill."

"Even without it being that cold, she would have lost a lot of blood already," Shawn added, "and been weak."

If Nicki closed her eyes, she could still see her little body with the dishtowels taped around her legs, the garbage bag bound around her waist. She'd done her best; it just hadn't been enough.

"The baby survived," Shawn said, giving his tea a stir. The clanking of the spoon against the porcelain was a surprisingly cheery sound–a reminder that *they* were alive and well.

Nicki nodded. Yes, the infant had lived but while that was somewhat of a consolation, it didn't take away from the fact that another child had died in a senseless, horrible way. A way that could have been avoided.

"You talked to Rosa then?"

Yes, she had. The other woman had accepted her friend request, and then her video chat, almost immediately.

"She didn't know that Ellen was her mother, Clark Johnson her father," Nicki said. "Though she'd started suspecting something was up there at the end."

"And her mother?"

"She'd lost a baby that fall. It wasn't something that a lot of people talked about back then, though you know that a lot would've known," Nicki added. "She was on bedrest for the end of the pregnancy. When she had the stillborn, she remained in the house, unable to get out of bed. It wasn't until the dorm mother called and asked her to accompany her to the campus that she finally got up."

"Ellen had lied?"

He'd heard the story twice already but continued to humor Nicki as she went over it again.

"Told her granny that she was going home with her friend, her friend that she was going home with her granny..." Nicki sighed. It was a tale as old as time. Only her family had figured it out when Ellen's parents had made a surprise trip home from Tennessee and had been unable to find their daughter at her friend's house.

"What made the dorm mother think to go look at the campus? In the kitchen?"

Nicki shrugged. "I don't know for sure. I think she may have known that Ellen was pregnant, or at least suspected. I guess she thought they'd just start looking there."

Shawn shook his head and emitted a long whistle. "I am still having trouble wrapping my head around the fact that the other girl was connected."

"Killed by Johnson's brother," Nicki agreed. "Dang, people and their reputations. He was so convinced that Taryn knew about the murder, knew that he'd been involved in Daisy's death. Even after all those years, Clark Johnson Reynolds was afraid that the truth would come out and everyone in town would know."

"And their little utopia would be destroyed."

Nicki nodded miserably.

"The bright side is that our girl helped tie some of that together," Shawn reminded her. "She was the catalyst that made it all come out. They were ugly truths, but they needed to be said."

"The only arrest that came out of it was Clark for threatening Taryn," Nicki said.

"I know," Shawn sighed. "Justice for Daisy's death may never come, not with all the key players gone. But I believe it comes around eventually."

Nicki got up from the table and poured herself another cup of tea.

"The buildings were demolished," she called over her shoulder. "They're gone."

"It may be for the best," Shawn said.

Nicki laughed. "Even after she'd learned that went on, Taryn still thought that they could been restored, and the place opened as an Appalachian folk center or retreat center."

"She had grand visions," Shawn smiled. "Too bad she didn't have the money. She'd have snatched up every old property she came across."

Yes, she would have, Nicki thought with a grin.

"Now sit," Shawn ordered, pointing back to her chair. "And let's talk about packing. We are off to Salem for the Danvers Mental Hospital job in a little under three weeks and it's going to take you that long to figure out what you're going to wear."

Nicki rejoined him at the table and smirked. "I already know what I'm going to wear," she said, "but it will take me that long to lose some weight. The camera *does* add ten pounds, you know."

"You're perfect just the way you are," he said, patting her on the hand.

"You're just looking to get lucky," she teased him.

"Yes I am."

Nicki glanced up at the grandfather clock that ticked away in the foyer. She wondered how long it had been there, how many things it had seen. "Matt will be here next week. You'll need to show him around, tell him how things work."

"I will," he nodded. "You think he'll be okay here?"

"I think so," Nicki replied. "He's looking forward to it."

"So everyone will be where they're meant to be then?"

"Yes," Nicki said, feeling as if a weight were lifting. "Everyone will be where they're meant to be."

FORTY-NINE

Library

HAZEL HILL, KENTUCKY 2014

Rosa's bright red, form fitting dress looked spectacular against her tanned skin. Her hair had never looked blonder or fluffier. Taryn thought she looked like a movie star. She was out of place with the tattered tennis court behind her.

"I just wanted to thank you again for the paintings," Rosa said. "They'll outlive us in the church and copies will be sent to the historical society."

They'll outlive us, Taryn repeated in her head. Chills zipped down her spine. All her paintings and photographs would outlive her. They were her immortality.

"Despite what happened, it's a beautiful place," Taryn said sincerely. "Peaceful."

"It is," Rosa agreed as she looked around the ragged campus and sighed. "But it's time for me to move on. It's time for me to find my own place."

Taryn knew that the other woman wasn't just talking about an apartment or new digs.

"Your mother?"

"She's agreed to go to the assist living facility in Lexington until she can get on in Nashville," Rosa said. "I think she'll like it. She's afraid, nervous about leaving Hazel Hill, but she's a sociable woman. She'll like being around other people. I can tell that she's getting excited, even though she won't admit it."

"You'll love Nashville," Taryn told her.

Rosa's eyes alit with anticipation. "The Grand Ol Opry every weekend and Printer's Alley on Saturday's night. I've already started packing."

Rosa would live out, if not the rest of her life then at least a solid portion of it, in Taryn's own hometown. She was chasing her dream of "big city living" and trying something outside of Hazel Hill and the academy. She was eager with possibilities, even though she was nearing retirement age. It was never too late to start over.

"I've felt tied to this place my whole life," Rosa sighed, suddenly serious. "Part of that was Mother's fault, part of it mine, but I've let it hold me back. I spent my childhood hearing about how I'd one day buy it and turn it into something and then I spent my adulthood feeling like a failure for not being able to do so. I've allowed my fear of it, and the fantasy of it, to keep me from trying anything else."

"Most of our chains are invisible," Taryn agreed.

Rosa nodded. "This isn't my place. It belonged to another time. It's time for me to live in *mine*."

"Logan knew that something bad had happened to Ellen," Taryn said suddenly, changing the subject. "He just couldn't prove it."

“I keep thinking about her in that cold room by herself,” Rosa shuddered, casting a glance at the dorm.

Taryn had not shown her the pictures, hadn’t told her of their existence. They were too heartbreaking. Rosa didn’t need to see the last hours of her little mother like that. Nobody did.

“The ceremony was lovely,” Taryn said.

It hadn’t taken Millie long to lead them to the spot in her rose garden where both Ellen and her infant, a girl she’d named Louisa, were buried. Now they had permanent resting spots in Rosa’s family graveyard.

“Mother spent a lot of time in that garden,” Rosa said, “but I always felt drawn to it as well. Whenever I’d fight with Mother and Daddy I used to go out there and hide, try to collect my thoughts. I had no idea that I was within feet of my *real* mother.”

The school had simply convinced Ellen’s parents that she’d ran away, and they’d had no reason to think otherwise. The academy may not have survived another scandal and so Miss Mollett had been instrumental in covering everything up. Millicent Lykins had her baby again, Ellen was laid to rest, and Clark Johnson Reynolds wasn’t speaking. Outside of his suspicions to what Clark’s brother, Jonah, had done to

Daisy, Logan had been unaware of anything that was going on.

Ironically, the school had closed just a few years after that anyway. Tragedies all the way around.

"Logan got his letters, all of them," Rosa said brightly. "He'd continued to leave them over break, thinking that Ellen would return and get them. She didn't, of course. I guess if Clark hadn't been so paranoid, hadn't found them first, they would've been destroyed by the elements and I wouldn't have them."

Logan had made copies for Rosa, copies of both his letters and Ellen's responses. Rosa was in the process of having some framed.

"At what point did you realize that something was off?"

Rosa shrugged, "At church. When Mother claimed that she was two months pregnant during the 'Our Town' production. I was born in January. Most pregnancies do not last eleven months."

"Maybe she was subconsciously ready to get the truth out," Taryn said.

"When we spoke about Clark, Mother grew nervous. She asked me to take her to your motel room. When you weren't there, we came straight to the school."

"I guess it's a good thing you were loaded," Taryn said thinly.

"Oh," Rosa laughed. "That wasn't mine, Mother's the one with the gun."

Both women were silent for several minutes. Taryn was glad that the church had liked her paintings, glad she'd been able to provide a service to them.

Glad the job was over.

"Well," Taryn said as she stuck out her hand, "it's been real."

Rosa laughed and grasped her fingers. "Thank you," she said. "I don't know how else to say it."

"Just look me up when you're in Nashville," she told her, "and we'll go honky tonking together."

"It's a plan," Rosa promised her.

FIFTY

NEW HAMPSHIRE, 2017

Nicki and Matt stood silently over Taryn's grave and gazed down upon the headstone. The words were simple, just her name and dates, but they'd had it engraved with musical notes, a palette, and a camera. Nicki thought Taryn would have approved.

"Sure you're ready to do this?" Nicki asked.

"Sure you're ready to go off and become a big TV star?" he teased her.

Matt was one of the best-looking men Nicki had ever seen. Tall and thin, his mixed Native American/Italian/Irish ancestry gave him olive skin and hair so black it looked blue. When they were out in public together, women turned and gave him second looks.

"I'm excited," he admitted. "I'm enjoying this project and I can do it from here as well as I could from anywhere else."

"Do you wonder if..."

Nicki stopped, realizing that it wasn't any of her business. Matt did not appear to take offense, however.

"Do I wonder if I should have pushed Taryn on it and come up here with her?"

Nicki nodded.

"Every day," he said. "But I tried. I tried talking her into it."

Did you really? Nicki wondered. *Did she truly know that you wanted to do it or was she afraid that you were simply running from your problems and using her as an escape?*

But she kept those thoughts to herself.

"I only wanted to take care of her," he said.

"And now you can."

"Now I can," he echoed.

"There were twelve-hundred murders here between 1750 and 1861," Nicki said.

"And then they stopped for a while?"

Nicki nodded. "When Nora Alderman were born, they stopped."

"And after she passed?"

"Infant mortality was the highest in the state. Half the town was destroyed by a tornado. There was an earthquake. A flood. Massive fires. People seemingly going crazy and others dropping dead like flies."

"Her husband and daughter?"

"Apparently killed by someone who worked for them, someone who had never done anything bad in his life before that," Nicki told him. "Things were bad."

"Until Taryn was born," Matt said. It wasn't a question but, rather, a statement.

"Until Taryn was born."

"Whatever thing is here, Taryn keeps it the area safe," Matt said. "Just the way that Nora did."

"Even in death," Nicki said.

Matt looked around and watched the wind ruffling the spring buds on the trees. A shadow crossed over the sun, darkening the sky for a moment, but then it was light again and everything was fine. "Maybe she's not gone."

"I think she's still here," Nicki agreed, "in some sense."

Indeed, whenever things started getting bad at the house, it never lasted for long. It would continue to keep trying to get out, to spread its nastiness however it could, but it would never fully win. Not if she was somehow around.

"I'm meant to be here," Matt stated firmly, "to take care of things."

By "things," Nicki knew he meant Taryn.

"What if," she said slowly, "Taryn found something in death that she didn't have in life? What if she's happy in death in a way that she couldn't be happy in life..."

She couldn't come right out and say what she was thinking, what she had come to believe. It would hurt him too much. She thought he understood what she was hinting at, however.

"It's okay," he said. "It doesn't matter how we're together. Or who she's with. I've always been meant to watch over her. And now I can."

Together, they departed the graveyard and started back across the lawn to the house. "So, what are you going to do," Matt began. "You know, when you're not busy becoming famous on TV?"

Nicki glanced up at the house. For a moment, she thought she saw a man and a woman standing together in the bedroom window, looking down upon the lawn, but then they disappeared, and she couldn't be sure she'd seen them at all.

"I don't know," she laughed. "I was thinking of taking up photography."

FIFTY-ONE

Bridge into Hazel Green, Kentucky

HAZEL HILL, KENTUCKY 2017

Taryn sat on her bed and looked around the dingy motel room. Her suitcases were packed, her car loaded up for the long drive home. She wasn't ready to leave yet, though. She was very tired, so much so that she thought that if she laid down and took a nap she may never wake up.

"I don't know that I can do these long drives anymore," she'd complained to her best friend, Nicki, on the phone earlier that day. "Any time I do something like that anymore, I wind up spending the next three days in bed paying for it."

"You need a break," Nicki had told her. "Come to the UK and Shawn and I will take care of you!"

"I'm not going to impose on you all," Taryn had laughed. "The last thing you need is me in the middle of your honeymoon period."

"Pfft," Nicki had snorted. "It would make it better. Come on, I'll bake pies!"

Taryn laughed, even now, thinking about it. The truth was, as tempting as it sounded she wasn't sure she could manage the flight. Sitting for long periods of time was part of what was bothering her. The pain in her back and hips became unbearable. Not even the "good" pain medication was helping anymore. She'd taken to using kratom, a foul-tasting and even worse-smelling tea that she ordered from online, and it was filling in the gaps but she still had moments in which she just wanted to curl up, close her eyes, and not awaken.

Her phone rang, and it was Matt.

"Hello there lovely," he said.

She could hear him rustling around in his kitchen. It was his lunchtime. She could imagine him making something exotic and delicious while she sat there with her Twinkies.

"You cooking?"

"Not, just eating," he replied. "Cookie dough ice cream. Straight out of the box."

Well, maybe not…

"You okay?" he asked. "You feel down."

"Just tired," she said.

Her blanket, the soft fluffy one that she traveled with, was folded in her lap. She ran her fingers over it and the downy material felt nice. She'd had that blanket forever; it was her favorite. Like Miss Dixie, she took it with her almost everywhere she went. It was always in her motel room. Her nana had made it.

"I cleaned up that audio from the kitchen, if you want it," Matt said. "It still creeps the hell out of me every time I listen to it."

She'd debated on letting Rosa listen to it. In the end, she'd decided not to. It was Rosa's mother, but it was Taryn's gift. Some things she wanted to keep close, not sharing it with anyone but Matt.

"Look, why don't you come down here and stay?" Matt asked. "Come visit. You can lie on the beach all day. You can take off your shoes and feel the sand under your feet. We'll dance at the bandstand there by the movie cinema. Take a vacation–and *not* a working one."

Taryn thought of returning to her dinky little apartment, the one with the elevator that always smelled like cheese, and then thought of being down in Florida with Matt. She did need to talk to him, they did need to figure out what they should do next.

And she *was* tired.

"Okay," Taryn said at last.

"I'll see you in a few days?"

Despite the ache in her lower back, Taryn shook her head and said, "No, I think I'll head on down right now. Once I get in the car, I may as well just keep driving."

She could hear the excitement in his voice as he went on to make plans for her arrival.

"Don't worry," he assured her before she hung up, "it's the right thing to do. You'll be glad that you're here."

When the room was quiet again and Taryn was left alone, she picked Miss Dixie up from off the nightstand and held her in her hand. She enjoyed feeling the weight of her electronic friend.

"We'll go see Matt," she told her camera, "but I can't keep avoiding it forever."

Each passing day, the desire to go to New Hampshire grew stronger and stronger. She couldn't explain it, could barely put it into words, but the call of her aunt Sarah's house had turned from a whisper into a shout.

"I'm meant to be there," she said to the room.

She just wasn't sure that she was ready; she knew deep inside that once she went, she'd never leave.

BLOODY MOOR

Return to the Welsh moor with Taryn, as she's hired to help restore Ceredigion House-the old, stately mansion that locals refer to as "The Cursed." With the help of newfound friends, Nicki and Shawn, they'll solve the centuries' old mystery that clings to the mansion and region.

https://www.amazon.com/Bloody-Moor-Ghost-Taryns-Camera-ebook/dp/B01MQXZEGY/

TARYN'S CAMERA BOOK 8

BLOODY MOOR

REBECCA PATRICK-HOWARD

SARAH'S HOUSE

What happened when Taryn moved to her aunt Sarah's house? What went on behind those closed door, in those isolated New Hampshire mountains?

https://www.amazon.com/gp/product/B01MU2LFGP/

TARYN'S CAMERA BOOK 9

SARAH'S HOUSE

REBECCA PATRICK-HOWARD

AUTHOR'S NOTE

This book is a complete work of fiction. The storyline and characters are all fictitious and not based on any real people, living or dead. With that being said, there are some parts of the book that were inspired by real places and events.

West Liberty, Kentucky is a real place in Morgan County. They really did have a tornado go through it several years ago and the downtown was almost completely destroyed. They've been slowly rebuilding.

Hazel Hill Academy is not a real school. However, it is highly based upon Hazel Green Academy, a former boarding school in Wolfe County, Kentucky. I grew up on the campus of Hazel Green. My mother was a student there, she graduated in 1965, and she later returned to be the bookkeeper. Even after the school closed in the early 1980s, we continued to live on the campus with all the empty buildings.

The photos in this book are all mine. The campus pictures truly are of HGA. I took them over the course of several years.

There were no murders associated with the school, no missing students. I grew up under the care of many of the former staff members and they're nothing but lovely people.

The campus is currently not in use and the buildings remain empty.

As far as I know, the campus is not haunted. However, you never really know, do you?

Rebecca's former home on the HGA campus

Rebecca, age 7, with Rita Robinson (Wolfe County librarian) in her red dress

ABOUT THE AUTHOR

Rebecca Patrick-Howard is the author of several books including the paranormal mystery series *Taryn's Camera*. She lives in eastern Kentucky with her husband and two children. To order copies of ALL of Rebecca's books, including autographed paperbacks, visit her website at:

www.rebeccaphoward.net

OTHER BOOKS BY REBECCA

Taryn's Camera Series

Windwood Farm (Book 1)

The locals call it the “devil's house” and Taryn's about to find out why!

Griffith Tavern (Book 2)

The old tavern has a dark secret and Taryn's camera's going to learn it soon.

Dark Hollow Road (Book 3)

Beautiful Cheyenne Willoughby has disappeared. Someone knows the truth.

Shaker Town (Book 4)

Taryn's camera is finally revealing a past to her that she's always longed to see-the mysterious Shakers as they were 100 years ago. But is she seeing a past she hadn't bargained for?

Jekyll Island (Book 5)

Jekyll Island is known for its ghosts, as well as its fascinating history, but now the two are about to take Taryn on a wild ride she'll never forget!

Black Raven Inn (Book 6)

The 1960's music scene...vibrant, electrifying, and sometimes even deadly...

Muddy Creek (Book 7)

Lucy did a bad, bad thing when she burned down the old school. Now it's up to Taryn to find out why.

Bloody Moor (Book 8)

The call it "the cursed" and the townspeople still fear the witch that reigned there a century ago. But this haunted Welsh mansion has more than meets the eye!

Sarah's House (Book 9)

Taryn's Pictures: Photos from Taryn's Camera

Taryn's Haunting

Kentucky Witches

A Broom with a View

She's your average witch next door, he's a Christmas tree farmer with sisters named after horses. Kudzu Valley will never be the same when Liza Jane comes to town!

Broommates

When Bryar Rose makes a fool of herself on national television, it's time for her to return to Kudzu Valley. But now that she's accused of murdering half the town, will anyone truly accept her?

A Broom of One's Own

What does a witch do when she can't get rid of the restless spirit that haunts the old cinema? Call for backup! (A Taryn's Camera/Kentucky Witches crossover)

Nothin' Says Lovin' Like Something from the Coven *(available now for preorder)*

General Fiction

Furnace Mountain: Or The Day President Roosevelt Came to Town

When Sam Walters invited the president to visit his Depression-era town, he never dreamed of what would happen next!

The Locusts (Coming Soon)

Things She Sees in the Dark

Mallory's cousin was kidnapped when she was eight years old and Mallory saw the whole thing happen. She's suffered amnesia ever since. Now, 25 years later, her memories are starting to return. Can she solve the case that no detective has been able to crack? And will she live through it, if she does?

Superstition Mountain

Superstition Mountain *(available now for pre-order)*

Wren has just taken a job in Superstition Mountain, Kentucky where the locals are friendly, the scenery gorgeous, and all the urban legends and folk stories come to life!

True Hauntings

Haunted Estill County

More Tales from Haunted Estill County

Haunted Estill County: The Children's Edition

Haunted Madison County

A Summer of Fear

The Maple House

Four Months of Terror

Two Weeks: A True Haunting

Three True Tales of Terror

The Visitors

Other Books

Coping with Grief: The Anti-Guide to Infant Loss

Three Minus Zero

Finding Henry: A Journey Into Eastern Europe

Estill County in Photos

Haunted: Ghost Children Stories from Beyond

CONNECT WITH REBECCA!

REBECCA'S LINKS

Pinterest: https://www.pinterest.com/rebeccapatrickh/

Website: www.rebeccaphoward.net

Email: rphwrites@gmail.com

Facebook:
https://www.facebook.com/rebeccaphowardwrites

Twitter: https://twitter.com/RPHWrites

Instagram: https://instagram.com/rphwrites/

KENTUCKY WITCHES

Like THIS book? Meet the Kentucky Witches!

https://www.amazon.com/gp/product/B01JM2TK 02/

Liza Jane Higginbotham is your average witch next door. Just a down home girl, she enjoys driving her truck, listening to country music and, oh yes, the occasional brew.

This witch just wants to enjoy the quiet life. When her no-good, hipster husband cheats on her with a tuba player, she moves back to take over the family farm in rural Eastern Kentucky. Here, she's expecting some peace, content to play in her garden, restore the dilapidated farmhouse, and throw her money away at the town auction house every Friday night.

But the town of Kudzu Valley just won't let a witch rest. From the high school football coach looking for a charm to help the team win the Homecoming game to Lola Ellen Pearson who wants to hex the local Pizza Hut for giving her food poisoning the night before her fourth wedding, everyone wants SOMETHING from the town's resident witch!

When Cotton Hashagen's dead body is found, though, all eyes turn to Liza Jane. After all, hadn't she JUST accused the local meter reader of a terrible crime? With the townspeople and police turning their eyes to Liza Jane, it's going to take a lot for her to prove that she didn't put a "whammy" on him AND solve the mystery to find the real culprit!

www.rebeccaphoward.net

Published by Mistletoe Press

First Edition: December 2017

Printed in the United States of America

All photography by Rebecca Patrick-Howard

66290966R00272

Made in the USA
Middletown, DE
09 March 2018